AFTER THE PURGE: VENDETTA

SAM SISAVATH

Published by Road to Babylon Media LLC
www.roadtobabylon.com

Edited by Jennifer Jensen & Wendy Chan
Cover Art by Deranged Doctor Design

ISBN-13: 978-0997894653
ISBN-10: 0997894652

BOOKS IN THE AFTER THE PURGE:
VENDETTA TRILOGY

Requiem

Tokens

Remains

ALSO BY SAM SISAVATH

Huge thanks go out to George and Susan for their invaluable insights. Thank you!

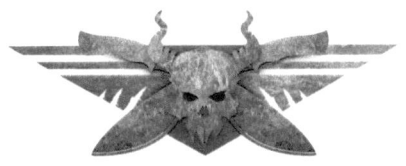

ABOUT REQUIEM

THE WORLD WAS NOT READY.

Six years ago, the world was plunged into darkness.

Five years ago, it got a second chance.

Now the fight for what's left begins...

They Called It The Purge...

History books call it The Purge, and it altered the course of human history. A breed of seemingly unkillable creatures that once lurked in the shadows of mankind's past finally revealed themselves. Driven by an insatiable lust for human blood, these monsters—dubbed "ghouls" by some—consumed the globe in one bloody, awful night. Their numbers growing exponentially through infection, they felled the unprepared governments of the world with hardly any resistance.

In the yearlong nightmare that followed, survivors were turned into chattel for the generations of ghouls to come. Most chose to cooperate, but a brave few fought back, and thanks to their sacrifice, the ghouls were defeated and driven back into the darkness.

The End was Just the Beginning...

Humanity was given a second chance, but the world post-Purge will never be the same. The cities have been abandoned, technology is limited, law and order is nonexistent, and survivors live off the land in small, isolated communities in the countryside. Nightfall is no longer the harbinger of doom it once was, but the night will never be completely terror-free. Though vastly smaller in number and weaker than they've ever been, the ghoul menace lingers.

But the monsters are now the hunted. Men and women who suffered unimaginable horrors under the yearlong Purge roam the land, seeking out the creatures wherever they hide. They call themselves slayers. They are skilled, dangerous, and they have scores to settle.

Two Strangers on a Dangerous Road...

Wash is a young slayer scouring what's left of America in search of one very specific ghoul. He will find it even if he has to brave hell itself to do so. Ana is a woman who is not what she seems—cunning, smart, and far more capable than she lets on. Forced into an alliance, the two strangers must learn to trust one another if they are to accomplish their goals—defeat the monsters, both inhuman and human, and get out alive.

ONE

The monsters were taking their time tonight, so there was nothing for Wash to do but wait. That was fine. He was used to waiting.

His breathing was slowed, his heartbeat barely audible to his own ears, and small, thin clouds formed in front of him. Aside from the nightlife around him, there was just the very faint *tick-tick-tick-tick* of the automatic on his left wrist to keep him company. Most people couldn't detect the different beats unless they held the wristwatch right up to their ear, but Wash knew them like a second heartbeat. There were exactly four *ticks* per second. No more, no less.

Tick-tick-tick-tick...

Wash waited because this was the easiest path to town, and the monsters always chose the straightest and fastest route. Just like they had the previous three nights, according to his intel. They were base creatures that way, as complicated as a cockroach—and just as persistent and fearful of the light. They hid from the sun, moved in the darkness, and survived to feed.

Their existence was simplicity itself. If he weren't here to kill them (*again*), he might have even admired them.

But instead of undead things, the girl showed up.

What the hell?

She was about to die but didn't seem to recognize it. Wash did, because he could smell the blood in the air. He'd sniffed it too many times before not to recognize it instantly. He wasn't the only one who knew she was out here. *They* knew, too. And they didn't have to see her, either. They could smell her. They could *hear* the blood in her veins.

Except there was a hitch: The girl wasn't afraid. He saw the fearlessness in the fluid way she moved, gliding through bushes and ducking under low-hanging branches. There was no panic, nothing to indicate she had entered the dark woods unwillingly.

She should have been afraid, though. Only an idiot strayed from the sanctuary and protection of the towns and wandered alone into the dark woods in the middle of the night. Even now, years after The Walk Out, there were still ghouls out here. Wash knew for a fact there were at least a few of them in the area with him *right now*.

So why wasn't the girl afraid?

Wash couldn't answer that question. At least, not yet. All he could do was watch her just as he had for the last ten seconds as she moved from the right side of his peripheral vision toward his left.

He pegged her height at five-two or three, her weight at maybe one hundred and ten pounds soaking wet. Pale white skin stood out clear as day from the darkness around her, and she should have been wearing thicker clothing against the chilly night. The black leather jacket was too light for this time of year. It wasn't freezing, but it was cold enough that the skin across Wash's face tingled and the exposed parts of his body were slightly numb from lack of movement.

A ponytail bounced behind her as she moved. Bright red hair and jeans and boots.

Snap! as the girl stepped on a broken twig.

The sound reverberated, ricocheting off the trees around them.

Now you've done it...

Wash readied himself, flexing his fingers to get the blood flowing. His original plan was to wait for the monsters to reveal themselves, to make their way toward town like they had the previous three nights. Once he knew how many he was dealing with, then he could act accordingly.

"Have a plan," the Old Man always told him. *"That's what separates the living from the dead. Can you guess which one of them didn't have a plan?"*

Of course, the Old Man never said anything about having your perfectly good plan ruined by a stupid girl in a black leather jacket traipsing around the woods in the middle of the night.

What the hell is she doing out here?

Snap! as the girl broke another twig.

The sound hadn't even had a chance to echo before it lunged out of the bush to the right of her.

Here we go!

It was a sickly-looking thing, pruned black flesh coating bones that had been deformed by the same sickness that made it what it was—undead, inhuman, a *ghoul*. It should have been difficult to spot against the deep dark night around it, but Wash's eyes had already adjusted to the lack of light. And besides, he'd seen the damned things so many times he would recognize one with both eyes closed.

He could *smell* it.

For half a heartbeat Wash almost opened his mouth to scream out a warning, but he didn't. The girl had stopped and turned to face the oncoming creature, and she was going to be dead in seconds. Screaming would have cost him two seconds —the act of opening his mouth, then forcing the warning out. Maybe three seconds—possibly even four. The girl didn't have that much time.

Instead, Wash reached down for the kukri strapped to his left thigh even as he leaped off the branch and plummeted to the ground below. Twenty feet would have broken a lot of people's legs, but it was child's play to him. He hit the soft earth with a loud *crunch!*, then was straightening up while catapulting himself forward—all in the same fluid motion. He'd done it before. Too many times to count.

Wait, where's the screaming?

The question popped into his head even as he raced toward the startled figure. She stood twenty yards in front of him, turned in the direction of the nightcrawler as it charged. It was closer than Wash—

—Ten yards—nine—*eight*—

And there was no doubt it would reach her first. As fast as he was—and he was fast, he was *damn fast*—there was no way he would reach the girl in time to save her life. He felt sorry for her, but it was her fault for being out here all alone in the middle of the night. Everyone knew not to wander into the woods by yourself. What was she thinking?

Then the girl was turning toward him, clearly responding to the sound of his boots pounding on the soft, damp forest ground. Her eyes flashed a brilliant shade of green even as they widened in—anger? Was she angry?

At *him?*

What the hell?

He had expected fear at the sight of him running toward her with the kukri clutched in his hand. The kukri was a machete with an inwardly curved blade, over twenty inches long—fourteen of that razor-sharp steel—and was as menacing as it was effective. So why did she look *pissed off* instead of scared?

What the hell is going on here? he thought even as he gained more ground.

Fifteen yards—fourteen—*thirteen—*

But he would still never reach her in time, because the monster was already within five yards—four—*three—*

The girl spun away from Wash just as moonlight glinted off an object in her right hand.

Where did that come from?

It was a knife, sharp blade gleaming as it moved in a wide arc, slicing across the cold, chilly air from right to left in a dramatic diagonal slash that traveled from top to bottom.

Wash was still trying to understand where the knife had come from when the lunging creature's head detached from its bony shoulders.

What...

Dark black eyes widened in shock—or what someone who hadn't been in Wash's shoes hundreds of times would have mistaken for shock, anyway.

...the...

But it wasn't, because shock was a human emotion and these monsters had lost that the moment they turned.

...hell...

The head *plopped* to the ground and rolled away even as the body it was once attached to simply lost all momentum and pitched forward, stick-thin arms waving wildly in the air as its legs gave out underneath it.

...is going...

The creature fell in a pile of *clacking* bones next to the girl. It would have crashed right into her, except she had side-stepped as soon as she slashed with the knife.

...on here?

The way the nightcrawler had fallen—like a marionette with its strings snipped—told him that the girl's knife was either made of or coated with silver. The metal was radioactive to ghouls, and it didn't take much. All you needed was to make contact with their bloodstream and the monsters simply ceased to exist. Wash had seen them come at him without their heads, without limbs, even without half their bodies. But they couldn't do any of those things if you stabbed, shot, or broke their skin and made contact with the bloodstream underneath with a silver weapon. That was the reason his bullets, as well as the kukri in his right hand, all had silver in them. He didn't know how it worked, it just did.

"*You're wasting your time thinking about it,*" the Old Man used to always say. "*It is what it is, kid. Silver kills the monsters, so we use silver. If dirt took them down, we'd be using dirt. Let the eggheads spend their time thinking about the whys. That's not our job. Next!*"

Wash slowed down even as the girl whirled back around to face him.

Those green eyes flashed in his direction again. "What the

hell do you think you're doing, asshat? You almost got me killed!"

"What did you call me?" Wash asked.

"You heard me."

"What the hell are you doing out here?"

"What the hell are *you* doing out here?"

"My job—" Wash was saying, when the air shifted around them.

There they are. There's the rest of them!

He knew there'd be more than one out here tonight. He was expecting maybe two (the townspeople hadn't been very clear about the numbers), but the stench was all wrong for just two nightcrawlers. It was too thick. Too heavy. Too *much*.

They came out from behind the girl, except she didn't see them because she was too busy facing him, the knife in her hand dripping with thick black blood. She gripped the handle tightly—ready to slash again.

"Behind you!" he shouted.

She spun around, the knife moving from her side to in front of her even as her legs changed into a fighting stance.

She's had training, he thought even as he broke off into a run.

Her head turned, shocked to find him there—for the half a heartbeat he was there, anyway—before he was past her.

Wash changed up his grip on the thermoplastic rubber handle of the machete in his right hand as he cranked into second gear. Then third.

Faster, faster, *faster!*

You could never run too fast when facing a ghoul. The faster, the better when there were more than one, like now.

Time began to slow down like it always did when Wash

knew that the next few seconds were going to determine if he lived or died, and he saw:

There were three of them, emerging out of the darkness. It was a pack. They were small, like the first one, and moved low to the ground and almost on all fours, but not quite. "Knuckle draggers," a slayer Wash had crossed paths with in Montana called them. They saw him and immediately lost all interest in the girl. It wasn't that they thought he was less dangerous, an easier prey. No, it was simply that he had put himself closer to them. Put the blood pumping through his veins within easier reach.

Their eyes—hollowed and black, like soulless pits over-flowing with tar—focused on him, and they changed directions instantly. They were hairless and barefoot, fleshlike thin layers of film clinging to bodies that were devoid of anything resembling muscle or tone. Sickly looking, forcing open mouths that revealed jagged and yellow and brown teeth with saliva dripping from them as they became rabid at the sight of him—at the presence of the untainted blood in him.

Rays of moonlight splashed across their domed heads, falling over one of them in such a way that it put a glint into its eyes. For a split second, Wash almost thought it was human and wondered what it had been before its transformation. A man? A woman? Maybe even a child. All of that was gone now, replaced by this skin-and-bones childlike revenant.

"*Stop it,*" he imagined the Old Man chastising him. "*Whatever they once were, they're not anymore. This is what they are now. This is the world. There is no going back. For them, or for us. Kill them all, and move on to the next one.*"

Wash lunged, slashing with the machete.

TWO

He caught the first one across the face with the kukri, gashing it from temple to jawline, and popping one of its eyeballs at the same time. Blood splattered the front of his thermal sweater, but the viscous, dark liquid was mostly lost in the black of its fabric.

One down...

Instead of stopping or pausing for even a second, Wash pushed through the falling nightcrawler as the other two attacked.

He felt sorry for them. He really did. They were pathetic things—thin and frail and twisted from the inside out—and the chest of the second one folded like papier-mâché when he punched his gloved left hand through it, the silver studs along the knuckles and finger joints raking its flesh with the ease of a knife through butter. He saw the lights go out of its eyes, what-ever remnants of humanity doused in a blink, and the body simply sagged even as his hand exited its back.

Two down...

Wash realized his mistake as soon as the creature fell to the ground and almost took his left hand, embedded through its chest, down with it. But he was strong enough that he refused to let it and gravity slow him down, and despite being one-handed, he swung and decapitated the third ghoul with the kukri.

It wasn't the best of swings, and he actually got more of the lower jaw than he wanted, not that the extra bone provided any added resistance to the machete's curved blade. He lopped the creature's head cleanly off at the neck.

And three makes a full day's work!

The headless nightcrawler went limp, but its momentum carried it forward and into Wash. He backhanded it across the chest just in time to knock its trajectory slightly astray, and it toppled past him, but it still jettisoned enough inky black liquid from its severed neck into the air. Wash snapped his eyes and mouth shut just as the creature's blood sprayed his face and shoulder before it fell with a lifeless *thump* to the ground behind him.

And just like that, the world resumed its normal speed.

Wash held his breath and slid the ghoul off his left hand, then spent some time cleaning the blood off the machete using the grass before slipping it back into a sheath on his left hip. His right was reserved for the Beretta, still nestled in its holster. He was carrying a light load—kukri and 9mm—because he knew he'd need the extra speed. Had there been more than four, he would have been in trouble. A little trouble, anyway, and nothing Wash hadn't gotten himself out of before. Of course, if he were here, the Old Man would have offered up a completely different assessment.

"You got lucky, kid," he would say. *"Just remember: Luck has a bad way of coming and going."*

I'm still alive, old timer. That's all that matters.

He pulled the rag from one of his cargo pants pockets and wiped at the sludge on his cheeks and forehead. He was covered in the filth, but the contact of ghoul blood on his skin wasn't anywhere close to the abhorrent smell of it clinging to him. The blood was tainted like the creatures it sprayed out of, and washing it off...

There goes another wardrobe.

He swiped the blood off the silver studs on the glove—or "gauntlet," as a kid in Wyoming called it. Wash preferred gloves, because that was what they were—black leather motorcycle riding gloves he had repurposed for this very specific usage.

While he cleaned himself up, Wash looked down at the bodies, at the identical faces. He would think it was the same nightcrawler copied three times over, but of course he knew better. The same thing that turned them into ghouls, that changed their eyes to solid black, robbed them of every hair follicle and made them little more than bags of deformed bones also made them into a single homogenous species. But there were exceptions. There were the ones with blue eyes...

"Don't fuck with them," the Old Man always said. *"If you see those blue-eyed fucks coming, you run the other way, you understand? I don't care how many slayers you got with you; I don't care how loud or big they talk, you run the fuck the other way."*

I can't do that, old timer, Wash thought as he used the toe of one boot to turn a severed head over so he could see the front of its face.

Black eyes, mouth open wide in a comical O shape. Wash didn't really blame this one. It was the same nightcrawler the girl—

The girl. Where's the girl?

No sooner did the question pop into his head than Wash heard her moving behind him. He turned around and got another good look at those wild green eyes—they were impossible to miss against the night background—as she walked over to where he stood.

"Hey, you okay?" he asked, just before she hit him in the face.

It was a nice punch, but he'd been hit by bigger and stronger men, and compared to them, a balled fist from a five-two-something girl just stunned him. Even so, he hadn't seen it coming, which was the part that stuck out to him.

Wash took a couple of steps back before gathering himself. "What the fuck!" he shouted, even as he felt along the bridge of his nose to make sure nothing was broken. It stung, but everything was still where they should be. "What is your problem, kid?"

"My problem?" the girl said. "And did you just call me a 'kid,' you asshat?"

Again with the asshat, Wash thought even as he hopped another step back and brushed at her fist as she swung at him a second time.

He was more than ready for this one and pushed her to the side, using her forward momentum against her while he skipped out of her path. He could have hit her back—she was wide open for a blow to the back of the head or neck, or even the kidney, if he were feeling vicious—but Wash had never hit a woman before, and he wasn't about to start now. Especially someone who barely came up to his chin.

"Calm the fuck down, kid!" Wash shouted.

She whirled back on him. "Stop calling me *kid*, you asshat!"

"I will if you stop calling me asshat!" he shouted back.

She pursed her lips at him, her hands making fists at her sides. He waited for her to try again (*Third time's the charm, right?*), but she thought better of it and allowed herself to relax —slightly. She was still in her fighting stance, even if she was trying to hide it. But Wash had been in too many fights to be fooled.

"Who the hell are you, anyway?" she asked. "What are you doing out here?"

"I could ask you the same thing."

She glanced up at one of the trees. "Were you sitting up there the whole time, like some weirdo?"

"Weirdo?" He grunted. "I was surveying the area."

"For what?"

"What do you think, genius?"

He rubbed at his nose again, then took another couple of steps away from her. It wasn't that he was afraid, but she was such a tiny thing that if she insisted on trying to deck him a third time, he'd have no choice but to put her down. The only other option was to let her hit him, and he wasn't about to do that.

"Women are men with tits," the Old Man liked to say, usually when he was drunk, which was often. *"They can stab you in the back or take you out from the front just as quick as any guy. Remember that."*

He remembered, just as he remembered everything else the Old Man had said to him. Sometimes it amazed Wash how well he could recall the old timer's little sayings as if they were recordings playing in an endless loop inside his head. Sometimes he even mixed them up with the things he imagined the old man saying.

Wash took another quick step back when the girl took one forward in his direction, but instead of assaulting him, she crouched next to one of the severed heads on the ground. She leaned over the pruned black face and stared down at its twin hollow eyes.

"What are you doing?" Wash asked.

She ignored him and got up, then walked over to the one he'd punched through the chest with his glove.

"What are you doing?" he asked again.

The girl stood up and put her hands on her hips. She shook her head, but Wash thought she looked almost...relieved?

"It's not them," she said.

"Not who?" he asked.

"Not *whom*."

"Whatever."

"If a question's worth asking, it's worth asking correctly."

"What are you, an English teacher?"

"If I were, I'd fail your ass on the first day of class."

She turned to look at him. Really, really stare at him from head to toe, and Wash took the opportunity to respond in kind.

She was a lot older than he had first thought, even though age was a difficult thing to pin down these days. The Purge made you grow up fast, or you didn't grow up at all. Mid-twenties, maybe late twenties, but she hadn't hit her thirties yet; he was sure of that. She was older than him by a few years, which he guessed might have been why she was so annoyed at him for calling her *kid*.

That doesn't excuse the whole asshat *thing, though.*

He had guessed five-two or three, but now that he could see her standing still for longer than a few seconds, he thought those small black boots of hers probably gave her an additional few inches. So five foot nothing, really. Her hair looked redder at the moment, and for some reason he didn't think her green eyes quite meshed with her color of her pale skin.

"What do you think you're doing?" she asked.

"What?"

"You're staring."

He smirked. "You were doing the same thing. Don't get all high and mighty on me, kid."

"I told you to stop calling me *kid*."

"What are you, fifteen?" he asked. He couldn't help himself; it was easy, and he got some satisfaction in watching her nostrils flare in annoyance.

She pursed her lips again but didn't respond. Instead, she walked over to the two remaining nightcrawlers and looked down at the first one's face. "Where's your partner?"

"My what?" Wash said.

"Your partner. Don't you slayers always work in pairs?"

"I don't have a partner."

"That's a first."

"What are you looking for?" Wash asked.

She glanced over at him and might have snickered, like she knew he was changing the subject on purpose. She still didn't answer him, though, and instead moved on to the fourth and final one.

"They all look the same," Wash said. "You know that, right? One nightcrawler's the same as another."

"Not all of them."

"You talking about the blue eyes?"

She kept quiet and crouched next to the last ghoul, turning its head over so she could see its face better.

"Have you seen them?" Wash asked. "The blue eyes? Have you run into them around here?"

She continued to ignore him and took out her knife and wiped the five-inch blade on the grass to clean it before sliding it back into her jacket's shirt sleeve.

So that's where that came from.

He wondered how she did that. Some kind of wrist rig, maybe. It was worth looking into later. Wash was always looking for a fresh method for arming himself. Innovating kept you ahead of the monsters.

"Hey," Wash said. "I asked you a question. Have you seen one of those blue eyes around here or not?"

She glanced over. "Maybe I have. What's it to you?"

"I'm looking for one of them."

She stared at him with something that almost looked like amusement. "You're *looking* for one of them? No one looks for the blue eyes."

"The one I'm looking for's got one eye. The right one. Have you seen it or heard someone seeing something like that around here?"

"What makes you think I'm from around here?"

"Aren't you?"

She shrugged. "So you were sitting in a tree in the middle of the night looking for a blue-eyed ghoul with one eye, is that it?"

Close enough, he thought, but said, "Have you seen or heard about it or not?"

She continued giving him that curious look for a brief second or two before shaking her head. "No."

"No what? No, you haven't heard about anyone seeing something like that, or no, you haven't seen it yourself?"

"Both. But then again, I don't hang around idiots that go around hunting blue-eyed ghouls. You suicidal or something?"

"I can ask you the same thing. What are you doing out here? You from Harrisonville?"

She shrugged again and stood up. "You're a slayer."

"Gee, you figured that out yourself?"

She smirked. "See you around, slayer boy."

She was turning to go when he reached over for her arm, but she spun away before he could get a grip.

She took a couple of steps away and scowled. "What the fuck do you think you're doing, asshat?"

"Jesus, you kiss your mom with that mouth?"

"No, just yours."

"Jesus, woman, I'm trying to be civilized here. I saved your life."

"I didn't need you to save my life."

"There were four of them. You telling me you knew that?"

She didn't answer, but he read it in her face anyway. She *didn't* know that.

Instead of confirming it, she said, "Sorry. I just don't like guys touching me without permission."

"Maybe it's your attitude."

"Maybe. There are a lot of dangerous people out there these days. You can never be too careful."

Then she smiled at him. It came out of nowhere, as if they

hadn't been bickering like children seconds ago, or that she wasn't seriously ready to cut him if he'd gotten too close. He had seen the way she held her right hand, with the palm open, ready to receive the knife hidden inside her sleeve.

"Nice gauntlet," she said, looking down at his left hand.

"It's a glove," Wash said.

"Looks like a gauntlet to me. You make that yourself?"

"It's a glove. And yeah."

"Poh-tay-to, poh-tah-to."

She turned and jogged off.

"Hey!" Wash said.

But she didn't stop or look back.

"Hey, who are you?" he shouted after her.

She didn't answer and slipped under a branch. He stared after her, at the way she moved, the way she slid around tree trunks before simply vanishing a few seconds later. She was going in the opposite direction of Harrisonville, which meant she wasn't from the town.

"See you later, lady," he said quietly to himself, even though he knew the chances of that happening were slim, especially if she was going to make a habit of walking around out here in the dark by herself.

Wash turned back to the dead ghouls on the ground. He took out the kukri and crouched next to the one with the hole in its chest. He could have used the sawback on the blade to cut his way through the neck, but he didn't have to. The bone was fragile underneath the thin layer of flesh, and all it took was one easy swing to chop his way clean through.

He picked up the head by the nostrils and walked back to the tree where he'd been camped out, and pulled his pack from the bush nearby. He dug out the plain gray sack and tossed the severed head inside, then returned to collect the others. People sometimes didn't feel like paying up unless you showed them irrefutable evidence you'd done the job they hired you for.

"Another day, another dollar," the Old Man used to say. It was something from the old days before The Purge made idioms like it, along with so many things people used to think were important, obsolete.

"Another day, another dollar," Wash said quietly to the empty night around him.

THREE

Harrisonville was twenty miles from the closest abandoned city. It was a small town of about four hundred people, almost all of them brought there against their will six years ago during the height of The Purge. Some left after The Walk Out, but many chose to stay and make the place a real home.

"Make lemonade out of lemons," as the Old Man would say.

It wasn't a bad home, especially considering what was out there. These days if you could find four walls and a roof, enough food to get by, and friends to watch your back during the night (and sometimes in the day), you were ahead of a lot of other people.

Despite all that, Wash wasn't even close to saying yes when the mayor made the offer for him to stay.

"Can't," he said. "I got things to do down south."

"Oklahoma?" the mayor asked.

"Texas."

"What're you gonna find in Texas that you can't find here?"

A one-eyed, blue-eyed ghoul, Wash thought, but he shook his head and remembered how badly the conversation had gone with the woman in the woods. He said instead, "Just something I gotta do, that's all. No offense."

The older man nodded. He was in his fifties, balding, a half-hearted attempt at a comb-over, and a paunch underneath his sweater that poked out like a pregnant woman's belly. Wash thought of him as Harrisonville's mayor even though the man didn't call himself that. He had a name, but Wash had forgotten it, mostly because he hadn't paid that close attention when they first met yesterday morning. Remembering people's names took too much effort, especially when you were probably never going to see them again anyway.

"That's all of them?" the older man asked as he looked across the room at the brown bag sitting in the corner. Creamy black blood had leaked and formed underneath and around the bundle.

"It was a pack," Wash said. "They wouldn't leave one behind. That's all of them."

"You sure?"

"Yes."

"Are you *sure*?"

Wash nodded. "Yes," he lied.

The truth was he wasn't sure, because there was no such thing as being "sure" when it came to nightcrawlers. While it was true that they always traveled in packs when there were more than one of them around, there were exceptions. He didn't give voice to that, though, because it would have just delayed his exit in the morning.

The major let out a relieved sigh, which told Wash he'd been convincing enough. "They've really been making a mess of the livestock, and we weren't quite sure how to handle them," the man said. "I guess it's been a while."

"How long is a while?"

"Long enough that we were having trouble getting people to volunteer to go look for them."

"You have silver in town?"

"Weapons aren't the problem. The *will* to go out there to use them is."

Job security, old timer, Wash thought, and hoped he'd hidden the smirk well enough.

He said out loud, "They're not going to be any more trouble from now on."

"Thank you," the man said, and reached across the desk. "Thank God you showed up when you did."

Wash shook the man's hand. "It was good timing for both of us. I needed some supplies, and you needed a hand."

"I think we got the better end of the deal, if you ask me." The mayor took a piece of paper out of his shirt pocket and briefly glanced at it. "This is everything?"

"That's everything."

"Most of what's on here is no problem. The only thing we don't have is coffee. Sorry. There hasn't been coffee around here for years."

"And everything else?"

"We can spare everything else." He put the paper away. "When do you need them?"

"I'm leaving tomorrow, so whenever you can put them together for me."

"So soon?"

"Like I said, I have to get going."

"Texas."

"Uh huh."

"I'll make sure we have it ready for you by morning, then."

"Thank you."

The mayor stood up and walked around his desk, then nodded for Wash to follow him. Wash sighed. He could feel a sales pitch coming from a mile away, but he let the mayor lead him out of the one-room office and out onto the front porch anyway. It wasn't like he could do anything or go anywhere until morning anyway.

Harrisonville, like every other ghoul collaborator town Wash had been through, was small and self-contained, with a single main street and a handful of alleyways and side roads. It wasn't anywhere close to a main highway and was surrounded by walls of trees to one side and a lake behind it. The water made it ideal and allowed the town to be self-sustaining as the resettled population learned to farm and raise livestock. It was as "country" as you could get, and Wash had crossed hundreds like it since he began traveling the country with the Old Man almost five years ago.

And yet, despite his familiarity with places like Harrisonville, the alienness of his surroundings lingered. He didn't belong here. Not with these people trying to carve some semblance of a life for themselves the best they could. He wasn't like them, and he would never be.

"You're a slayer, son," the Old Man once said to him. *"You don't have the scars like the rest of us, but you're a slayer through and through. You were made for this. I knew you were a natural the day I met you."*

Wash wasn't sure how much of that was true, especially

since he hadn't killed a thing—living or unliving—before he met the Old Man. But there was no denying that the old timer had been right. Wash was good at this. *Really* good. So good, in fact, that sometimes it scared him when he allowed himself to think about it for too long. Which was why he tried not to.

The *tick-tick-tick-tick* of the watch on his left wrist, hidden underneath his sleeve, echoed softly in his ears, pushing away the questions and doubts like they always did.

"How old are you, son?" the mayor was asking him.

Wash flinched at the word *son*, but the older man probably didn't notice because he was too busy lighting a homemade pipe. He took a long draw from it, then pushed out a puff of smoke into the chilly night air around them. The older man shivered slightly and clutched his sweater tighter around him, but Wash had been knee-deep in the temperature for so long during the last twenty-four hours that he hardly felt it.

"Twenty-five," Wash lied. It wasn't too far from the truth, and he had the grizzled face of experience to sell it to most people. At night, it was even easier.

He leaned against one of the poles holding up the awning while the mayor sat on an uncomfortable-looking wooden chair and puffed away. Harrisonville resembled towns in all those cowboy movies that the Old Man loved so much. Except for the lightbulbs, cars, and every technology invented since the horse and buggy that didn't need 24/7 electricity to run them. There were enough lights in Harrisonville thanks to the strategically placed solar-powered LEDs to see with, but they were dimmed to conserve energy.

Wash's eyes were drawn to the windows of a big brown apartment directly in front of them, each one fastened with rebars on the outside. The place was almost completely dark except for a couple of windows, and in one of them, along the second floor, Wash watched a woman moving around on the other side. An early riser. It was easy enough to tell she was a woman when she pulled her nightgown over her head and the shape of her breasts were revealed, just before she turned and open a dresser to sift through its contents.

Wash pulled back his sleeve to check his watch: A few minutes past five. It would be sunup in thirty minutes or so.

He returned his gaze to the woman on the second floor as she slipped a long-sleeved shirt on and did the buttons. The way she stood, the outline of her feminine frame perfectly exposed to the window by the candlelight behind her, made him wonder if she was putting on a show for his benefit.

"Twenty-five," the mayor was saying. "Isn't that too young to be doing what you're doing?"

Wash smiled. "You haven't met a lot of slayers, have you?"

"Can't say that I have. Why?"

"Twenty-five isn't young. It's old."

"Is that right?"

"Most slayers are in their twenties. I've met a few in their teens. The ones in their thirties are far and few. The ones older than that..." He paused before continuing. "It's not the kind of life that lends itself to retirement plans."

"I guess not."

Wash wondered if the mayor was being naïve on purpose, but he quickly dismissed that possibility. Most people didn't know what it took to do what he did; they just knew that he *did* it so they didn't have to.

Just like the woman on the other side of the second-floor window. She would never know what it was like to voluntarily go out into the darkness and wait for the monsters. She would never get close enough to smell them, get so close so often that she instinctively knew if they were around when there was even the slightest shift in the air.

The mayor had gone quiet next to him and seemed content to sit there, puffing on his pipe in silence.

Wash shuffled his feet. "What's on your mind?"

"You could stay here," the mayor said. "We need people like you."

"You expecting more ghoul trouble?"

"That's one reason. They're never really going to go away, are they?"

Wash shook his head. He liked the way the mayor had said that, with certainty. He'd met too many people who had their heads in the sand and tried to pretend The Walk Out solved everyone's problems. It did—a lot of it, in fact—but the monsters didn't all go away in the blink of an eye. Some of them stayed behind. And some of the ones that refused to vanish were even more dangerous than the black-eyed ones.

"No, they're not," Wash said.

"I don't expect so," the mayor said. "But the reason I say we need you isn't for your abilities, son."

Wash flinched again at the word.

"We need men," the mayor continued, as if that should explain everything.

And Wash guessed it did. Women outnumbered men by a healthy margin everywhere he went. Most of them were single moms, and everyone knew why. Just as everyone knew the reason the vast majority of children across the world were either five years old or under. Harrisonville had its share of those. Everyone did.

"I gotta get to Texas," Wash said. "There's something down there I gotta do, that I can't put off."

"You can have your pick," the mayor said. "You're not a bad-looking young man. Women would be throwing themselves at you."

Wash smiled at that. He knew a few slayers who would beg to disagree. Even the woman from earlier, in the woods, who kept calling him an *asshat* might have a different opinion of his looks.

"You wouldn't have to know anything about farming or ranching," the mayor continued. "You could learn those skills if you wanted, or you could do something else. There's plenty of work around here, but it'd be your choice. I'm opening the world to you here, son. Just say yes."

It was tempting, Wash had to admit, even as he watched the silhouette of the woman on the second-floor apartment sit down on the edge of her bed and slip on a pair of pants. She was tall, with long hair, and from what he'd seen of her outline, slim and athletic. He wondered what she looked like in real life.

"There are plenty of single women who don't have kids yet," the mayor said. "You have choices, is what I'm saying. A lot more than what's out there, I'd bet. A lot more than what's down south in Texas. Think about it. Harrisonville can use someone like you; you could make a good home here."

"It's not about choices..."

"Isn't it?"

"No. I gotta go south. That's not a choice. That's just something that is."

"You *have* to, or you *want* to?"

"I have to."

"That's too bad."

Yeah, it is too bad, Wash thought as the woman blew out the candle and her apartment went dark, her figure vanishing along with the light.

He heard the Old Man's voice in his head, saying to him, *"The job's done. It's time to move on to the next one. Next!"*

Next...

Wash looked over at the mayor. "When you hired me to clear out those ghouls in the woods, you said you hadn't seen another slayer in years. Is that right?"

The mayor nodded. "Yes. Why?"

"There was someone else in the woods at the same time as me. A woman."

"Another slayer?"

"I don't know. Maybe."

The mayor seemed to think about it for a moment. "We didn't hire anyone else. Just you. If there was another slayer out there, she was on her own. Did she say what she was doing around here?"

"She didn't stick around to answer my questions."

"Sorry I can't help you, son," the mayor said. "I don't know why anyone would be out there at night, alone." Then, with a grin, "Well, you know what I mean."

Wash grinned back. "Yeah, I know what you mean."

But his mind was already back to a few hours ago, when he got his first glimpse of the ginger as she moved through the woods without any semblance of fear.

Who are you?

The question nagged at Wash long after he collected his payment and rode out of town a few hours later, with the morning sunlight in his face. He knew a dangerous person when he met one, and the redhead was that. Not only because she could handle herself out there with just a knife, but the way she had gone from looking like she wanted to kill him to smiling at him a moment later.

Which made what she'd said to him even more ironic:

"There are a lot of dangerous people out there these days. You can never be too careful."

FOUR

He walked into Harrisonville on foot with supplies that barely filled out half of his pack's available space and rode out on a big brown-orange horse while pulling a light black one behind him as a pack mule. It wasn't a bad haul for a day's work, and being mounted instead of walking was going to greatly increase his speed heading south.

"You have choices, is what I'm saying," the mayor had said. *"A lot more than what's out there, I'd bet. A lot more than what's down south in Texas. Think about it. Harrisonville can use someone like you; you could make a good home here."*

He had thought about it, during the conversation and again afterward as he waited for them to saddle his horses. It was a tempting offer, and it still was now as he put the town behind him, the sounds of doors slamming, horse hooves, and people getting ready for another day ringing in the crisp morning air. The mayor had wanted him to stay, but in a day or two they would forget about him as life continued. It was just how it is; he had made peace with that a long time ago, ever since the Old Man first showed him how to fight.

"You were made for this. I knew you were a natural the day I met you."

Was that a good thing? He wondered what his mother would say if she knew about the path he'd taken, or the one he was on now. Like so many others, she hadn't survived that first night of The Purge. Wash could hardly remember what she looked like six years later. It was something he hated to admit, but it was the truth. Maybe, he thought, that was for the best. Would she approve of what he had become now?

It doesn't matter. She's gone. Just like a whole lot of other people...

He rode along a dirt path barely larger than a single road lane flanked by thick towering trees on both sides. Harrisonville was isolated from the main roads, which was exactly how they liked it. Wash only knew it existed because of the map he carried. Without it, he would have passed the town by, clueless of its existence and vice versa.

The temperature was still low enough that he was glad for his thermal clothing, but warm enough that he couldn't see his breath. He'd hated to burn the shirt and pants from last night, but there was no use in trying to wash out ghoul blood. It always lingered, even when you thought you had gotten every last bit of it. Maybe most people didn't notice, but Wash did.

"I gotta go south," he had told the mayor, and that was the direction he pointed the big brown-orange horse now, while the black carried most of his supplies behind him. A lead rope attached to the black's bridle and wrapped around Wash's saddle horn ensured the animal wouldn't take off.

Horsepower was the preferred mode of transportation

these days, with gasoline being a pain in the ass to find. That hadn't been the case during The Purge year, but the five or so since The Walk Out had seen survivors scattering across the country gobbling up what hadn't rotted or become unusable. Hoarders were everywhere, and people in towns like Harrisonville had collected everything they could around them, some even sending searchers far and wide to claim what was left behind before someone else could stumble across them.

Someone like him, for instance.

Wash got around that, as did most slayers, by providing services in return for payment. *"You got a ghoul problem? We'll kill them for you. For a price."* Someone in Iowa had even made a song from that, based on some horror movie Wash had never seen but heard the Old Man talk about once or twice. Something about ghosts...

He had put a good five or so miles on Harrisonville when he felt that familiar sensation, like a gnat nipping at the edge of his peripheral vision. It was hard to explain, but Wash always had a good sense when someone was watching him, like now.

He remained poised in the saddle and kept the orange-brown moving forward at the same unhurried pace he'd been on for the last hour or so. He kept his head straight while his eyes snapped left and right; the problem was that he couldn't see behind him. The black animal was quiet back there, its unshod hooves *plop-plop-plopping* against the uneven dirt underneath them. The horse Wash was sitting on was similarly unshod, which was common because of the lack of skilled blacksmiths. It was just easier to let them move unencumbered by loud clopping steel shoes.

Wash calmed down his breathing—his heartbeat had accel-

erated slightly—so he could hear better. Gradually, the deliberate *plop-plop-plop* of the horse under him and the one
behind him quieted. Even the familiar *tick-tick-tick-tick* of the
watch began to fade into the background.

He listened, and heard...

Nothing.

He couldn't hear a single thing coming from either his left
or his right, or from behind him that shouldn't have been there.
The only noises other than his own breathing and the animals'
were the birds in the trees. A flock of them, forming a V, flew
by overhead.

Maybe I'm wrong...

If he were, it would be a first. He'd never been wrong
before, and Wash had learned to trust his instincts. It had
saved his life too many times for him to start doubting it now.
There was someone—or some*ones*—out there, watching, and
following him.

"That's what instincts are for," the Old Man once said.
"Either you trust it, or you don't. There's no in-between."

Wash's left hand held the reins while his right rested lazily
on his thigh. The holstered Beretta was within easy reach, and
that was the weapon he would go for first. The Mossberg
590A1 tactical shotgun slung behind him from a strap would
have to remain a backup since unslinging it would take too
much time and effort. The sheathed kukri on his left hip was
also a good weapon as long as whoever was following him
didn't have a gun of their own.

So it had to be the Beretta. The M9 had seventeen silver-
tipped rounds in the magazine with an additional bullet in the
pipe. Eighteen in all. That was more than enough to deal with
whoever was out there...as long as they didn't already have him

sighted with their own gun. In which case he was a dead man, regardless of what weapon he grabbed first.

It wasn't a very appealing conclusion, but wishing for something better didn't make it come true. He'd learned that from the Old Man, too.

Wash took some comfort in the knowledge that if there were guns already pointed at him, they could have shot him anytime and he wouldn't have seen it coming. People got killed on the roads on a regular basis. It wasn't just the complete lack of law enforcement, but also the abundant availability of weapons everywhere. That was just one of many reasons why people like the ones in Harrisonville rarely ventured outside their comfort zone. Only a fool would do that.

He had already planned to stop and let the two horses graze in another hour, but whoever was out there (*Unless you're wrong*) didn't know that. Still using the same unhurried pace, he pulled the orange-brown off to the side of the path and calmly climbed down from the saddle. He tied the reins to a large branch nearby, even though he was pretty sure the horse could snap it if it wanted to. The animals immediately knew what stopping meant and began chewing on nearby green grass while standing side by side.

Wash began stretching, his ears opened for every sound besides his own quickening heartbeat and the chirping of birds in the trees around him. There was a time when birds were too scared to make any noise, but The Walk Out had changed everything for them, just as it had for Wash and the rest of humanity.

When he was done stretching, Wash unzipped his pants with one hand while walking away from the road. He didn't go completely through the charade and pull himself out to take a leak, but he made the motions. He hoped it was enough to convince anyone who might be watching from nearby.

He kept his left hand in front of him while his right drifted over to the Beretta. The pump-action shotgun with the adjustable stock and pistol grip thumped against his back, and Wash was very aware of the loud *crunching* sounds he made with every step he took—

He stopped and spun and drew the 9mm.

It was a fast draw, helped by the advance positioning of the holster along his thigh. What a slayer in North Dakota, after getting a look at it, had laughingly called "a gunfighter's rig." Wash didn't know anything about that; the holster was strapped that low because of experience and trial and error.

He had twisted a full 180 degrees and was once again looking out at the road and the two grazing animals. His forefinger was in the trigger guard while his thumb worked back the hammer even as the handgun swung up to chest level. Wash would have pulled the trigger if he saw danger.

But there wasn't any.

At least, no immediate danger.

There was just the girl—the redhead from last night— standing next to the black horse and rubbing down its thick black mane as she looked across at him. "I thought you were going to the bathroom."

"Jesus Christ," Wash said. "I almost blew your damn head off, kid."

She frowned. "Why do you keep calling me that?"

"Why shouldn't I?"

"I'm twenty-five."

"Bull."

"You wanna see my driver's license?"

He shook his head and gave the adrenaline a few seconds to come down. Finally, he lowered his gun hand and walked back over to her. "You saying you have a driver's license?"

"Don't you?" Before he could answer, she smiled. "Your fly's open."

Dammit, Wash thought and quickly stopped to zip himself up.

He might have caught her smirking when he looked back up, but that couldn't have been true, because her back was already turned to him as if she didn't feel any threat coming from him whatsoever.

I could have shot you. You have no idea how close you came to dying, lady.

Or maybe she did know and was just really good at hiding it. He wouldn't put anything past this one.

The animals in front of the woman continued to graze, oblivious to the almost-violence.

"These are your payment?" the woman asked. In the light of day she was definitely not a *kid*, but he'd already known that after last night and only called her one anyway because of how annoyed she seemed by it. "For killing those ghouls?"

"Yeah," Wash said. He untied the black horse's reins and led it away from her. "You were following me. Don't deny it."

"I won't."

"Why?"

"I made camp outside of town after our run-in. Heard you walking by with your loot."

"It's not 'loot.' I earned them."

"I helped. I killed one of them, remember?"

"I didn't ask you to, so it doesn't count."

"Is this why your partner left? Because you don't like sharing?"

He grunted but didn't give her the satisfaction of an answer. He knew a probing question disguised as a snarky remark when he heard one.

You're not that smart, lady.

She walked over to the orange-brown and began rubbing its mane. The horse lifted its head slightly to look at her before letting out a soft whinny of approval and returning to its breakfast. "He's a beautiful quarter horse."

"He's worth more than a quarter," Wash said.

"Funny."

"What was?"

She squinted across the saddle at him. "Oh. You weren't trying to be funny." She smiled. "I was referring to the horse. It's a quarter horse breed."

"I knew that."

"Of course you did."

"Not that I care what it is. I just ride them."

"You should care precisely because you ride them. You depend on them. We all do, now."

Wash walked over to the orange-brown and looked across the saddle at her from the other side, and for a second he forgot what he was going to say.

It was her eyes. They were amazingly green, even more so now in the morning sunlight. Her skin was just as pale and her hair just as bright red as they had been last night, but they also looked...different somehow. Even that sharp, impish nose of hers—

She was smiling at him. "I know I'm pretty, but I'm not *that* pretty."

"Usually people wait to be complimented," Wash said.

"I have a feeling neither one of us has time to wait for something to happen."

They spent the next few seconds staring at each other in silence. He waited for her to flinch or look away first, but she didn't. Instead, she busied herself rubbing down the orange-brown while holding his gaze. He wished he could say she was unattractive, but she wasn't wrong. She was right, though; she was pretty, just not *that* pretty. He'd seen prettier.

"What do you want?" he finally asked. "It better be good, because you almost got yourself killed for it."

"Don't be so dramatic. I knew you weren't going to shoot me."

"People get shot all the time out here and no one ever finds out because their bodies disappear when night falls. What makes you so special?"

"I'm not, but I knew you wouldn't shoot me." She touched her nose. "Not after I punched you and you didn't hit back. You have a lot of self-control, even after fighting those ghouls. Most people wouldn't have been able to resist after all that adrenaline." She smiled. "You're good at what you do. That's obvious to anyone with eyes."

He squinted back at her, not exactly sure what was happening. Was she trying to play some kind of mind games with him? Was this all a prelude to something else?

But it was hard to read her face. It didn't help that he kept being drawn back to her eyes and that easy smile. That *too* easy smile.

"What do you *want*, lady?" he asked, injecting just enough menace to let her know he wasn't going to play her games—and hoped it was at least partially convincing.

"You're headed south. So am I."

"So? What's that to me?"

"You have two horses."

"That's right. *I* have two horses."

"You don't need two horses."

"I have supplies."

"You can spread them out between the two animals. Besides, a Tennessee Walker isn't bred to be used as someone's pack mule."

"You're giving my horses names now?"

Again, that smile that could have been condescension or amusement, or maybe both. "The black one's a Tennessee Walker breed."

Dammit, Wash thought, and said, "We're not in Tennessee."

"And you can find Arabian horses in America, too. What's your point?"

"My point is, you're not getting it. Or the quarter horse."

"Why not?"

"For one, you nearly got me killed last night."

"You nearly got *me* killed last night."

"I saved your life."

"I didn't need saving."

"There were four of them."

"I was prepared to fight double that."

He narrowed his eyes at her, unable to decide if that was all false bravado coming out of her mouth or if she actually believed it. Like the last time, she held his gaze, and he had a feeling it wouldn't matter how long he stared, because she wasn't going anywhere.

"You're headed south, and so am I," the woman said. "We

can travel together. It's safer that way. Like you said, people get killed on the road all the time."

"You don't even know where I'm going."

"South."

"South is a wide, wide direction, lady."

She smiled again.

"What?" Wash said, and that time the irritation came easily.

"*Lady* is better than *kid*."

"Who cares."

"I'm Ana."

"I don't care."

"What's your name?"

"It doesn't matter what my name is or where I'm going. You're not coming with me or getting one of my horses."

"I'll trade you."

"With what?" Wash asked, and before he realized what he was doing, he looked her up and down.

She was still wearing that black leather jacket from last night, a plain white T-shirt underneath it, and the same denim jeans that were probably a little too tight. It was the first time Wash had met a slayer who didn't outfit themselves in cargo pants or the kind of clothes that came with a lot of pockets for extra supplies. He was pretty sure the woman couldn't have fit anything beyond a pack of gum into those blues.

She wasn't wearing a gun belt and had nothing that looked like a gun on her that he could see. Not that she was unarmed, because he remembered how that knife had slid into her palm from inside her jacket sleeve last night. She carried a tactical pack behind her that was clearly carrying dwindling supplies. If he'd met her this morning for the first time, he wouldn't have believed she was anything other than a frightened woman looking for some company on the road, and maybe he would have bought her story.

Maybe that's her game. Lure the threat in, then take them out at close range.

"How long have you been out here by yourself?" the woman who called herself Ana asked.

Too long, Wash thought, but he said, "Long enough to know better than to give one of my horses away for nothing."

"When was the last time you rode with someone?"

Wash smirked, because he understood what she was trying to do with the question. It was her third attempt to figure out what he was doing out here without a partner.

He said instead, "Answer my question. What do you have to trade?"

"I have something you want. Kopiko."

He gave her a confused look. "I thought your name was Ana."

She unslung her backpack and unzipped it, then pulled something out before tossing it across the saddle to him.

Wash snatched it out of the air. It was a bag with the words *Kopiko Instant 3 in 1 Brown Coffee* written across it, along with a picture of a steaming mug of coffee.

"Coffee?" Wash said.

"What did you think I was offering?"

He ignored the question and asked her instead, "How do I know it's not expired?"

"Open it and find out."

"I will. How many do you have?"

"That's for me to know. But I'll give you one every

morning as long as we're riding together. When we decide to go our separate ways, I'll split whatever I have with you."

"How do you know I don't already have coffee? Or that I even drink it?"

She smiled.

"You were in Harrisonville," Wash said. "The mayor told you."

She shrugged. "Maybe. Do we have a deal or not?"

"Mind as well tag along."

"Might as well."

"What?"

"It's 'might as well,' not 'mind as well.' Common mistake."

Wash grunted. "I want two bags every morning now."

"Two?"

"Yeah, two. Just for being so annoying."

"One."

"Two."

She sighed. "All right. Two."

Wash pocketed the bag. "And you take the Georgia Runner."

"Tennessee Walker."

"Poh-tay-to, poh-tah-to," Wash said.

He turned around and grinned to himself. He'd entered Harrisonville on foot with an almost empty pack and ended up with two horses and enough food, water, and ammo to keep him from having to hire out again as he made his way down to Texas.

And now he had coffee, so things were definitely starting to look up.

"I saw that," Ana said behind him.

Dammit.

FIVE

"What's your name?"

He didn't answer her when she asked the first time.

Or the second time.

On number three, he finally broke down.

"Wash."

She might have almost laughed. Almost. But she caught herself in time and just allowed a small smile to slip through.

"Like car wash?" she asked.

He sighed. "Yeah. Like car wash."

"Is that short for something?"

"Yup."

"It's not washateria, is it?"

He shot her a quick look, and she laughed.

"I'm sorry," she said.

"No, you're not."

"I am. Really, I am. It's not polite to laugh at someone's name, and I was raised better than this. So I'm sorry."

He shook his head and faced forward and wondered how long this nascent partnership of theirs was going to last before he lost it. Were bags of instant coffee really worth all the hassle he was going to have to endure? He hadn't even tasted the one she gave him yet, so he didn't know if her part of the bargain was even any good. Instant coffee could last for years—sometimes decades—but the flavor was always the first to go. And without flavor, what was the point?

They had been riding for about ten minutes with Ana on the Walker to his right. He had shifted some of the bags over to his big orange-brown to lessen the load on the other animal, and he no longer had its reins cinched to his saddle horn. So what exactly was keeping her from kicking the horse's flanks and taking off? Well, there was the Beretta in his holster...

Right. As if you could actually shoot her if she did take off.

But she didn't try to run with the horse or the supplies, and he didn't understand why. It wasn't because she wasn't a risk-taker. Everything he knew about her since last night pointed to the exact opposite.

So why was she still riding next to him?

She wants something, obviously.

What, is the question.

He didn't buy that she just needed someone to ride south with her. While it was true that the roads were dangerous, and people did die or go missing on them often, she didn't strike him as someone who feared the unknown. So what was she? What was her end game?

Wash had a feeling, though, that he was only going to find out the answer to that one when she wanted him to know.

"What about you?" he asked.

"What about me?" Ana said.

"What's Ana short for?"

She didn't answer, but she did smile at him. She did that a lot, and he couldn't help but ask himself how much of it was genuine. The lack of overt weapons on her, the tight jeans, the easy smile... How many of those things were all part of her *I'm not dangerous, come a little closer so I can stab you in the neck with my hidden knife* presentation?

"I'll make you a deal," Ana said. "I'll tell you everything you want to know about me when we get to know each other a little better."

"What makes you think I want to know everything about you?"

"Don't you?"

"You think way too highly of yourself, lady."

"It's human nature to be curious."

"I'm not the curious type."

"I don't believe you. They call it 'human nature' for a reason. It's in all of us."

"Not me."

"Uh huh."

He gave her an annoyed look. Maybe he didn't *want* to wait to find out her end game. "What's your deal?"

"Deal? I don't have any deals that I'm aware of."

"Yeah, you do. Last night you were ready to cut my throat. This morning you're begging to be my friend."

"'Begging?'"

"Basically."

That smile again. "Things change."

"Like what?"

"Harrisonville gave you horses."

That's it? I don't buy it, he thought, but said, "So that's all it takes, huh? Get something you want, and suddenly you're all nice and friendly?"

"That's how the world works, Wash. Or haven't you noticed?"

"What were you doing out there last night, anyway?"

"You first."

"You know what I was doing. My job."

"And that's all it was?"

Wash didn't answer right away and tried to recall all the things he might have said to her last night.

Dammit. I asked her about One-Eye, didn't I?

Shit. Should have kept my big mouth shut.

"That's all it was," Wash said anyway. "Now it's your turn, so spill it."

She flashed him that amused look that told him she didn't believe him for even a second and wanted him to know it. But she said instead, "You know where Omaha, Nebraska, is?"

"Home of the Little League World Series?"

"You've been there?"

"I've been around pretty much everywhere once or twice."

"I was resettled in a town nearby, alongside the Platte River. It was called N15 during the occupation, but the residents changed the name to Newton after The Walk Out. A friend of mine from there went missing, and I came down here looking for her."

"Was that what you were doing last night? Looking for your friend?"

"Yes, in a manner of speaking. My friend stopped at a campsite near the Nebraska-Kansas border a few days ago. I found ghoul tracks there. That's how I followed them down here into Kansas, then outside of Harrisonville."

Wash recalled the way she was going from nightcrawler to nightcrawler, staring at their faces.

"You thought she might have been turned," Wash said.

"She, or some of the other people that were with her."

"You know you can't tell even if she had been. The transformation—"

"I know," Ana cut him off. Then, with less conviction, "That's what they say, anyway."

"Because it's true. Once you turn, you don't look like yourself anymore. You're just another black-skinned bag of bones. A husk of what you once were. That's it. End of story. Next."

She shot him a quick, annoyed look. "It's not that simple. She's my friend. I'm going to find out what happened to her, one way or another. Whether she was turned or not, I'm going to find out. I can't go back to Newton until I do that."

Then you're going to be spending a lot of time running around out here, lady.

But he said, "So you're a tough chick on a mission, is that it?"

"And what are you?"

"I'm not a chick."

"No, but you're a tough something on a mission, too, aren't you? What were all those questions about a one-eyed ghoul? I didn't even know they could lose an eye. I thought they always regenerated. I mean, they can do that with entire limbs, for God's sake. Why not an eyeball?"

It was a good question, and Wash hadn't known it was possible, either, until he had seen it with his own eyes.

But Wash didn't say anything.

"I told you my story," Ana said. "Not fair you're keeping quiet. You haven't even told me why you're running around out here alone. Slayers always work in pairs."

"Not always."

"No, not always. But almost always."

"I bet half of what you told me isn't true. Maybe more than half."

She shrugged. "That's your prerogative to think that. All I know is that you asked me about a one-eyed ghoul last night. One of those blue eyes."

He focused on the road and continued to ignore her.

"Fine," Ana said. "Keep being an asshat."

"Act your age, lady. Calling people *asshats* is what a ten-year-old would do."

"Don't want me to call you an asshat? Stop acting like an asshat, then."

Wash sighed and tried to come up with a perfectly good reason why he didn't just shoot her now, take back the Tennessee Walker, and continue south alone again. Except this time he would be able to add a backpack full of instant coffee to his inventory.

Stop pretending like you could actually shoot her in cold blood. You couldn't even hit her back after she punched you last night, for God's sake.

"Did it kill someone you loved?" she was asking him.

He glanced over at her. "Seriously?"

"What? You thought I'd just give up?"

"Well, yeah."

"I don't give up that easily. I never have, and I never will."

"Just let it go."

But she didn't. "I know silver doesn't kill them. The blue eyes, I mean. Not the way it does the black-eyed ones. Was that how it lost its eye? Did you or someone shoot or stab it in the eyeball with silver? That must have been something."

He didn't answer, not that she seemed to care. Ana tilted her head as she ruminated over her own questions, and he got the sense she wasn't even talking to him anymore.

"We still don't know all that much about the ghouls," she continued. "They have three weaknesses. Silver, sunlight, and bodies of water. Someone told me it was something in the water. A combination of mercury and chemicals and who knows what else that sinks them like stones if it gets down their throats. I saw it, you know, a couple of them in the Platte River. They looked like those gargoyles you see perched on the edge of rooftops in the cities. Their skin had turned rock hard, like granite."

Ana paused for a moment, the Tennessee Walker moving casually underneath her. She wasn't even looking at him as she kept talking.

"There are so many things we still don't know about them. Why does silver kill the black-eyed ones just like"—she snapped her fingers—"that, but barely slows down the blue eyes? Why does a headshot have almost no impact on the black eyes, but is the only thing that can kill the blue eyes?" This time, she turned in his direction. "Do you know?"

He shook his head. "No."

"I don't know why I asked. You're just a slayer. I haven't met a slayer yet who gave two cents about what makes the ghouls tick. You guys aren't in it for answers. It's all about revenge, isn't it?"

He narrowed his eyes at her. "You talk about us as if you're not one of us."

"I'm not."

"Bullshit."

She shrugged. "Believe what you want, but I'm not one of you."

"I saw what you did last night. You may not dress like us, but you're definitely one of us."

"Why? Because I know how to use a knife?"

"Because you weren't scared. You walked into those woods *looking* for nightcrawlers."

"A lot of people aren't afraid of the night anymore. The Walk Out changed everything."

"And a lot of people can't do what you did."

"Just because I didn't devote the rest of my life to going around the country looking for monsters to kill doesn't mean I can't defend myself."

Wash let out a short laugh. "You're full of shit, lady, and you know—"

He didn't get the chance to finish. It wasn't even the pain—it was the *shock*.

The shock of being *shot*.

The first bullet knocked him off his saddle, and the second one sailed over his head because he was already tumbling to the ground when it was fired.

Wash hadn't heard a gunshot either time, but before he could fully grasp what had happened (*I've been shot. Jesus Christ, I've been shot!*), he was crashing to the dirt road, and the sharp edges of the Mossberg slung over his back was digging into his flesh from a dozen different points.

"Wash!" Ana screamed.

Her voice was echoing in his ears as he managed to roll over onto his stomach and reached for the Beretta, wrapping his fingers around its cold grip. He lifted his head and looked down the road at the same time, just as dark-clad figures emerged out of the trees on the left side.

At first he thought the ground had come alive, but his mind quickly adjusted and saw them for what they were: Men in ghillie suits. The barrels of their rifles were abnormally long, and he thought, *Suppressors. They're using suppressed weapons. That's why I didn't hear the gunshots! It's an ambush!*

The word *ambush!* was still reverberating around in his skull as he pulled the Beretta and at the same time attempted to focus on the attackers. Why was it so damn hard to focus? Because he'd been shot, and there was a pretty good chance his body was, at this very second, going into shock from blood loss.

But he managed to get the 9mm out anyway and was trying to point it when something stopped him. His hand simply froze, and he wasn't sure why—

Ana was crouching next to him (*How'd she get down here so fast?*), and one of her knees was pressed against his gun hand, pinning it to the ground while her other hand frantically groped at his side. He wasn't sure what she was doing until he saw bright red liquid squirting through her fingers.

Blood. That's my *blood.*

Wash looked up at her as he struggled to comprehend what was happening. Everything was still moving at regular speed—that slowing down of time that he'd come to rely on so often to save his life hadn't kicked in and he couldn't understand why.

Ana's eyes were fixed on him, and strands of red hair had fallen loose over her face.

"What...?" he managed to get out.

"Don't," she said, shaking her head. "They'll kill you."

He had difficulty processing what she was saying. Of *course* the men in ghillie suits charging up the road toward them right now were going to kill him. They had already made that blatantly clear when they shot him off his saddle. And when they finally reached them (*Any minute now*), they were going to finish the job.

So why was Ana not letting him fight back before that happened?

She had leaned down and was whispering. "Trust me, Wash. *Trust me.*"

Trust you? he wanted to reply. He didn't know her, had just found out her name less than an hour ago, so why did she expect him to "trust" her?

And yet, and yet there was something about the way she was looking at him that made him want to believe her. That *did* make him believe her.

Don't trust her. She can't be trusted.

Don't trust her!

Not that he could put those doubts into words. He had a hard enough time just keeping his eyes open, much less getting anything more than a slight wheezing sound through his gaping mouth.

Growls, more animal than men, approaching them. The ghillie suits. They were coming, shaking the ground with their heavy footsteps. They were shouting something, but he couldn't decipher any of it.

Ana seemed to understand just fine, and she turned away from him and looked up the road. Her face changed in the blink of an eye, morphing from the confident woman who had just told to him to trust her to a suddenly terrified redhead who should have been hiding behind closed doors in a town somewhere in Nebraska instead of out here traveling a dangerous backcountry road with him.

"Don't shoot!" Ana cried, tears streaming down her cheeks. "Don't shoot! Oh God, please don't shoot!"

SIX

Wash opened his eyes to Ana hovering over him. There was light behind her, but it was pale and fading and splashed across what looked like a wooden ceiling.

I'm alive. How am I still alive?

They were in some kind of room, but he couldn't turn his head to see the rest of it. It was hard enough just keeping his eyes open, and doing anything more was beyond his ability.

"Don't move," Ana whispered. "You've been shot."

He winced as pain lanced through his entire body.

"It's not bad," Ana said. "It was a through-and-through. I got them to let me stop the bleeding and bandage it up. You owe me, Washateria."

"That's not my name," he groaned out.

"I know, I'm just messing with you." She glanced up at something nearby. "He's awake. Can you help me?"

Not something, but some*one*.

Shuffling sounds as that someone approached them,

followed by a new voice. "His name's Washateria?" Soft and small, and female.

"Yes, but he likes to be called Wash," Ana said.

"I don't blame him. Washateria. Now that's a name."

Ana looked back down at him, that teasing smile on her lips. "Don't try to move. I couldn't get them to give you anything for the pain, so it's going to hurt for a while. But at least you were unconscious on the way here."

If he could get another groan out, it would have been *I've been shot before, and I'm still alive*, but he was too weak to make the attempt. Instead, he continued looking up—not that he could do anything else; he wasn't even sure he could move his head—as the owner of the female voice appeared next to Ana.

Young, maybe still in her teens, dirty blonde hair draped over an oval-shaped face. She would have been amazingly attractive if not for the dirt on her cheeks and cracked lips.

"Hey, Wash," the girl said. "I'm Marla." She turned to Ana. "Are you sure he'll be okay if we do this?"

"He'll be fine," Ana said.

"But he doesn't look very good."

"He's tougher than he looks."

"Okay, if you say so." Marla didn't look convinced, though. "How are we gonna do it again?"

"We need to roll him over onto his side so I can take off his bandage," Ana said. "I need you to hold him still while I clean and apply some ointment to the wounds and swap in some new gauze. You look pretty strong."

"I'm really not."

"Just make sure he doesn't fall forward or backward while I'm working on him."

Marla frowned. "I'll try."

"Don't try. I'm counting on you."

"Okay," Marla said again, with so little confidence that even Wash, in his current delirious state, could see through. "How did you get them to give you all of this stuff, anyway?"

"I'm very convincing."

"They wouldn't give me anything."

"You probably didn't ask the right way."

"What's the right way?"

"The way that makes them say yes." Then, a slight edge to her voice, "Now, hold him still, okay?"

Ana's face leaned in closer, her green eyes focusing in on him. "I have to move you. It's going to hurt."

He might have nodded, but he couldn't be sure.

"Okay," Ana said, this time to Marla.

"What if I drop him?" Marla asked.

"Don't do that. Just push him up onto his side. *Slowly* and carefully."

"God, this is..."

"Don't think about it. He's a tough guy. He'll survive." She looked back down at Wash. "Easy does it..."

He wasn't sure how "easy" the whole thing went because as soon as he felt a pair of warm hands on his shoulders, his body began moving and the lancing pain became a throbbing tidal wave, and then there was just darkness.

***

"I thought for sure Marla was right and you were going to die," Ana said when he opened his eyes a second time. "You put a real scare into me, Washateria."

"How long...?" he managed to moan out.

"Just a few hours."

"No. Since I was shot."

"Half a day."

That explains the fading light, he thought as he tried to concentrate on Ana's face, using her vibrant eyes to help him focus. He'd never met anyone with green eyes before, and wondered if they were all this spectacular.

"I'm pretty, but I'm not *that* pretty," Ana smiled.

He was staring at her again. He couldn't help it. Besides the fact that her face encompassed pretty much everything he could see at the moment, she was...nice to look at.

"Where...?" he asked, because it was still too hard to turn his head to get a better look at his surroundings. Besides, that would mean turning away from her face, and he didn't want to do that right now.

Ana glanced up and around for him. "Some kind of dirt basement. They took us about another five or so miles through the woods after the ambush. I walked, and you were tossed over the Tennessee Walker. They were kind enough to let me take off your shirt and use it as a tourniquet so you wouldn't bleed to death on the way over here. I'm not sure where we are, exactly. I've never been to Kansas before. I didn't see anything that looked even remotely close to a landmark, though." She shook her head. "Right now, we're under a big building. Some kind of warehouse. Can you smell it?"

He shook his head. Or did he?

"Grease and oil," Ana said. "It's stronger topside. I can smell them through the walls even from down here. I didn't see any big machineries when they were walking us through the place, so maybe it was abandoned before The Purge. Not anymore, though."

Wash tried to get a whiff of what she was talking about, but he came up with nothing. It didn't help that his senses were impaired, which, when he really thought about it, was a blessing. He'd been shot before, and the lingering pain was always the worst part.

Almost, because the really worst part was the absence of the familiar *tick-tick-tick-tick* from his left wrist. It wasn't there anymore, and the sudden realization made him try to sit up.

"Stop it," Ana said. "What are you doing?"

"They took my watch," he groaned.

"Yeah, so? They took everything."

"My watch..."

"It's just a watch."

"It's not."

"There are watches all over this country, Wash. Rolexes, Swiss-this, Swiss-that. You won't even have to pay taxes on them anymore."

"Not like mine."

"What makes yours so special?"

"It just is."

"If you say so." Ana sighed. "Look, don't try to move, okay? You'll just aggravate the wound. Marla and I didn't go through all that trouble and get our hands dirty for nothing. Especially me. I've been covered in your blood since the road. I'm frankly sick of it. Anyway, give yourself time to heal. Here." She picked up a cheap plastic spoon filled with something that looked and smelled incredibly unappealing and held it up to his lips. "It's not exactly gourmet, but you need it more than I do."

He didn't argue and opened his mouth to let the food slip through. His tongue tasted oat and wheat and little else. He would have gagged at the taste if he weren't starving. He forced it down his throat and into his empty stomach, even as he tried to shake the absurd feeling of loss at the watch's absence.

"Is he okay?" a voice asked. Wash recognized it as Marla's, the pretty blonde who had helped Ana change his bandages earlier.

"He will be, as long as we keep them away from him," Ana said. She held another spoon to his lips.

"What if we can't do that?" Marla asked.

"We'll have to, Marla."

"But what if we can't?"

"We'll *have* to," Ana said. There was something in her voice—part confidence and part aggression—that made Marla stop short of asking the same question a third time. "Besides, they're not going to do anything. If they were, they wouldn't have given me medicine and bandages for him."

"Are you sure about that?" Marla asked. "They took Kenny..."

Who's Kenny? Wash thought, but the only thing he got out was a labored wheeze.

"Just remember what I said, okay?" Ana said to Marla. "Do your part, and we'll get through this. I promise."

She promises, Wash thought, watching Ana's face as it was turned toward Marla somewhere else in the basement with them. *And I'll be damned if she doesn't mean it. Holy Christ, can she be convincing.*

He replayed the image of Ana, out in the road, telling him to trust her just before she turned toward the men who had shot him and began crying. The sight of tears streaming down her cheeks had shocked him. *Where did those come from?* he remembered asking himself just before he lost consciousness.

She's one hell of a convincing actress, Wash thought now as he opened his mouth for another spoonful of disgusting gruel. *Thank God she's on my side, or I'd be just another corpse in a backwater road waiting for nightfall to vanish.*

At least, I think she's on my side...

"Who are they?" he whispered, surprised he managed to get out all three words without wincing with the effort.

Ana didn't need him to elaborate on who "they" were. She shook her head. "I don't know. I haven't even seen their faces. They were wearing those things..."

"Ghillie suits."

"Is that what they're called?" Then, not waiting for him to confirm, "They had their faces painted, too. Kind of scary, actually. Like swamp monsters come to life. Except for the guns, of course."

Wash wanted to say, *"I don't think anything scares you easily, lady,"* but decided his strength was better used parting his lips for another spoonful.

"How many?" he asked.

"Four. All men." She pursed her lips. "They were going to kill you, Wash. They were going to finish you on that road."

"They didn't...because of you."

"I cried and clung to you, and generally made a real pain in the ass of myself until they agreed to let me bandage you up. After that, I wouldn't leave your side. I guess they thought I was worth putting up with. Either that, or they have plans for the both of us." She paused again, maybe replaying the events of the day over in her head. "They didn't say anything on the way here, to me or to each other. They must have been together for a while, the way they were communicating with just looks." She smiled down at him. "You're very lucky. I wasn't sure they'd buckle to my demands."

"You took a risk..."

"I played the odds."

"Still risky..."

"Life's a risk these days, Wash. You know that. It doesn't matter who you are or where you live, or how safe you think you are. The risk is always there. It's always real. Only a fool thinks the world is safe again."

Wash stared at her, at the hardness on her face, the maturity in eyes that told him she'd been through more than he'd ever know. It was the very first time he'd glimpsed the real her, and he was almost certain she had let it slip by accident.

And then it was gone, replaced by curiosity pointed squarely at him. "But I'm still trying to figure you out, Wash."

Me? You're trying to figure me *out? Lady, I still don't know who you really are!*

But the only thing that came out of his mouth was, "Why?"

"I've met slayers before, but you're...different. I expected to see scars on you. I expected bite marks all over you. But you don't have them. Your body is clean." She tilted her head slightly. "How is that possible?"

"We're not made in a factory..."

"Yeah, but I haven't just *met* slayers before, Wash. I've sewn a couple of them back to life. I've seen their scars up close. You don't have any. You're the first slayer I've met who hasn't been fed on. Ever, from the looks of it."

"Don't ever let them know you're different," the Old Man

once told him. *"This isn't the kind of business where being different is a good thing, kid."*

Different meant not having the scars of The Purge. For a slayer, that was teeth marks, eternal reminders of what they had gone through. It had been hell on earth for many of them —it had been, for the Old Man. Every slayer Wash had met since had the markings over their bodies—some could hide them with large shirt collars and long-sleeved shirts, but not everyone had that choice. For Wash, it had been a matter of never talking about it, never bringing up the topic. Most slayers weren't nosy anyway, and those who were, you gave wide berths to.

"Who are you, Mr. Wash?" Ana asked, her eyes still trained intently on him.

"My things," he said, hoping to change the topic. "They took them?"

"They're gone. Your guns, that weird-looking knife of yours, even our horses. But we can get them back. Later, when you're better."

If I survive the rest of the day, you mean.

"What do they want?" he asked.

"I don't know. Marla doesn't know, either. She's been down here for two weeks and all they've done is feed her." Ana glanced up (at Marla, Wash guessed), before looking back down at him. "She wasn't taken alone. She was traveling with a friend, Kenny, but they took him a week ago. She hasn't heard from him since."

"Did they...?" he asked, and let the rest trail off.

Ana shook her head. "Not yet. And I'm not sure they will."

He gave her a confused look and could tell Ana shared it. Not just that, but she had probably been thinking about it for even longer than him, because she had been awake this entire time, and it wasn't the kind of question that could be ignored.

"They're...different," Ana said. "They weren't staring at me. It was as if they couldn't care less who I am. *What* I am. You understand?"

He nodded. He understood, even if he didn't, truly.

He said instead, "Be careful, Ana. Be really careful, until we find out what they want."

"Yeah, I know. Trust me, Wash, I know. I'll deal with it when the time comes. You need to just concentrate on not dying on me."

He made an effort to nod and thought it was mostly successful.

After another spoon of tasteless oat and wheat went down just as difficult as the last few times, he said, "Are you sure there's just four of them?"

"So far." She glanced up toward the ceiling. "They don't make a lot of noises up there. I think they've been at this for a while. They've probably gotten really good at it by now."

Wash found the look on her face, even with most of it partially hidden by shadows, and the clear sound of her voice fascinating. She *wasn't scared at all.* He couldn't detect anything that even resembled fear coming from any part of her. It had been the same back in the woods outside of Harrisonville, and again on the dirt road this morning when he'd almost shot her.

Who are you?

Ana looked back at him. "Last one," she said, holding the spoon up. "Marla said they give her three meals a day. But unfortunately, they're all the same thing."

"Did you eat?"

"I had a big breakfast before I caught up to you on the road. Besides, you need it a lot more than me right now. I don't have to keep reminding you, but you're no good to me dead, Wash."

I'm no good to me dead, either, he thought as he forced down the last of the gruel. It was just as disgusting as the first spoonful.

"You feeling better?" she asked.

"Better," he lied. His stomach was still a big empty canyon waiting to be filled. He was so tired and weak (*Can't even turn my head, for God's sake*) he could have kept eating for days and not been full.

"Liar," she said.

And, of course, she can read me like a book, too.

Wash wanted to believe that was because he was too tired to put up a convincing front, but maybe she really was just that good.

"We'll get out of this," Ana said. "But I'm going to need your help to do that." She glanced away, probably at Marla, before saying to him in a quiet, almost conspiratorial voice, "Marla may not be up to it, I don't know. I just know that if we're going to survive this, I'm going to need you."

"Be careful," he whispered.

She smiled at him. "Are you worried about me?"

"Yes..."

"This morning you almost shot me."

"You tried to steal my horse."

"Not true. If I'd wanted to steal your horse, I would have kept following you and waited for you to do something dumb like wander off, and then taken both of your horses."

He narrowed his eyes at her but didn't doubt her for one second.

Ana leaned down even further and whispered into his ear. "Can you keep a secret?"

Do I have any choice?

She sat back and glanced around briefly before her right hand dipped out of frame. It returned a few seconds later, her fingers pinching the black handle of a knife. It wasn't the same one that she'd used on the ghoul last night. This one was smaller, thinner, and she could have been hiding it anywhere.

Just as quickly as she revealed the blade to him, it vanished a heartbeat later.

He mouthed the word (because he was too scared of being overheard), *"How?"*

"That's the problem with carrying around too many weapons; sometimes you lose one and don't realize it until much later," Ana whispered. "He's already come down here and searched me twice looking for it. I doubt he'll do it a third time. He probably thinks he lost it on the way back here earlier, maybe even when he was helping to put you on the horse. Don't tell him, but that's when I took it."

Ana smiled and put a finger to her lips.

Wash grinned up at her, not sure if he was impressed with Ana or scared shitless of what she was capable of.

Oh, who are you kidding. It's definitely a little of both...

...maybe even slightly more of the latter...

SEVEN

He drifted off, though he didn't know when or how, but at least it wasn't because he had lost consciousness like the last two times. The slop he'd forced down his stomach had given him some strength back, but it hadn't been enough to keep him awake. It was for the best anyway, since being awake only meant enduring unnecessary pain.

When he opened his eyes a third time, he expected to hear the *tick-tick-tick-tick* coming from his left wrist, the watch having miraculously returned somehow, but it was instead to the sound of a gunshot—the *bang!* so loud that it seemed to shake the walls, ceiling, and floor underneath him simultaneously.

Gunshot! his mind screamed as he sat up—and instantly grimaced as every inch of him burst with regret.

Too fast. Moved too fast!

He pushed himself up the rest of the way, both palms feeling damp from...dirt? Yes, dirt. He was in a dirt basement, according to Ana. It was underneath and behind him as he forced his way into a sitting position, clenching his teeth the entire time to keep from crying out.

Stop moving, you idiot. Stop moving! his mind screamed, but Wash didn't, because he couldn't. He had definitely heard a gunshot, and that was the signal that something had gone very, very wrong if he ever heard one.

His skull was on the verge of imploding, but he gritted through it and got his best (*first*) look at the basement. He was surrounded by dark packed earth, some of it still clinging to his palms and pants legs and was probably in his hair, too. He couldn't tell the size of the room without a source of light to work with, but it had been big enough to accommodate him, Ana, and Marla all at the same time. It was also big enough that Ana had, on more than one occasion, dropped to a whisper when she didn't want Marla to overhear.

He looked up at the ceiling and could barely make out the wooden boards above. Wash glanced around him, but there were no signs of Ana or Marla. His exposed skin tingled against the cold, and he wrapped his arms around his chest before remembering the wounds. He gingerly pulled up the hem of his thick thermal shirt, careful not to antagonize the holes he knew were down there from the ambush. He couldn't see much of anything except a fresh layer of gauze tape that wrapped all around his waist, its dull color standing out against the near pitch darkness. But just because he couldn't see it didn't mean he couldn't feel—

Bang!

A second gunshot, this one also coming from above him. The first one might have originated from the same location, but he had no way of knowing that. The second shot wasn't loud enough for Wash to think it was directly above him but near enough to be heard—

Bang-bang!

Two more shots, squeezed off in a row, and close enough together that they almost blended into one.

What the hell was going on up there?

Where were Ana and Marla?

He remembered Ana with the knife and recalled telling her to *"be careful,"* and her response of *"trust me."*

Wash trusted her. He did. Not only because he didn't have any choice, but the way she had said it, while looking at him with those green eyes—

Bam! as what sounded like a door slammed, *and it was very close.*

Someone's coming.

Wash tried to get up. It took three tries, and he nearly fell over each time, but he managed to keep pushing upward anyway, using the dirt wall behind him for leverage, until he was finally standing on both feet. He kept one hand on the wall at all times while willing his legs to become steady, to not keel back over...

There. Thank God.

Thank God...

Now that he was (*barely*) up, he wasn't sure what he was going to do next—or if he even could do anything other than stand here pressed against the wall like an idiot. His hair was matted against his forehead, thick with sweat and dirt. He was pretty sure his shirt and pants had blood on them, but he was grateful for the semidarkness that hid the stains. He'd dealt with being stabbed and shot and hurt badly before, but it was always easier when you couldn't see the full extent of the injuries.

"Ignorance ain't always bliss, kid," the Old Man would say.

Tap-tap-tap! as someone raced across the floorboards above him, moving from left to right, and Wash tracked the hurried footsteps to a trapdoor near the center of the room. He hadn't spotted it before because it was made of the same material as the ceiling.

What were the chances it was Ana? Or Marla? They weren't in the room with him, so they had to be up there. How long had it been since he fell asleep? An hour? Two? It had been getting darker when he was last awake, but he couldn't be sure. He could have been asleep for more than a day, for all he knew. That was the problem with getting shot. Time had a habit of slipping through your fingers.

Wash pushed off the wall, stumbling and trying pathetically not to trip on his own legs as he made a jagged line toward the trapdoor. He angled toward the back of the basement so when someone opened the door and peered down, he wouldn't immediately be spotted. Beyond that, Wash didn't have any other plans, which went against everything the Old Man had taught him.

Sometimes you just have to improvise, old timer!

He scanned the place as he moved, looking for weapons. Any weapon. Anything at all. But there was just dirt. Nothing but dirt. Where was the plate that Ana had been feeding him the gruel from earlier? Where was the plastic spoon? Where was *anything at all* that he could use to stab someone with? Either his night eyes were still too poor to make out anything worthwhile, or there really was nothing of value. He wasn't sure which explanation made him feel better. Or if either could.

The ceiling was about ten feet above him. A full story. There was nothing that looked like stairs or a ladder to access the trapdoor from down here, so the only way up was if someone already topside gave you a hand.

A prison. This is definitely a prison.

Clank! as a deadbolt moved on the other side of the trapdoor. Someone was definitely coming down, and they were in a hurry. He thought he could hear heavy breathing, but maybe that was just—

Him. He was hearing himself breathing.

Get control of yourself. Remember what the Old Man taught you!

He watched as the square-shaped door began to move. It lifted slowly, almost grudgingly, allowing shafts of soft white light to flood into the formerly dark basement an inch at a time. Soon, Wash was able to see parts of the black dirt that made up the floor and some of the wall in front of him, but little else. He glanced around, hoping the light would yield something resembling a weapon, but there was still nothing to be found.

I would settle for a plastic plate right about now...

Finally, the door flipped over and landed back down with a *bam!* and Wash glimpsed high rafters in the background. His angle was limited by his position, at the back of the room and too far from the opening to get a good look at what was up there. He couldn't see who had opened the door, but he could hear them moving around. The footsteps were frantic, maybe even slightly desperate—

"Wash!" a voice called from above.

Ana!

He hurried forward and stood underneath the soft lights and peered up. She appeared, looking down through the hole back at him. Sweat clung to her temple, and her face was flushed, as if she'd been running.

"Step back," Ana said. "I'm dropping the ladder down."

He nodded and did as he was told. The ladder slid down through the hole and struck the dirt ground with a nice, solid *thunk*. The steps were painted silver, but the sides were bright red, which Wash guessed made it easier to see in the semidarkness of the basement since there wasn't anything that looked like artificial lights down here.

"Can you climb?" Ana asked.

"Yeah," he said, and hoped it was convincing.

The first rung hurt, as did the second and third and every one after that. He clung onto the ladder and felt it quivering underneath him as if it would come undone against his shaky weight with every step he managed without falling back down to the basement's damp floor. He forced himself up anyway, grimacing and grunting with every inch.

Get up there or you're going to die down here. And you can't die down here because you have things to do. You have things to kill.

Get up there!

Wash thought about the Old Man and how much he owed him, and that forced him to keep moving despite everything.

Because he did owe the Old Man too much to die down here.

Too much to just give up now.

Too much.

Too much!

Ana was there to help him up the final rung. He didn't so

much as step off the ladder as he rolled over and onto his back, and spent the next ten seconds or so trying to regain his breath, to keep his pounding heartbeat from bursting through his chest like some space parasite in one of those movies the Old Man once told him about.

After a while, he finally noticed that he was sitting in dirt and that there were heavy shoe prints all around him, some fresher than others. It didn't take very long for Wash to put two and two together—he, Ana, and Marla weren't the base-ment's first guests. There had been others before them. Others who were ambushed on the road, just like he and Ana had been. How many more? And where were they now?

What the hell is this place?

"You okay?" Ana was asking him. "Wash? Are you okay? Wash, answer me." She was crouched on one knee next to him, holding him up with both hands. "Wash? Wash!"

He nodded and attempted to slow down his breathing so he wasn't hyperventilating. It didn't help with the pain, but it got him over the hump. "I feel like I'm drowning."

He took a second to glance down at his waist and didn't like what he saw. Now that he had lights to see with, he couldn't ignore all the splatters of dry blood soaked into his shirt and pants. God, there was a lot of blood. How was he even still alive?

"Well, suck it up, buttercup," Ana said. "Here, this will help."

He looked over at her, thinking, *Buttercup?* But he forgot all about the insult when he saw what she was holding out toward him.

It was a 1911 model semiautomatic pistol. Black all over, except for the brown walnut grip. There was heft to it when

Wash took the gun, which told him the magazine was either fully loaded or close enough.

"Can you shoot?" she asked.

He nodded. "Yeah."

"I mean, *really* shoot?"

He nodded again. "Yeah, I can."

"Good, because I can't hit the broad side of a barn with those things."

For the first time since he climbed up from the basement, Wash got a good look at Ana.

Loose strands of hair fanned around her small face, the red against her pale skin a stark contrast against the soft lights. Her face was still flushed and there were drying smears (*Blood. That's blood.*) across both her cheeks and lower jaw. The part of her neck that he could see had dark swaths of purple across them, almost in the shape of...hands? When she'd reached over to help him up, he had also glimpsed drying red spots over both hands and their fingers.

"You okay?" he asked.

She nodded and pursed her lips. "I'll be better when we leave this place far behind us."

Ana helped him up, but Wash was glad his back was mostly turned to her so she couldn't see the world of hurt on his face as he staggered onto wobbly feet. He concentrated on his grip on the gun to keep his mind off the pain. He was glad to have the pistol. Hell, he was glad to have any weapon after coming up with goose eggs earlier.

Now that he was (*barely, again*) on his feet, Wash looked around him. They were in some kind of back room lit by a couple of soft white lightbulbs—one on the ceiling and one next to a door in front of them. The place was barren and devoid of decorations, as if its entire reason for existing was to provide access to the basement below.

Basement? That's a prison.

"Come on, we're not safe yet," Ana said. She slipped one arm around him—high up and above his bandages—before taking the first tentative step toward the door. "Put your other arm around me."

Wash obeyed but kept his right hand, with the gun, free. Except for the 1911 she'd given him, Ana didn't look like she'd found any other weapons.

"What happened?" Wash asked.

"Let's talk about that later."

"Ana, *what happened?*"

"Later," she said, and the look on her face told him she wasn't going to change her mind anytime soon.

He sighed. "Where's Marla?"

"She's gone."

"Gone where?"

"I made sure she got out before I came back for you."

"She's out there? Outside? Alone?"

"Don't worry about her. She's got a gun."

"The gunshots I heard..."

Ana nodded. "That was her."

"Who was she shooting at?" was his next question, but he never got it out because the door in front of them snapped open first and a large man with a thick, bushy gray beard filled out the doorframe.

He was massive—at least six-five, and it might have been the pain Wash was trying to battle through, but he swore the guy was at least as wide as a mountain. He was wearing some kind of long johns and a nightshirt, which would have made Wash chuckle if it weren't for the weapon in his hands.

Ana's entire body went suddenly stiff next to Wash, and he thought she was about to say something—maybe shout out a warning—but if she were able to get it out, it would have been lost in the—

Bang-bang-bang! as the Model 1911 bucked in Wash's hand as he squeezed the trigger three times as fast as he could, which was pretty damn fast. He'd been shooting since he was seventeen, and even with two bullet holes in him it was all about instinct.

"Slow is smooth, and smooth is fast," was one of the first things the Old Man said to him when they began his training.

Three rounds should have been enough to take down the mountain man, but they weren't. Instead, the massive figure seemed to stumble as he leaned against one side of the door-frame, and he was still trying to lift the weapon in his hands. It looked like a rifle and had a rifle buttstock, but when the man aimed it at Wash, he got an eyeful of two barrels instead of one. It was a shotgun with two barrels side by side.

"Wash!" Ana shouted.

She didn't have to, because Wash had already decided to shoot the man again, putting three more rounds into his chest as more words of wisdom from the Old Man ran through his head: *"Rules to live by when it comes to gunfights, kid, especially if you want to keep living: Keep shooting until they stop moving."*

That did it, and the man finally lowered his double-barreled shotgun before slowly sliding down to the floor, his large bulk taking up almost all of the open door space.

Wash stared at the dead man along with Ana, neither one of them saying anything for a moment.

Five seconds...

Ten...

"Jesus, I didn't think he was ever going to go down," Ana finally said, before she started them moving toward the door again.

"Grab it," Wash said.

"What?"

"The shotgun."

"That's a shotgun?"

"Looks like a shotgun."

"Let me get you outside first. I don't want you to fall when I let go."

"Good idea. I don't want to fall, either."

Ana helped him get by the dead man. He looked to be in his fifties, dark eyes staring at Wash as they stepped over his splayed legs. The man had bled very little for someone who had been shot six times, and if not for the blank expression on his face, Wash might think he was just really good at holding his breath and not blinking.

They made it onto the other side, a long hallway with concrete floors and walls constructed from heavy metal sheets. Wash leaned back against the cold steel so he wouldn't fall down and flexed his grip on the 1911 again. The gun felt lighter than before, which wasn't good. He'd wasted six shots shooting one man, which left him with...how many? He couldn't tell and didn't trust himself to take out the magazine and count bullets right now.

"God, it weighs a ton," Ana said as she stepped back out through the door with the shotgun. She was going to hand it over to him but quickly realized he wasn't going to be able to carry it, and instead slung it over her left shoulder. "I'll hold onto it."

"Now what?" he asked.

She slipped her arm around him again. "There should be only one of them left, but I don't know where he is. They might have split up"—She glanced briefly back at the mountain man—"and one went after Marla."

"And if he didn't?"

"Then I guess you should shoot him, too, if he pops up."

Wash grinned and nodded. "Yes, ma'am."

EIGHT

"Are you sure this is a warehouse?"

"Yeah. Why?"

"I don't know. It doesn't look like a warehouse."

"What does a warehouse look like?"

"More...warehouse-y."

"That's not very specific, Wash." Ana shrugged. "I guess they had a lot of time on their hands since they took the place over. I'd bet that underground dungeon wasn't in the original floor plans."

"Yeah, I wouldn't take that bet," Wash said.

Wash concentrated on what was ahead instead of what was behind them. His body ached, and every step he took sent slashes of pain through every one of his limbs. He had to keep clutching and unclutching the pistol to make sure he didn't drop it, thankful for the distraction from his physical misery. Ana had the mountain man's double-barreled shotgun hanging off one shoulder, but if they ran into trouble, it was up to him.

Her every focus at the moment was keeping him upright and the two of them moving forward.

Wash tried to think what the Old Man would say if he were here to see the state Wash had found himself in. He imagined a chuckle and a joke, followed by a word of warning. The Old Man was not the most trusting type, and that paranoia had rubbed off on Wash to some extent. It was only normal, given how much time they spent alongside one another.

Except Wash didn't have any choice right now but to trust Ana, because without her he wouldn't have made it out of the basement, much less survived the road ambush. And he was sure the mountain men would have caught him out there by himself. These assholes had a well-oiled operation from years of trial and error. Even if his instincts kicked in and he sniffed them out, would he have survived against four heavily armed men that had gotten the drop on him?

I'm good, but I'm not that good.

He sneaked a peek over at Ana, gritting her teeth as she shouldered him with one arm. She looked even smaller pressed up against his body, but there was nothing weak about her fortitude. He could see that in her eyes—that refusal to give in despite how much she was struggling to keep them both upright.

Ana glanced over and caught him staring. Her smile temporarily replaced the strain on her face. "Eyes forward, buddy. There's at least one more still out there. Maybe even two."

"Two?"

"Maybe two. I'm not sure. It depends on what one of them did."

"Okay, so maybe two, but definitely one?"

"Yes. Maybe two, but definitely one more. So be ready for anything."

"Understood."

"And by that, I mean shoot anything that isn't Marla."

"Yeah, that's what I figured you meant, Ana."

"Just wanted to make sure, that's all."

They hadn't been walking for very long—maybe only a few minutes, maybe not even that—and the corridor was about to come to an end. There was a door on the other end; it was metal like the rest of the building, with the only exception being the basement where he had been held.

"You said Marla escaped?" Wash asked.

Ana nodded. "She's somewhere out there. The faster we get out of here, the faster we can go looking for her."

"Those gunshots..."

"What about them?"

"They were loud."

"And?"

"It's quiet out there, Ana. Loud sounds attract attention, remember?"

It didn't take her very long to grasp what he was trying to say. "Shit. I forgot about that."

Most people do, he thought, thinking about all the townspeople he'd worked for over the years. Men and women who should have known better but still somehow let their guards down enough to need his help. Sometimes there were just one or two ghouls in the area, feeding on the rare livestock that wandered outside at night, and sometimes it was more serious. Wash always hated it when kids were involved.

"She wouldn't have fired those shots if she didn't have to,"

Ana said. "Marla's not a dummy. She knows what's out there, too. Everyone does."

But not everyone remembers in the heat of the moment, he thought, but said, "You said there could be one or two more out there. That means you're sure there's only four of them?"

"I think so."

"So you're *not* sure?"

Ana shook her head and thought about it for a moment. Then, "I didn't see anyone else other than the four that ambushed us on the road."

"This is after they brought us here?"

"Yeah."

"There's no women? Just men?"

"Just men, like the one you shot."

"Like him how?"

"Big. Shaggy beards. They looked like mountain men."

Wash nodded and smiled. He'd thought *mountain man*, too, when he first saw the big one he'd shot earlier.

He glanced back over his shoulder. "If they're all like him, I'm going to need more bullets."

"I have the shotgun," Ana said. "How do you shoot this thing, anyway?"

Wash squinted at the double-barreled weapon slung over her shoulder. It looked just as odd now as it had the first time he saw it, and he wouldn't be surprised if it was something the dead man had cooked up himself. It looked somewhat homemade. There were no hammers that Wash could see, and he could only make out one trigger. That meant every shot either unleashed both barrels at once, or one at a time. He cringed at the possible recoil, but maybe that was why there was such a generous buttstock—to absorb the kick. The weapon didn't have optics mounted on it, even though it did have a rail system on top. Then again, a scope was probably overkill when you could shoot two barrels at once, quickly reload, and fire again. There was a grip attached underneath the forend for easier reloading and, he guessed, stability when firing both barrels.

"Is it heavy?" he asked.

"Like carrying ten logs." Ana grunted.

"Can you use it?"

She gave it a quick glance. "I guess I'm going to have to."

"It looks pretty basic. Pull the trigger, and it fires either both barrels at once or one at a time."

"Which one is it?"

"I don't know; I've never seen that model before. Either way, just keep it aimed at your target until it stops shooting."

"And how long would I need to do that? Keep it aimed?"

"Shouldn't be more than a second."

"'Shouldn't be?'"

He shrugged. "Usually about one second. Use the pistol grip under the barrel to rack it after the shot."

"'Rack it?'"

"Reload a fresh round. Pull the pistol grip back as hard as you can, hear the sound of it reloading, then let it snap back forward."

"Okay..."

"You've never used a pump-action shotgun before?"

"I have. I just never bothered to learn the lingo." She sighed. "I don't like guns."

"Why not?"

"I just don't. Don't ask me to explain."

He couldn't help but chuckle. "After everything that's happened? The Purge? The last five years?"

"Is that weird?"

"Kinda, yeah."

"I guess I'm a little weird."

"I guess so," Wash said when they finally reached the end of the hallway. "Hold on. Let me see if I can hear anything."

She pulled her arm out from around him. Wash quickly grabbed the wall to keep himself upright, then pushed his ear against the cold slab of metal. He slowed down his breathing, then stopped it entirely in order to concentrate on listening for anything—anything at all—coming from the other side.

Ana had unslung the shotgun and now had it cradled in front of her as she stood next to him. The weapon looked way too big for her, but then most rifle-length guns probably would have, given her slight stature. She didn't say anything while he tried to listen for sounds and just watched his face for signs.

Wash finally pulled back and shook his head. "I don't hear anything," he said, dropping his voice to almost a whisper just in case he was wrong.

Ana moved closer and leaned against the door before pulling back after a few seconds. "Me neither."

"What's on the other side?"

"The main part of the warehouse, including the front doors. The rooms they were staying in—their living quarters—are on the other side."

"This is just one part of the building?"

She nodded.

"What else did you see?" he asked.

"Some ATVs and a stable."

"Stable?"

"With about a half dozen horses inside. Including ours. There were also bundles of stuff covered with heavy tarp. I don't know what's underneath them. Probably just boxes with extra supplies."

"How many times did you walk through this place?"

"The whole place from end to end? Twice. When they came for me and Marla, and later when I ran back for you."

He thought about what she'd told him, before saying, "Living quarters, stables, vehicles. I guess they really have been here awhile."

"Who knows for how long."

He turned back to the door before pushing slightly off the wall. He changed up his grip on the 1911. "I'll go through first."

"Are you sure?"

"Yeah."

"You can barely stand. You almost fell down a second ago."

"Almost only counts in horseshoes and grenades."

She gave him an amused look.

"What?" Wash said.

"Sounds like something an old man would say."

"I got it from an old man."

"Well, that explains it." Then, with her serious face, "But are you sure you're not going to fall right through that door as soon as it opens?"

"I'll be fine."

She gave him a doubtful look but didn't say anything.

He nodded at the weapon in her hand. "You come out behind me, then move to my left side with that thing."

She glanced down at the shotgun, then gave him the least confident look he'd seen on her since they'd met.

"Remember," Wash said, "if it fires both barrels at once, you can move the gun immediately. Most shotguns give you a twenty-five yard maximum range. Assuming it's got buckshot and not slug rounds."

"I don't know what that means, Wash."

"Basically, just keep shooting until whatever's in front of you goes down. Put the buttstock against your shoulder to help with the recoil. That's what it's for."

She sighed. "I really don't want to use this."

"Suck it up, buttercup."

She smirked. "What did I tell you about being an asshat?"

He grinned before turning back to the door.

Wash regripped the pistol, then put his free hand on the lever. Like the door itself, it was cold to the touch, but he quickly got over it.

He looked over at Ana one last time.

She had positioned herself next to him, clutching and unclutching the forend grip of the unwieldy-looking shotgun in front of her. She returned his nod, but it was impossible to miss the apprehensive look on her face.

Wash faced the door again. He sighed and wondered what was going to kill him first: Whatever was waiting for them on the other side or just the act of moving on his own without Ana's assistance.

Fuck it, he thought and didn't bother counting down before he jerked on the lever, felt the door starting to open, and helped it by pushing hard and stepping through at the same time.

Too fast, as it turned out, and pain screamed through every part of him, but Wash clenched his teeth and kept moving anyway. He lifted the 1911 to chest level and took aim, thankful for the lights inside the adjoining rooms that allowed him to see. It wasn't just the artificial kind, either, but also a large swatch of moonlight coming through an open door.

Time slowed, and his every heartbeat became sledgehammers pounding away against asphalt in his chest. His breath formed small clouds in front of his face as Wash saw, in the next few seconds:

Two doors to his right—a regular-size one and a much larger garage door next to it that could slide up to the ceiling. Even if Ana hadn't already told him they were somewhere in a forested area, Wash would have figured it out just by looking through the *open door* and spotting the field of trees beyond.

Two ghouls feasting on the remains of a man wearing a thick black coat lying on the floor about a couple of meters from the door. The creatures were hunched over the body, one of them practically buried in the man's thick black beard. The *slurp-slurp-slurp* was the only sound in the entire place, but that was quickly broken by the loud whinny of a horse.

A small motor pool of ATVs to his left—but nothing bigger than a four-wheeled off-roader—and a makeshift stable near the back. Horses—a big orange-brown one among them—were locked behind iron bars that looked more like a prison cell than housing. The bars were the only reason why two more ghouls couldn't get inside at the animals, not that that was stopping them from trying anyway. One of the nightcrawlers had almost successfully squeezed itself through two of the bars, even as the Quarter Horse and another smaller brown kicked at its defenseless head with their hind legs.

He would have opened fire immediately, except there were no reasons to. The ghouls bent over the dead body were oblivious to his and Ana's presence, as were the two trying to get into the stables at the back.

His heartbeat returned to normal, as did the movements of the cold air around him, and Wash exchanged a quick look with Ana. "Silver bullets?" he asked.

She shook her head. "I don't know. Has to be, right?"

"Has to be." He nodded, but thought, *Please be. Please be!*

Wash looked back over at the ghouls in front of the door just as one of them lifted its head and glanced back. *At him.* A paint of fresh blood coated the area around its mouth and dripped from its chin, and though Wash had accepted long ago that the monsters were no longer capable of emotions, he swore there was something that almost looked like...bliss (?) in the creature's hollowed black eyes.

It saw him, but it didn't get up to attack. Instead, the night-crawler returned to its victim and was bending down to rejoin its companion, chewing and slurping loudly on the man's neck, when Wash shot it in the back of the head.

The ghoul collapsed forward and lay still on the dead man's chest, and Wash thought, *Yup. Silver bullets.*

The second creature lifted its head, its face almost completely covered in a sheen of thick red wetness. It seemed to almost scowl at Wash just before he shot it in the face—the bullet punched through its weak skull and *pinged!* off the metal wall behind it—and this ghoul, too, collapsed over the dead man it had been feasting on.

Wash stared at the body buried underneath the two ghouls for a moment, but he couldn't tell what the man looked like. Most of his face was gone, with just a hole where his nostrils once were, and a lump where—

Boom!

The entire warehouse shook with the explosion coming from next to him. It was so close that Wash was pretty sure every part of him could feel it, including his bandaged side.

Another ear-splitting *boom!* rang out almost exactly half a second later.

Wash looked to his left. Ana, holding the shotgun with the buttstock against her shoulder. She was staring forward, wide-eyed, at one of the ghouls. Or what was left of it. The top part of the undead thing's head was gone, and there was a hole the size of Wash's fist in its chest. It lay on the floor where it had fallen, halfway between them and the stable.

She turned to him, lowering the shotgun, her entire body trembling slightly. "It fires one at a time."

Wash smiled. "How's the kick?"

"Actually not bad. The second shot surprised the hell out of me, though." Ana nodded toward the stable. "What about that one?"

The last ghoul was still attempting to squeeze itself through the bars, oblivious to the violence behind it or its dead fellow ghouls. It was trying, but it couldn't quite get its entire head past the available space, not that it let that little inconvenience stop it from continuing to push, and push... The horses were still kicking at it, landing blow after blow on its arms and legs and skull. But that, too, didn't deter the creature for one second.

Stubborn bastard.

Wash took aim at the ghoul's back, but he didn't pull the trigger. He lowered the 1911 instead. "I can't shoot it. The bullet's just going to go right through it and hit one of the horses."

Ana slung the shotgun and walked forward, and suddenly

she had the same knife she'd stolen from one of the mountain men in her right hand.

Where the hell did that come from?

Wash tried to remember if he'd seen her holding the knife earlier, but he couldn't. If he was surprised, he wondered how much more shocked the mountain man had been when Ana plunged it into him. The blood on her face, the bruising around her neck...

She's impressive. And scary.

God, is she scary.

Ana walked right up behind the lodged ghoul, and without hesitation, stabbed it in the back of the skull. The undead thing went limp, its body trapped between the bars. The horses on the other side quickly settled down, but Wash didn't think any of them—five in all, three wisely keeping to the back —were completely relaxed.

Ana turned and headed for the door. She glanced over in his direction as she passed him by. "Sit down. You look like you're about to fall."

"That's because I am," Wash said.

"So sit down."

"Yes, ma'am."

He took a couple of steps back until he found the wall behind him, then slid gratefully down to the floor. He peeked under his shirt at the bandages. The sight of bloodless gauze allowed him to let out a relieved sigh.

Ana stepped around the bloody mess in front of the door in order to get to the door itself. She closed it, then locked it using the deadbolt before scooting over to the large garage door next to it. When she was satisfied, Ana walked back to the three bodies and crouched next to the pile. She stabbed the dead man in the forehead, then stood up—but didn't go anywhere.

"What's wrong?" Wash asked.

"The body," Ana said, staring at the black-clad figure under the two unmoving ghouls. From a distance, their size could almost convince him they were two children lying in their father's arms.

"Which one?"

"The mountain man." Ana crouched and grabbed the dead man by the forehead and turned his head side to side. "I don't recognize him."

"How can you tell? Ana, he doesn't even have a face anymore."

"It's not his face, it's his hair." She glanced toward the door. "It's blond."

Wash had to squint to see what she was talking about. The dead man's hair *looked* blond, but there was so much blood and wetness that it was hard to tell from across the room.

"So?" Wash said.

"There were four of them, and they all had dark hair." Ana stood up and looked around the warehouse before quickly, nervously unslinging the double-barreled shotgun and racking it, the *clack-clack!* of the shells reloading echoing off the metal walls. "Wash, there's still one more unaccounted for. He might still be in the building..."

NINE

Ana might have been right and there might have been one more mountain man running around somewhere in the building with them, but he hadn't shown his face even after all the noise they had made. Wash's gunshots would have traveled to every inch of the place, never mind the double blasts from her double-barreled shotgun.

And yet, no one appeared from the other side of the warehouse or tried to bang their way back in through the front doors. According to Ana, there was no back way in or out that she was aware of, but she made sure to emphasize the *that she was aware of* part.

Wash remained in the same spot where he had sat down, next to the door that led into the west side of the warehouse, while Ana disappeared into the hallway across the wide open space. She hadn't hesitated and hadn't even given him the option of talking her out of it.

"Stay here. I'll be back as soon as I can," she had said before taking off.

As if I could stop her, Wash thought as he watched her slip through another door a good fifty yards or so across from him.

It was a large place, but how much of it had been here before the mountain men added to its size over the years? He could see signs of recent construction everywhere, from the not-quite-finishing along the walls all the way up to the rafters.

Wash laid the 1911 semiautomatic on his lap and let himself enjoy the peace and quiet, all the while listening for evidence that Ana had stumbled across her prey. If the fifth mountain man existed in the first place, anyway. But Ana was so sure, and he was leaning toward believing her. After all, she was the only reason he was still alive, and he guessed he owed her the benefit of the doubt.

And then some.

He glanced over at the thick puddle of blood, where the blond and his killers lay in front of the door. All the signs pointed to the poor sap opening the door and being pounced on immediately. That was the only explanation for the lack of blood, anyway, except at the spot where he currently lay. If Ana was right, then that would mean there were five of them instead of four.

"That has to be it," she had said. "I only saw four, but there could easily have been a fifth one somewhere doing something else while they were taking me back and forth."

He had to admit, Ana was an impressive woman. It was too bad she also scared the shit out of him. He hadn't asked how she'd gotten away from their captors and managed not only to help Marla escape, but come back for him. Maybe, just maybe, he was a little afraid to find out the answer.

What are you so scared of? She's barely five-something and weighs less than a ten-year-old, for God's sake.

And yet, and yet...

Wash suddenly looked up and lifted the pistol at the same time when he heard footsteps approaching.

It was just Ana, coming out of the door on the other side. She had a backpack in one hand and the shotgun in the other.

Already?

Wasn't it just a few minutes ago that he watched her walk through that same door? It felt like it, but Wash didn't discount the possibility he might have dozed off and didn't realize it. Either that, or getting shot was playing havoc with his grasp of time.

"Did you find him?" Wash called over.

Ana shook her head. "If he's still here, he's got a pretty good hiding place."

"Why would he be hiding?"

"I don't know. Maybe he's scared of me."

Wash smiled, but he thought, *And I wouldn't blame him one bit.*

"Or maybe he's out there chasing Marla with the other one," he said instead.

"Or that," Ana nodded. She glanced over at the closed door. "Marla has a gun, so she's not completely helpless."

Out there, at night by herself, she's going to need more than a gun, Wash thought, but he said instead, "What's in the bag?"

"Something to keep you alive," Ana said as she crouched in front of him. She put down the shotgun and unzipped the bag.

"That's good. I like staying alive."

"Who doesn't?" She took out a half-empty sheet of pills and popped out two of them. "Ultracet. You know what those are?"

"Do I look like a pharmacist?"

"Tramadol and Acetaminophen." She handed the pills to him, along with a bottle of water, then slipped the rest of the pill sheet into one of his cargo pants pockets. "Two every four hours as long as you need them. Eight per twenty-four hours maximum."

Wash made a face. "You know I've been shot, right?"

"Don't go over eight a day."

"Whatever you say, doc."

She squinted back at him. "I'm serious."

He gave her a mock salute before downing the pills and chasing them with the water. "How much water do we have?"

"More than enough. Drink it all."

He didn't argue and finished off the bottle. It was warm, but warm was better than none.

Ana had produced a large roll of gauze and placed it on the floor next to him, along with scissors and a small white first-aid kit. "I'm going to have to suture your wounds after this."

"You know how to do that?"

She frowned. "Yes, but it's not fun."

"Hey, I'm the one you'll be sticking needles into."

"That's true, but you'll be so doped up when that happens you won't notice any of it. Me, on the other hand, I'll have to actually *do* it."

He chuckled. "Wanna trade places?"

"Pass."

"What else you got in there?"

She fished out another bottle of water, along with a Beretta 9mm that looked familiar.

"You found my gun," Wash said, taking the pistol from her. "What else?"

"Your shotgun and our supplies. But I left those behind

and only carried over what I could fit in here." She took out two magazines for the Beretta, and Wash pocketed them. "And, oh, this." She held up one of his gloves, with the silver studs along the knuckles. "You made this yourself?"

"Yeah." He took the glove, then its partner, and dropped them next to the 1911. "For close quarters."

"Wouldn't a knife be better?"

"You can't wear a knife."

"Depends on what kind of knife," she said with a grin. Ana next pulled out a see-through bag with jerky inside. "Here. You'll need to get your strength back."

The contents smelled glorious when she opened the bag, but Wash didn't reach for it immediately.

"What's wrong?" Ana asked.

"You said you didn't know what the mountain men wanted."

"And?"

Wash glanced at the bag, then at her, but he didn't say anything.

It took Ana a few seconds, but she finally understood. "You think it's...?"

He shrugged. "I don't know what it is. It could be venison or some other animal. Plenty of them out there now, if you know how to hunt. Did they say anything when they came to get you and Marla earlier?"

She shook her head. "Nothing."

"Where were they taking you, exactly?"

"Somewhere on the other side of the warehouse, but I didn't feel like waiting to find out where exactly."

"Before you made your move..."

She nodded. "I couldn't have done it without Marla. She

was brave, and I guess desperate to get out of here. You can do amazing things when you're desperate."

"You said you got one of them with the knife?"

"I killed one of them and wounded another, but he managed to get away."

"One of those mountain men *ran* from you?"

"He was young. I think he was only a few years older than Marla. Anyway, Marla got his gun during the fight, and he fled up the hallway. After we split up and I was on my way back to you, I saw him running out the door after Marla." Ana looked like she was reliving everything she was telling him. "It was chaotic. I'm not sure why he chased her but not me."

"The one I shot," Wash said. "They probably decided to split up."

"Maybe," Ana said, but she didn't look convinced. He could see her mind working behind her green eyes, trying to piece everything together.

Finally, she looked down at the bag of jerky before holding it up to her nose and sniffing it.

"What does it smell like?" Wash asked.

"Meat," Ana said.

"What kind of meat?"

"I don't know. Is there a difference in smell between deer meat and...something that's not deer meat?"

"You'd have to taste it." Then, "Did you...?"

Ana's face paled. "I wasn't hungry. Too much adrenaline."

"Where did you find it?"

"There's a big pantry in the back. Next to the kitchen."

"What else did you find in there?"

"Just things you'd find in any kitchen."

"Fridge?"

"No."

"They have electricity, so why don't they have a fridge? Did you look everywhere?"

Instead of answering him, Ana threw the bag across the room. It skidded along the concrete floor and slid into a corner where it lay crumpled.

"It could just be venison," Wash said.

"It could be," Ana said. "But they didn't grab Marla because she was a woman. Or me."

"Are you sure about that? I mean, *really* sure?"

She nodded. "Besides what Marla told me—about how they took her friend Kenny but never came back for her—I didn't see it in their eyes, Wash."

"See what?"

"You know what. That thing that all men have." She stared back at him. "That you had when you first saw me in the woods. Then again, on the road. And you still have now," she added with a slight smile.

"Maybe they have another room. A hidden one, like the dungeon in the back."

"Besides the kitchen, I found a game room and an armory. There may be more rooms that I haven't gotten around to yet. I wanted to bring some things back to you first." She snapped another quick look over at the bag of jerky. "There were a dozen of those things back there..."

"There has to be a fridge. Maybe another underground room like that dungeon of theirs. Where would they put all the meat they haven't gotten a chance to dry out yet?"

"I don't know." She shivered slightly and didn't try to hide it. "And I'm not too excited about looking for it, either."

"Don't you wanna know?"

"I don't know. Do you?"

Wash didn't answer her. He wasn't sure he needed all the grisly details, either.

Ana had begun glancing around the warehouse, as if expecting that mysterious fifth man to suddenly appear.

"Forget about the food," Wash finally said.

She turned back to him. "You're not hungry?"

"Not anymore," he lied.

She scooted over and sat down next to him, laying the shotgun across her lap.

"You comfortable with that thing yet?" Wash asked.

"I don't think that's ever going to happen. I like that I don't have to aim, though."

"Shooting takes practice."

"I've done that. A lot."

"And?"

"I got blisters from pulling the trigger so many times."

"There are shooting gloves..."

"That's not the point." She sighed and stared across the room. "If he's still out there, and he's alive, he'll make his way back here..."

"You still think that dead guy's not him?"

"Yes."

"Because you saw four guys with dark hair, and that one's a blondie."

"Exactly."

"If you're right, then there's definitely five of them instead of four. *If* you're right."

She sighed. "I could be wrong. I guess we'll find out for sure by morning. If he doesn't come out by then..."

"Yeah. Morning's good."

Wash leaned his head back against the cold wall and fought through a new surge of pain. He reached down and placed his hand over his side, then glanced over at the bag in the corner. Did it really matter if the meat in there was deer or...something else? He was hungry, and he needed protein in the worst way.

So did it *really* matter?

Hell yeah, it matters.

"You okay?" Ana asked. She was looking at him intently, trying to gauge his reaction.

"If I'm still alive by morning, you can ask me that question again."

"That's not very reassuring, Wash."

"Sorry. I didn't know reassuring you was my job."

"I'm a girl. You're a guy. That is your job."

He smirked. "Yeah, right."

She grinned, before returning her eyes to the door that led into the other side of the warehouse.

"Does it hurt?" Wash asked, touching his neck.

"Shit, I forgot all about that," Ana said, reaching up to caress the redness around her throat. She flinched a bit. "I have blood on my face, too, don't I?"

"Cheeks and jaw."

She took out another bottle of water, then dampened one of her shirtsleeves and wiped at the blood on her face before doing the same to her fingers and palm.

"Marla was okay?" Wash asked.

"She was alive the last time I saw her. I'll try to see if I can find her tomorrow morning. Maybe pick up her tracks."

Ana went suddenly quiet and stared off.

"What?" Wash asked.

"Nothing," Ana said.

"What is it?" he pressed.

Ana didn't answer right away. Then finally, "She reminds me of someone."

"Your friend?"

"Yes."

Wash had been watching her closely, and he caught the glimmer of uncertainty on her face. "Tell me the truth. All of it."

She looked over and they locked eyes.

"The truth," Wash said.

Ana nodded. "Her name's Emily."

"Your friend..."

"My sister."

"Who took her?"

She stared at him for a moment. Then, "You don't care that I lied to you? That I didn't tell you I was looking for my sister in the first place?"

Wash shrugged. It wasn't that he didn't care, but that he always assumed she was lying, that there were things she wasn't telling him. To find out that he'd been right all along wasn't all that surprising as a result. It wasn't about her, but about the world they lived in, where everyone lied. *Everyone.*

"Not really," Wash said.

She smiled. "You're full of surprises, Washateria."

"I thought we went over this."

"You know you like it."

"Goes to show you don't know me that well."

"Yeah, I do."

"Tell me what happened with your sister."

Ana's face grew noticeably darker under the warehouse's soft lights. "Some people took her, along with three others."

"When was this?"

"Over a month ago."

"You've been chasing them for a month?"

"One month, three weeks, and five days. Sometimes it feels like it's been years since I left home."

"How exactly have you been surviving out here with nothing but that little knife of yours?"

"It's easier than you think."

"How's that?"

"I have certain advantages that you don't."

He sneaked a sideways look at her, but he didn't have to think about it for very long. She was pretty, and young, and very capable—he'd since come to learn—of talking her way out of just about anything.

"The closest I've gotten to them was two—no, three days, now—about two miles north of Harrisonville," Ana was saying. "I found their campsite, and those ghoul tracks that led me to the woods outside Harrisonville."

"Where we met."

"Uh huh."

"You told me you were headed south. So that means you know where they're going."

"I have a pretty good idea. They traded with some guys at a cabin, and one of the asshats let slip that they were heading south. I guess they were all drunk on bourbon at the time."

"South is a big place."

"They're going all the way down to the Texas-Mexico border. Some place called Brownsville, close to the Gulf of Mexico. It's their final stop."

"Brownsville..."

"Have you been there?"

"No, but I know where it is. It's a long way south."

"That's why I needed one of your horses. I knew you were headed south, too. Texas, to be precise, so the odds were in my favor."

He snapped her a quick, alarmed glance. "How did you know that?"

"Harrisonville told me."

"They *told* you?"

"Well, the guy who runs the place. I went in there right after you left."

"And he just told you where I was headed?"

"Wash, I'm just an unarmed and helpless young woman traveling alone in a very dangerous world. He thought he was helping me. Even suggested I hurry to catch up to you before you got too far ahead."

"How did you catch up to me, anyway?"

"I ran."

"You ran?"

"I'm faster than I look. Actually, I'm a lot faster than most people. Anyway, it wasn't like you were moving very fast up that road. Still, it wasn't easy running through the woods so you wouldn't see me coming."

He sighed. "Tell me something. You used to be an actress before all of this or something?"

"What makes you say that?"

"You're really good at it."

"At what?"

"Convincing people of whatever you want them to believe. Some would even call it being manipulative."

"And what would you call it?"

"Let me get back to you on that."

She smiled. "No, I wasn't an actress. I worked in an office."

"Now why don't I believe you?"

"I'm hurt, Wash. Really hurt."

"Uh huh."

His stomach growled, and he looked across Ana at the bag of beef. What were the chances...?

No. No way in hell.

"So what's the plan?" he asked instead, hoping to take his mind off his hunger. "Try to catch them on the way down to Brownsville?"

"That's the best-case scenario. If that doesn't happen, at least I know where they'll be eventually."

"Unless those guys at the cabin lied to you."

"They didn't lie to me."

"How are you so sure? People lie all the time, Ana. Especially out here."

She stared across the room at the dead man lying underneath the two nightcrawlers. "They didn't lie to me, Wash. I made sure of that."

"How?" he was going to ask, but decided to keep his mouth shut.

He said instead, "What are you going to do when you finally catch up to them?"

She didn't answer, but she didn't really have to. The answer was so obvious Wash didn't know why he bothered to ask in the first place.

They sat still, backs against the cold metal wall, and listened to the hum of the light bulbs around them. It was still dark outside—Wash could feel it without having to see it—but it would be light soon.

"I need your help," Ana finally said.

"Yeah, I figured," Wash said, and pictured the Old Man grinning at him:

"Everyone wants something, kid. Sometimes you'll realize you knew what they wanted even before they say it; and sometimes you won't see it coming. But always remember: No one does anything for free. Everyone always wants something in return."

TEN

The fifth guy never materialized—if he ever existed in the first place. Which was just fine with Wash. He didn't have the time or inclination—never mind the strength—to get into another gunfight, anyway. The painkillers he'd taken were doing their job (it helped that he'd popped two more about three hours after the first couple), and he was feeling better. A lot better. Ana found bags of nuts and berries to replace the uneaten jerky still lying crumpled in the corner, and Wash devoured them while she wandered off again.

He fell asleep sometime after Ana left and didn't wake up until the next morning. When he picked himself from the cold concrete floor, he found himself alone inside the large room. Sunlight peeked inside through the high windows above the doors, and the acrid smell of vaporized ghoul flesh stung his nostrils.

Wash looked toward the trio of bodies near the door and wasn't surprised to find nothing left of the ghouls but bleached white bones lying on top of the dead mountain man, as if some pranksters had stolen a pair of science lab skeletons and draped them over a drunken frat boy. It didn't matter how many times Wash saw it, it always seemed like such a magic trick. The sun simply stripped away every inch of flesh that covered the creatures, reducing skin and muscle to gray dust that still hung in the air and flitted across the fields of sunlight. The blood, too, was gone, but only the tainted fluids that had leaked out of the ghouls. Their victim still lay where Wash last saw him, as dead this morning as he had been last night.

"There you go again, wasting your time thinking about it," the Old Man would say whenever he brought it up. *"It is what it is, kid. Why does the sun destroy them? Why does silver kill the black eyes but not the blue eyes? That's just how it is. That's the world we live in. Next!"*

It wasn't much of an explanation, but then Wash never really expected one from the Old Man. The old timer rarely wasted a second thinking about things he couldn't control. That didn't mean he was stupid. Far from it. The Old Man was one of the smartest men Wash knew. But he was someone who also accepted his limitations. And understanding how and why ghouls reacted to sunlight the way they did, or why silver dropped the black eyes when decapitating them did nothing, wasn't something that concerned him. He was too busy killing ghouls.

If someone told me six years ago it was black magic, I'd have believed them, Wash thought as the thick stench in the room stung his eyes. *Next!*

He wiped at his eyes before picking up a half-empty bottle of water nearby and drank the rest of it. He looked toward the stable at the back, where the nightcrawler that was hanging between the bars last night had fallen to the floor in a pile of bones. The horses were standing around looking bored.

There wasn't much about the warehouse that Wash could see in the morning that he hadn't already gotten a good look at last night, including the stacks of moving crates underneath the heavy tarps. They were filled with vehicle parts and horse equipment, as well as bags, blankets, and backpacks. Maybe some of those—or maybe all of them—came from all the poor bastards that'd had the misfortune of stumbling across the building's previous owners before Wash did.

The ATVs and off-road vehicles next to the boxes might come in handy. That is, if there was fuel for them. There was a reason horsepower had become the preferred mode of transportation for a lot of people. Horses didn't need still-usable gasoline, which was harder and harder to come by these days. But Wash preferred horses anyway; all they needed was a patch of grass to keep them going.

The loud, almost echoing *clank!* of the front door opening made him glance over, at the same time reaching down for the Beretta lying on the floor next to him, beside the 1911. He relaxed when Ana stepped back inside the warehouse.

She had found her black leather jacket, and her hair was tied back in a ponytail, and she would have looked identical to the woman he'd run across in the woods outside of Harrisonville two nights ago if not for the heavy shotgun thumping against her back and the gun belt she had hanging off her slim hips.

"Finally awake, huh?" Ana called over.

"How long ago did you leave?" Wash asked, putting the handgun back down.

"Sunup." Ana left the door open behind her—to help filter

out the smell, he guessed—before stepping around the dead body and bones on the way over to him. She sat down with a tired sigh and placed the shotgun on her lap. "I found Marla's tracks, but I lost them about half a mile from here when she crossed a small stream."

"There's water nearby?"

"Uh huh. Probably the reason the mountain men decided to set up shop here. It looked pretty hidden, like the warehouse. I'm sure that was the other big selling point."

"You think she got away?"

"I didn't see any blood, so that's a good sign."

"What about the guy you saw chasing after her? The young one?"

"He followed her all the way to the stream, but I lost him after that, too. I thought about crossing over to see if I could pick them back up, but I didn't want to risk it."

"You think she made it?"

"I don't know. I hope so."

"Would she come back if she thinks it's safe?"

"After everything she's been through? Getting abducted and losing her boyfriend?" Ana shook her head. "I wouldn't, if I were her. She hardly knows us."

"You saved her life."

"I did, but she played her part. As far as I'm concerned, we're even." Ana paused. Then, "Maybe she'll end up at Harrisonville. It's what, ten miles from here?"

"Give or take," Wash said. "You think the folks at Harrisonville knew the mountain men were out here all this time?"

"Did the mayor say anything to you about them?"

"No. You?"

"No. Then again, we didn't ask him, did we?"

"No, I guess we didn't."

"So you can't really blame him for not mentioning them."

"Fuck him. I'll blame him anyway."

"Hey, it's your prerogative, tough guy. Until then..." Ana took out another small see-through bag from her pocket and handed it to him. "Flax seeds. They're good for you, and you're going to need a lot of them until we can find some variety in their pantry."

"How big is that pantry, anyway?" Wash asked as he scooped out a handful of seeds.

"A whole room. Almost as big as their armory."

"Did you find the rest of my stuff?"

"Yours and God knows how many other people's stuff." She picked out some seeds and popped them into her mouth. "Clothes, too. A lot of it. I don't know why they're still keeping them."

So what happened to their owners? Wash thought, glancing past Ana at the bag of jerky crumpled in the corner.

"You're still thinking about that?" Ana asked.

"Aren't you?"

"Yeah. I guess I am, too. All night."

"Did you find anything that might give us any clues about what they've been doing out here?"

"I thought we already know what they've been doing out here."

"I mean, evidence. Something that confirms what we think."

She shook her head. "No, and I'm not sure I want to, either." She grabbed another handful of seeds and chewed on them. "I just want to get out of this place as fast as possible, Wash."

He shared her discomfort, and maybe he didn't really want to know, too. It wasn't just the clothes, the piles of unused and seemingly superfluous supplies, or even the mysterious meat. It was everything.

Wash glanced down at his empty wrist. "Did you find my watch while you were looking around?"

"Again with the watch," Ana said.

"Did you find it or not?"

"I only saw it for a second when they first took everything else, so I wouldn't recognize it if I saw it again. But there is a lot of jewelry in a box back there. You can look for it yourself later." She eyed him curiously. "What's so special about that watch, anyway?"

"Someone gave it to me. I promised them I'd never lose it."

"What's her name?"

"I didn't say it was a her."

"I assumed."

"You know what happens when you assume."

"Yeah, yeah."

They sat quietly and chewed on the flax seed in silence for a moment. With the door open, the smell of evaporated ghoul flesh had begun to dissipate, but it still hung in the air like a permanent marker. The stench should have made him uncomfortable, but Wash was too used to it by now to be too bothered. He wasn't sure, though, if that was a good or bad thing.

I've been doing this too long. Way too long...

"Who were they?" he finally asked. "The ones who took your sister?"

Ana stared across the warehouse intensely as she talked,

as if she could look back into the past and relive the moment. "I don't know all their names, but I know the one who's leading them. Mathison. He and his friends showed up in Newton about a week before everything happened. I knew they were trouble as soon as I saw them. As soon as I saw *him*. I wanted them to keep going, leave town, but I was outvoted."

"Outvoted?"

"We do everything in Newton by votes. Majority rules. It's a regular democracy. The system worked just fine until a bunch of asshats with something a lot of people in town wanted showed up. I got outvoted, and Mathison and his crew were allowed to stay. By the time the others realized I was right, Mathison had already fled with Emily and three other women. They left in the middle of the night and left a lot of blood and tears in their wake."

"Were they on horseback?"

She shook her head. "They showed up on foot and left the same way. We have the stables guarded at night, and I guess they decided not to risk it."

"So why were you also on foot out there?"

"The horses belonged to the town, not me. They couldn't spare to loan me one to chase Mathison."

"Couldn't or wouldn't?"

"Does it matter which?"

"I guess not. At least they're not moving any faster than you. Who else is chasing them?"

"You're looking at her."

"Just you? But they took three other people besides your sister."

"Yeah, they did."

Wash watched her somber face carefully. "Let me guess: You were outvoted."

"Yeah," Ana nodded. "Mathison's crew killed three people on their way out. Gutted them like fishes. I guess they didn't want to use their guns and wake everyone up, so they used their knives. It was bloody, and a lot of people in town hadn't encountered that kind of violence in a long time. It shocked Newton to the core. Even when we hired slayers to deal with ghouls that would wander into our area, the others never had to see it. Their hands were always clean."

I've heard that story before...

"So you're out here all by your little lonesome hunting a band of killers, is that it?" he asked.

She looked over at him and smiled. "I was."

Morning came and went, and Marla never returned. Neither did the missing mountain man. Wash was glad no one showed up, because it meant he could just sit in the same spot and not have to move. But that changed when Ana decided it was time to suture his wounds. He would have argued if he thought it would have done any good. Besides, he knew she was right. Having bandages on was one thing, but he could still feel himself bleeding underneath them.

Before she went to work, Ana took out a bottle from one of the backpacks she'd stuffed full of supplies and shook out two pills. They were brightly colored and had the letter *M* stamped on one side and the number 30 on the other.

"What are those?" Wash asked.

"Morphine," Ana said.

"You know what morphine pills look like?"

"Don't you?"

He shook his head. "Never came up."

"You'll need them for the pain."

Again, he didn't argue, and chased the pills down with some water while Ana got ready. She placed the first-aid kit next to her, along with a needle and scissors on top of a clean rag. The warehouse provided everything she needed. Everything except the answers that neither one of them were sure they really wanted to know.

"You've done this before?" he asked.

"Yes."

"How many times?"

"More than I'd like."

"What exactly did you do before all of this? And don't give me the office bullshit."

"Not this, I can assure you."

"So how do you know about pills, sutures, all those neat tricks with small knives?"

"It's been six years since the world went to shit, Wash. I had to pick up a few new skills to survive. It was that or sign up to get some stranger's semen put inside me so I can squeeze out a kid for the ghouls to feed on. No thanks."

Wash chuckled. She was talking about being a collaborator during The Purge. Men and women who voluntarily chose to cooperate with the monsters. They were resettled into towns like Harrisonville, where the men gave blood and served the wills of the new overlords while the women allowed themselves to be impregnated by strangers. It was the reason why almost every child he came across these days were five-year-olds.

The fact that Ana hadn't been one of those collaborators wasn't a surprise to him. It was going to take a lot more than just some monsters to make this woman do something she didn't want to.

"You know this is going to hurt, right?" Ana was asking.

He sighed. "I know."

She glanced over her shoulder, toward the other side of the warehouse. "The living quarters are back there. There are beds..."

Wash shook his head. "I'm not lying down on the same bed as those fuckers. Do it here. I'll be fine."

She gave him a doubtful look. "Are you sure?"

"Yes," Wash said. "But just in case I don't see you again after this, you can have my horses."

It hurt, and he managed not to cry out. At least, he thought he did. By the time she was almost done, he was fighting back tears and hoping she didn't notice. She probably did, even if Ana didn't say anything. But she could just have been too busy with the actual bloody work—and trying to keep him alive while she did it—and didn't have time to enjoy his misery.

When she was done, Wash lay down on top of a blanket Ana had rolled out earlier and stared up at all the cobwebs that had taken over the rafters. Sunlight pooled along the ceiling, reflecting off the heavy metal siding and the chrome from the vehicles in the back. It was impossibly peaceful beyond the warehouse walls, and for a moment he forgot about the mountain men and all the bags of mystery meat Ana had discovered.

"You okay?" Ana asked. He heard her voice but couldn't tell where she was exactly. Nearby? She had to be nearby.

"Yeah," Wash said.

"You sure?"

"Yeah," he said again.

"Try not to move unless you have to. You're not bleeding, but things like bullet holes don't magically seal themselves up overnight. We'll have to stay here for at least another day, maybe longer if you can't travel by then."

He traced her voice to somewhere on his right, and Wash turned his head in that direction. She was sitting on the floor next to him, her hands draped over her bent knees, watching him back. She had been wearing surgical gloves earlier, but Ana had taken them off. There was still some blood along her wrists.

"The longer I hold you back, the farther Mathison's getting away," Wash said. "You should think about taking off."

"And just leave you here?"

"I'll catch up when I can."

"He's widening the distance, but I know where he's going. Sooner or later, we'll both get there."

"Brownsville."

She nodded.

Unless the guys at the cabin lied to you, Wash thought, but he said, "If they're still on foot, we can make up the lost time on horseback. Unless, of course, they've picked up horsepower themselves since you found their last campsite."

"It doesn't matter. I'll catch up to them eventually. When that happens, I'll need you by my side."

"You mean my trigger finger."

"That, too."

He chuckled. "I'll be there. If I don't die tonight, I mean."

"You're not going to die, Washateria. Not if I have anything to say about it."

He tossed her an annoyed glare. "Seriously? Still with that?"

"Admit it, you like it."

"I don't."

"You do. You just don't know it yet."

"Thank God you're here to tell me what I know and don't know. I didn't realize I've been missing that all my life."

"You're welcome."

"I was being sarcastic."

"I don't think you were doing it correctly. Otherwise I would have gotten it."

Wash groaned and closed his eyes. "Tell me about your sister."

"Why?"

"It'll help pass the time. And I'd like to get to know her if I'm going to be risking my life to save her."

"I don't know where to start..."

"Start anywhere. How old is she? What does she look like? What's her favorite color? Is she as pretty as you?"

He couldn't see her, but he imagined Ana smiling when she said, "So you admit it. You think I'm pretty."

"Don't let it get to your head. I'm delirious with pain and meds. I'm pretty sure I think unicorns are real, too. Now, tell me about Emily before I fall asleep."

He heard her taking a deep breath before finally speaking.

"She's nineteen. She was just a kid when The Purge happened..."

ELEVEN

Wash slept and woke up throughout the day, but the meds kept him from staying awake for very long. He was fine with that and willingly allowed the sweet, sweet bliss of sleep to draw him back into its embrace each time.

Ana came and went, including dragging the bones and dead bodies out of the warehouse. When she was done with that, she returned for a shovel and spent another two hours or so outside digging graves in the woods. Later, she took the horses out in pairs to let them graze on the grass.

Wash considered getting up and going through all the supplies that the mountain men had left behind to see if he could find anything of value, but each time the idea came up, his body rebelled. Instead, he spent his time staring at the spiders spinning cobwebs along the rafters, before eventually falling asleep again.

The supplies Ana had laid on the floor next to him had doubled in size when he next opened his eyes. Then it was triple. Ana was still going through the warehouse room by room, bringing out what they would need and leaving what they didn't. His things, including the Mossberg 590A1 tactical shotgun, were among the pile, along with his pack.

"Fuel?" he remembered asking her during one of his brief awake interludes.

She had shaken her head. "I don't think they've used those vehicles for a while now. Every gas tank is empty and has been for some time."

"Too bad."

"Yeah, too bad."

He thought about asking her if she'd discovered any new hints as to what the mountain men had been doing to their prisoners, but never followed through with it. He decided he didn't just *not* want to know, but that it didn't matter anymore. The men were dead, and along with them, their evil deeds.

Then he slept again.

When he next opened his eyes, feeling as alive as he had in quite some time, Ana was sitting next to him Indian style with his kukri machete in her hands.

"What time?" he asked.

"Half an hour before nightfall."

"Already?"

"For you. For me, it's been a slow day."

Wash guessed that explained the darkening rafters. The light bulbs hadn't been turned on yet, and Ana had told him earlier about the solar panels on the roof and in a big field behind the building, which was how the mountain men got their electricity. Which still didn't explain where they kept their fridge, because Wash knew they had one. How else would they store their...goods?

"What is this thing?" Ana was asking as she took a few practice swings with the kukri.

"It's a machete."

"I can see that. But what's it called? I've never seen something like this before."

"It's called a kukri."

"Sounds Japanese."

"Nepalese."

"From Nepal?"

"That's usually where you find Nepalese stuff, yeah."

"Asshat." She held the blade in her palm and weighed it. "It's got nice balance. No wonder you like using it. It feels like a knife but has the reach of a short sword. The best of both worlds. Is the blade...?"

"It's got silver in it."

"Of course it does. Where did you get something like this? Somehow I have a hard time envisioning you traveling to Nepal for one."

"Why? You want one?"

"I wouldn't say no, if you're offering."

"If I have time, I'll make you one."

"You know how?"

"The same person who made that one for me taught me how. Kukris aren't supposed to be that long."

"Did he make it himself?"

"What makes you think it was a he?"

She rolled her eyes. "Girls don't run around making machetes, Wash."

He smiled. "Yeah, he did. He was good with his hands. He's the one who taught me how to shoot, too."

"'Was?'"

"He's dead."

She put the kukri down. "I'm sorry."

"It happens."

Ana didn't say anything for a while and seemed content to sit there staring at him. She had tied her hair back in a ponytail again, which was disappointing. He remembered the sight of her red hair fanning around her face and decided that he missed the look.

"What?" he said. "I'm pretty, but I'm not *that* pretty."

She smiled. "Touché."

"So what is it?"

"I think you're going to need another day, Wash."

"I'm feeling better. I'm feeling a lot better, actually."

She shook her head. "But you're not. Physically, anyway. And I'm going to need you at your best—or damn close—before we go back out there again. Mathison and his people aren't going to give Emily back to me without a fight. You know that, right?"

"I know."

"It's going to get bloody..."

"I know that, too." He reached over and took her hand and squeezed, and was rewarded with an amusingly surprised look on her face. "We'll get her back. I promise."

"Thank you," Ana said, almost hesitantly. He really had caught her by surprise, which was something Wash didn't think was possible.

He pulled his hand back to spare both of them the awkwardness. "You never told me how many men Mathison has with him."

"Ten."

"Ten?"

"Does that make a difference?"

"I was hoping for...less."

"That's not counting Mathison."

"So, eleven total."

"Uh huh. Are you having second thoughts now?"

"More like third or fourth thoughts," Wash said.

He slept peacefully, either because of the meds or the fatigue of the last few days catching up to him, but by the time he woke up to morning sunlight the following day, Wash felt like he could take on the world again. As long as the world didn't come at him with four-by-fours swinging at his midsection, anyway.

He pushed up from the blanket he'd been lying on for the last two days to find Ana sound asleep on something that almost looked like a futon next to him. She lay on her side facing him, her arms protectively across her chest. The duvet she had been using was bunched around her knees, and Wash picked it up and placed it back over her. She shifted in her sleep, turning over onto her back, but didn't wake up.

Wash stood up and fought the instinct to stretch. That wouldn't have done his stitched side any good. It was healing, and he could feel the relief coming from down there, but that didn't stop him from taking two more painkillers anyway. (*Just in case...*) That left six more pills in the sheet, which wasn't too alarming since the mountain men had plenty more stocked up. He had a feeling he was going to be finding out if the rest were as good as the ones he'd been taking soon enough.

He took a moment to pick up his gun belt and slipped it

on, then dropped the Beretta into the holster on his right hip and the kukri into its sheath on his left. He left the 1911 semi-automatic on the floor and walked to the stable, where he opened it and took out two of the horses—the orange-brown Quarter Horse and the Tennessee Walker—and led them outside for their morning breakfast. His stomach growled, but he pushed it off until he could raid the mountain men's pantry himself. There had to be more than just nuts in there. He would kill for some MREs right about now.

Once outside, Wash didn't have to go too far to see where Ana had dug the graves for the warehouse's former occupiers and the leftover ghoul bones. He walked the horses to a nice patch of green and tied them to a branch to let the animals eat. Wash stood nearby and enjoyed the simple act of standing on his two feet without feeling woozy or having the urge to sit down to rest. Even the cold morning barely had any effect on him. It was either the pills or the healthy dose of sleep. Or likely both.

The warehouse looked much bigger on the outside, its steel exterior giving it an almost impregnable aura. Besides the door and the big garage entrance next to it, there were just the high windows at the top. It didn't look welcoming at all—a big gray building in the middle of nowhere—and maybe that was the point.

As he waited for the horses to finish their breakfast, Wash heard the faint *pop-pop-pop* of gunshots in the distance. It was very far—much too far for him to be worried about them, even if his hand did dip instinctively toward the holstered Beretta. He listened to the shots echoing before they slowly faded into oblivion.

Gunfire wasn't uncommon out here, but that didn't mean you should ignore it. Everyone and their dads carried guns these days. Unless, of course, they were like Ana, who was more dangerous with that hidden knife of hers. And then there was that mind. You could lose a knife, but that brain of hers was always at her disposal.

He waited to hear more gunshots, for signs that whoever was doing the shooting might be coming in his direction, but there were just the birds chirping freely in the trees and the rustling of animals on nearby branches. He thought he might have glimpsed a buck somewhere in the woods behind him, but it was gone before he could make sure. Now *that* was meat he would gladly wolf down.

When the horses were done eating, Wash led them to the stream and let them drink their fill. He found that he enjoyed the slow walk to the stream and back to the warehouse, and by the time he reached the door, he wished he could have stayed outside longer.

Ana was sitting on the floor rubbing her eyes when he walked back inside. "What happened?"

"What happened where?"

"So nothing happened?"

"Depends on what you're talking about."

She paused for a moment, gathering her thoughts. "I heard gunshots in my dream."

"It wasn't in your dream. Someone was shooting out there."

"Nearby?"

"Not nearby enough to be worried about."

"You think it might have been Marla?"

"Maybe, but what would she still be doing around here after two days?"

"She wouldn't," Ana said. "Unless she didn't have any choice. That other mountain man—mountain *boy*—could still be chasing her. That would explain why he hadn't come back yet."

"Unless she got him first."

"There's that, I guess."

Wash put the animals back into the stable, then took out the remaining three. "I'll be back."

"Are you okay?"

"Feeling better than I have all week."

"I doubt that."

"Better than the last two days."

"That's more believable." She stood up and stretched. "How much of the Tramadol did you take?"

"Two more."

"Remember to go easy on that. It can be habit forming. You don't want to become an addict out here, Wash. No rehab to check into."

"I'll keep that in mind, Mom."

She frowned. "Don't make me kick your ass, Washateria."

He chuckled, and they exchanged a brief smile that was, Wash thought, not nearly as awkward as when he had touched her hand earlier.

"It's nice, isn't it?" Ana said. She stood next to him, watching the three horses grazing on the thriving grass spread out all around them. A cool breeze ran through the trees, rustling strands of her long red hair that had come loose from the pony-tail. "I can see why they chose this place. It's hidden, but at the same time, there's something peaceful about it."

"It's not bad," Wash said. He drank some water and passed the bottle to her. "You could always come back here after you get your sister back."

Ana shook her head. "That's not going to happen. Not in this lifetime." She glanced back at the warehouse. "Not after what they've been using this place for."

"We don't know for sure what they've been using this place for."

"It wasn't to make friends, Wash. That dungeon they put us in is proof of that. Shooting you on the road was the biggest proof of all."

"It was just a thought," Wash said. He took the bottle of water back and finished it off. "We should get going soon."

"Can you ride?"

"I'll manage."

"Wash," she said, focusing on him, "I need you to be absolutely sure."

"I'm sure."

"Sure, sure?"

He smiled. "As sure as sure can be, sure."

She returned it. "Okay. In another hour or two?"

"Let's make that two." Wash looked back at the building. "You said they have an armory in there?"

"Next to the living quarters on the other side. Why?"

"The Mossberg I'm carrying is good for nightcrawlers, but if we're going up against men, I'll need something with better range. And, I need to find my watch."

"Again with the watch."

"It's important to me."

"Yeah, I'm starting to see that," Ana said.

The armory was an appropriate name for the room Wash found himself in. Even with just a single squiggly light bulb spraying its weak yellow light on the place, he was amazed by how much armament the mountain men had put together. There were racks of rifles, walls of handguns, and shelf after shelf of ammo.

There were too many guns to choose from, half of which Wash had never laid eyes on before, and he'd seen more than his share while traveling the country with the Old Man. There were exotic models from around the world in front of him, including plenty of what looked like custom-made battle rifles.

But rifles were rifles, and it was the same for pistols.

He settled on the much more familiar M4 carbine with a pistol grip and a Trijicon ACOG mounted on top. Seven pounds, give or take, with a fourteen-and-a-half-inch barrel. The optic would give the weapon maximum range; at the same time, the length was "short" enough to maneuver in close quarters if necessary. The fire selector had an option for full-auto, and you never knew when that might come in handy.

Wash shoved a couple of spare magazines into his old tactical pack, then grabbed four more and put them into a second bag. Before he left, he snatched up a pair of pistols and magazines for those, along with two boxes of 12-gauge shells. He would have taken more, but the weight was already dragging him down noticeably.

Next, he went to the storage room where Ana had told him

about the box of jewelry. He sifted through clothing, shoes, and personal belongings of the mountain men's previous victims. There, on a shelf. It was a box, but Ana had failed to mention it was a green ammo box. Instead of bullets, there were rings, necklaces, and watches inside.

Wash tossed a couple of Rolexes, Omegas, and some TAG Heuers to the floor. He eventually found what he was looking for near the bottom. It had a smooth silver case around a white dial with a brown alligator leather strap. It was plain and unassuming, but he felt whole again as soon as he slapped it around his wrist. The hands were frozen, which was expected for an automatic watch after sitting still for the last few days. He got it moving again by motioning his hand up and down a couple of times. After that, he used one of the quartz watches to find the right time and reset his.

Ana was already outside the warehouse, cinching up the saddle on her Tennessee Walker when he rejoined her. They were going to take only four horses—with Wash riding the Quarter Horse—and using the remaining two to ferry their supplies. The fifth horse, which according to Ana was the oldest by far, was released back into the woods. The animal had hesitantly taken a couple of steps toward the tree line before stopping and glancing back at them, as if afraid this were some kind of trick. After it was satisfied it wasn't a trick, the animal took off and they didn't see it again.

"You should take one of these," Wash said, holding up the M4.

She gave him an amused look. "You're still saying that after what happened on the road last time? Why would anyone shoot little ol' me, in her tight jeans and jacket, and nothing that even looks remotely like a weapon on her, when there's you with all those guns?"

"So I'm just the diversion, is that it? They see us on the road, and it's a no-brainer to shoot me but not you?"

"You're just figuring that out now?"

He grunted, thought, *She's got a point*, and tossed his bags over the brown horse that he would be using to ferry his supplies, tying the animal's reins to the horn of his orange-brown's saddle. Ana said the horse was a Morgan breed, and it was small compared to the one he was riding.

"I'm only doing this because you saved my life," Wash said.

"Twice," Ana smiled.

"Technically, but since I only have one life to give, I'm only counting it once."

"You cheat at cards, too, Wash?"

"Only when the other guy's not looking."

Wash walked the short distance over to his horse, and when he was sure Ana wasn't watching, took a couple of deep breaths before swinging into the saddle. He probably did it too fast, if the sudden stabs of pain were any indication. He grimaced through them before looking back at Ana.

She was staring at him, but he didn't think it was because she had caught him in pain. It was something else.

"Thank you for doing this," Ana said.

He nodded. "Thank me when this is over."

"I'll do that, too."

She climbed into her saddle, and he couldn't help but feel a little envious at how easily she had done it. The horse attached to Ana's Tennessee Walker was also brown, but with large splashes of white paint, which, Wash guessed, explained why it was called an American Paint Horse.

"Did you find it?" Ana asked.

He pulled back the long sleeve of his left hand to show her the watch.

"That's it?" Ana said. She sounded disappointed.

"That's it."

"I saw a couple of Rolexes in there. Why didn't you swap for one of those? They were probably twenty grand each, easy."

"It's not about the price tag."

"What's it about?"

"Not dollars."

She waited for him to continue, and when he didn't, "Maybe you'll tell me the real reason some day."

Maybe some day, he thought.

Ana turned her horse around and started off. Wash gave his orange-brown a soft kick and quickly caught up to her. They rode side by side away from the warehouse and were back underneath the cool shade of the woods moments later.

"Why Texas?" Ana asked. "I know why I'm going, but why are you? What's down there that's so important you wouldn't take Harrisonville's very generous offer to get hitched to one of their eligible ladies and make beautiful babies?"

"Is that what the mayor told you?"

"He told me lots. He would have told me more, but I was in a hurry to catch up to you." When Wash hadn't answered her question, "So what's in Texas? It's not a woman, is it?"

"Why is it you think everything comes down to a woman?"

"It's just the woman in me. I'm biased."

He smirked. "No, it's not a woman."

"Then what is it?"

He kept silent.

"It's going to be a long ride down to Texas," Ana said. "You might as well tell me now, because you'll end up telling me later anyway."

"Leave it alone, Ana," Wash said. "Just...leave it alone."

TWELVE

A part of Wash wanted to stay at the warehouse until he could walk without feeling pain. He didn't like the idea of going up against *it* with two holes in him already. He was going to need everything he had (*and then some*) to kill the bastard, and the idea of facing off with it with one hand tied behind his back was not all that appealing.

Of course, he couldn't wait and heal up. He'd already held Ana back two days, and to make it three would have widened the gap between her and Mathison even further. Regardless of what she had told him—that it didn't matter how far ahead Mathison got because she knew where he was going—he didn't completely believe her. And there was a simple reason for that: Because it would have mattered to *him* if that were his sister out there.

But he'd be damned if he didn't feel the urge to hang back and wait, if only just another day.

"Wishing for it doesn't make it happen," the Old Man would say.

Yeah, I'm beginning to figure that one out, old timer.

They were only an hour into their journey when Wash snuck in a couple of painkillers. He made sure Ana was slightly ahead of him when he did it and quickly ground the pills between his teeth before swallowing them without water. The powder clung to his throat somewhat, but he worked some saliva around and got them down eventually.

The weather remained chilly, but not freezing cold. Wash was comfortable inside a new set of thermal clothing, one that wasn't covered in his blood. They were his last, because he wouldn't allow himself to make use of the mountain men's stash or the leftovers from their previous victims. Ana wasn't complaining despite only wearing jeans and that leather jacket of hers. The road was the same one they'd been traveling on before they were ambushed, a fact that kept Wash's attention on high alert.

Fat lot of good that did you the last time.

He wanted to blame it on Ana's sudden presence, how he was too busy arguing with her to notice the ambushers sneaking up on them. But the truth was, they were just that good. Which made sense considering how long they had been intercepting travelers on the road. How many people had crossed their paths and never saw it coming?

Yeah, keep telling yourself that. It's better than admitting your instincts failed you.

"It'll take us a day to reach the Oklahoma border," Ana was saying in front of him. She pointed to their right. "Interstate 35 is over there, about five miles away. All we have to do is continue south, which will take us through Oklahoma City. Dallas-Fort Worth is two hundred miles after that."

"How do you know that?" Wash asked.

"They're called maps, Wash. I made sure to know where I'm going at all times." She glanced back at him. "How were you going to get to Texas?"

"Keep heading south. Eventually I'd get to where I needed to be."

"You didn't have an itinerary?"

"Don't have to. Texas is a big state. Hard to miss."

"Still, it's never a bad thing to have a plan."

She sounds like you now, old timer.

Ana didn't say anything for a while after that. She had also stopped asking him about his reasons for going to Texas. Wash was hoping that was going to hold, but somehow he knew it wouldn't, so he wasn't surprised when she finally broached the subject again.

"It's down there, isn't it?" she asked. "One Eye. The blue-eyed ghoul you're looking for. It's in Texas."

He didn't answer her. At least not verbally, but he forgot that his silence was the same as an answer, because he didn't deny it.

"How were you going to find it?" she asked. "Like you said, Texas is a big place. It could be anywhere. If I've learned anything, it's that the blue eyes are good at hiding."

Wash kept quiet.

"I've heard stories about them out there," she went on anyway, "but I don't know anyone who's actually seen one of them with their own eyes since The Walk Out. Most people think they're bogeymen. Made up."

"Most people are wrong," Wash said.

"So you've seen them with your own eyes?"

"Yes. More than one."

"What happened?"

"We killed them."

"'We?'"

"It usually takes more than one slayer to kill a Blue Eye. Sometimes a lot more."

"And yet you're going down to Texas to take on one of them by yourself..."

He sighed. "Ana, I don't want to talk about it."

She pursed her lips at him, and he thought she would keep going, but she didn't. Instead, she said, "All right."

"All right?" he repeated.

"All right. You'll tell me when you're ready."

"I wouldn't hold my breath, if I were you."

"You will."

"If you say so."

They rode on in silence for a few more minutes, before Ana said, "You need to go easy on the pills."

He sat up straighter in his saddle. "What are you talking about?"

She slowed down until he caught up to her, and Ana flashed him a wry *I saw your hand in the cookie jar* glance.

"Let me guess: You have eyes in the back of your head, too?" Wash said.

"No, but you weren't being nearly as sly as you thought you were." Then, with a look of concern, "Are you okay?"

"Peachy."

"I'm being serious, Wash."

He nodded. "I'm fine. The pills were there; it seemed stupid not to use them. That's what they're for, right?"

"You have to be careful. I've seen people get addicted to them."

"I won't take any more until tonight. And only if I need them." *Which I probably will*, he thought, but didn't add.

"Okay," Ana said. "Just don't lie to me. I'm only looking out for you."

"I will, mo—"

She shot him a quick warning look. "*Don't* finish that word."

"What word?"

"You know what word."

He chuckled. "I was going to say, 'I will, Miss Ana.'"

"Sure you were."

"Swear."

"Uh huh."

Wash couldn't help but smile to himself. At least he knew of another thing that could ruffle her feathers. Maybe it was a little childish, but he filed the information away for future use anyway.

"What's that short for, anyway?" he asked. "Ana."

"I'll tell you if you tell me what Wash is short for."

"Agreed."

"Anastasia."

"Hunh."

"'Hunh?'"

He shrugged. "I didn't think it'd be that."

"What did you think it was?"

"Not that." Then, "So it's Ana. A-n-a?"

"Yes. Why?"

"I thought it was A-n-n-a."

"So what's Wash short for?"

"Washateria," Wash said.

She squinted at him.

Wash grinned. "True story."

"You bastard," Ana said.

Ana had said it would take a day for them to reach the Kansas-Oklahoma border, but she hadn't added why. Of course, Wash knew the answer anyway: Him. They were moving at a trot when they could have been going much faster. Certainly both their horses, after so much time to rest at the warehouse, could have cut the timetable in half. More than half, actually.

Except they couldn't go that fast, because Wash's wounds wouldn't allow it. Ana knew it, and so did he even if neither one of them said it out loud. He was grateful for that, but the gratitude was tempered by the knowledge that Ana couldn't risk losing him before they reached Mathison. She needed his trigger finger because her skills with a knife weren't going to do a lick of good against eleven men who had already slaughtered their way out of Newton.

That undeniable fact should have made him wary of her, but it didn't. It was more than just owing his life to her (twice now, even if he had joked about only having one to give earlier), or that they were heading in the same direction anyway. There was also the very real dislike Wash had for people like Mathison. Wash had crossed paths with plenty of men who did evil things because they *could*, and because there was no one to stop them. The existence of men like Mathison annoyed him to the core.

More than that: It pissed him off.

"Are you willing to die for your beliefs, kid?" the imaginary Old Man in the back of his mind asked. *"Are you willing to go*

up against eleven hardcore killers to keep them from doing more evil deeds?"

Do I have a choice?

"Yes, you always have a choice. Just remember that whatever you choose, you have to live with it. All of it. No regrets. No doubts. No second guesses. You do it, you live with it, and you move on. Next!"

They continued on for another two hours, stopping only to eat from the mountain men's stash of nuts. In a day or two he was going to get tired of nuts, but by then hopefully they'd have found something else to replace them with.

It was already midday, but the sun didn't do much to chase away the chill. Afterward, they climbed back into their saddles and pushed south, their pace still slowed by Wash's wounds. He felt guilty but also glad at the same time that he wasn't punishing himself. The time for that was still somewhere ahead of them.

Around hour four, Ana stopped and pointed. "Wash..."

He saw it, too: Smoke drifting lazily in the air. It was coming from in front and slightly to the left of them, which meant it was off the road and somewhere deep in the woods.

Ana glanced over at him. "What do you think?"

"It could be anything," Wash said. "A campsite. A cabin. Or even a town. I've never been down this road before. Have you?"

She shook her head. "Maybe someone in trouble."

"Or that."

"We should take a look."

"Are you sure you want to do that? It could delay us."

"Maybe, but if it's someone needing help, I don't want to just ride past them. Emily wouldn't want me to do that."

"It's your call." He drew the Mossberg from its holster along his horse's flank and thumbed off the safety. "You sure you don't want a gun?"

She shook her head before aiming her Tennessee Walker off the road. Wash followed behind her, the shotgun at his side with the muzzle pointed at the ground. It was a less aggressive posture than having the barrel aimed forward; at the same time, it wouldn't take much to tilt it up and pull the trigger.

The smoke was wood burning, and Wash could smell it clearly as they neared. It wasn't a raging forest fire but appeared to be contained. The question was: What had caused it? The trick was figuring out the answer before someone started shooting. The fact that he hadn't heard shooting *yet* was a good sign. But that was also the problem: You often didn't hear shooting until they were shooting *at* you. He'd relearned that cold, hard truth three days ago.

Ana stayed in front of him, and if he thought it would have done any good, Wash would have told her to let him take the lead. He had a feeling, though, that it wouldn't have made any difference, so he didn't. The Paint Horse trailed behind her while Wash pulled the Morgan along.

After about ten more minutes of slowly, cautiously pushing through the woods, the aroma of burning wood got noticeably stronger. They wound their way around trees, slipping under branches, and all the while Wash kept waiting to hear gunshots. Maybe it was paranoia, but what was that saying about it not being paranoia if people really were out to get you?

The smoke grew bigger and thicker as they got closer. Finally, they reached a clearing and Ana pulled up in front of him. Wash hurried over to her position, clutching the shotgun at his side with his finger next to the trigger guard, just in case.

He looked out at a two-story house in flames. The fire was more intense up close, consuming the entire building and sending thick columns of smoke into the air. It was some kind of ranch, with a barn and storage shed to the right of the large structure currently being swallowed by the raging fire. Wash had a difficult time identifying where the first floor ended and the second floor began. It just looked like one big wall of flames.

"Wash," Ana said.

He followed her gaze to the barn as one of its doors squeaked open and a lone figure stepped outside.

Wash slid his forefinger closer toward the shotgun's trigger.

It was a girl wearing dirty overalls with a white T-shirt underneath, her dark, short hair covered in dirt, sweat making them stick to her forehead. She was close enough to the heat radiating from the house burning nearby that her figure flickered in the air almost as if she were a mirage that didn't actually exist.

Ana must have thought the same thing, because she said, "Are you seeing this?"

"Yeah," Wash said.

The girl was barefoot as she walked toward them. Wash didn't think she could have been more than thirteen, and there was something odd about the way she moved. It was her pace, the very deliberate way she was approaching them, as if she'd been waiting for their arrival all this time. But of course that didn't make any sense.

Right?

Ana glanced over at him again and shook her head, and

Wash nodded back. He understood without having to be told. He kept the Mossberg next to him, the barrel pointed at the ground, but didn't put it away. Ana climbed off her horse and opened one of the supply packs slung over the saddle, took out a bottle of water, and walked to meet the girl.

The girl had stopped to stare at them, her arms dangling loosely at her sides as if she didn't quite know what to do with them. Now that she was closer, Wash realized he was wrong— she was much older than he had thought. Sixteen or seventeen, but her small, frail frame made her look younger from afar. He could make out blood on the front of her denim clothing, and he was pretty sure that instead of sweat, it was actually blood that plastered her hair to her forehead. Her feet were dirty, like the rest of her, her toes caked in mud and...something else. He had an easy time imagining her crawling around in a dark and dank tunnel before finally emerging into the light in order to greet them.

What the hell happened to her?

Ana stopped about ten feet from the teenager, probably because she didn't want the kid to run off. Not that the girl looked as if she could be scared away. Wash had seen it before: She was traumatized, and that look on her face wasn't fearless-ness—it was confusion. He wondered if she even remembered her own name.

"Hey, are you okay?" Ana asked.

The girl looked past Ana and at Wash.

Ana glanced back at him, but Wash shrugged.

She turned back at the girl. "My name's Ana. What's yours?"

The girl didn't answer her. Had she even heard Ana's questions?

Ana took one tentative step toward the kid, and when the teenager didn't immediately turn and flee, Ana took another one. Then another. She didn't stop until she was standing in front of the girl. Ana was taller, though not by very much.

"You want some water?" Ana asked. "You look like you could use some water."

The girl remained quiet and kept staring at Wash. She had big brown eyes and a round face, childlike in so many ways. All of that was a stark contrast against her filthy appearance, including the blood on her cheeks and forehead.

Blood. That is definitely blood.

"Hey," Ana said, snapping her fingers in front of the teenager to get her attention. "Are you okay? Are you hurt? What's your name?"

The girl still didn't answer. She didn't even look like she was capable of speaking, and for all they knew she couldn't—

"Wash," the girl in overalls finally said.

The word stunned both Ana and Wash.

"What did you just say?" Ana asked her.

"Wash," the girl said again, pointing at Wash.

Wash slowly climbed off his saddle as Ana looked back at him. "Did she just say your name?"

"I don't know," Wash said. "It sounded like it."

"Do you know her?"

"I've never seen her before in my life."

"Are you sure?"

"I'd remember her, Ana. I've never been through this part of the country."

"But she knows your name."

"She said 'Wash.' She could have meant anything."

But even as the words came out of his mouth, Wash didn't

believe any of it.

And the girl proved him right when she said, "Washington."

"'Washington?'" Ana said to the girl, who continued to look past her and at Wash. Ana turned back to Wash again. "Is that...?"

He nodded. "That's my full name. Washington."

He saw the hundreds of questions racing across Ana's face and imagined it probably mirrored his own at the moment.

Ana turned back to the girl. "Do you know him? Do you know who this is?"

Like the last few times, the girl ignored Ana and said to Wash while staring at him with those brown eyes of hers, "He was waiting for you. He said you'd come."

"What is she talking about, Wash?" Ana asked. "Who is 'he?'"

"I..." Wash began, but stopped himself.

"Wash?"

He shook his head.

Could it be? Was it possible?

No. It can't be.

Wash looked over at the enflamed house nearby as smoke continued to lick at the sky and the building's wood crackled even as its foundation threatened to buckle under the relentless assault.

Here? Was the bastard here this entire time? Was it *this close* and he never knew it?

Impossible. Why would—

A scream from behind him. It was Ana's voice, shouting out a single word: "*No!*"

Wash spun around in time to see Ana lunging at the girl,

who was stumbling away from her. The teenager's face had changed, the fear that wasn't there before was now every-where, from her eyes to her trembling pale lips to the quivering tip of her nose. At first Wash thought Ana was attacking the kid for some reason, but all that changed when he saw the gun.

The girl had a revolver in her hand (*Where did that come from?*), and she was holding it to her temple. The hammer was cocked back and her finger was on the trigger. The weapon looked like something from the 1800s, and there was engraving along the grip. The barrel was silver and polished, and sunlight gleamed off its smooth bore shape.

"He's going to come back for me," the girl said. "Tomorrow. Next week. Next month. He told me he'd come back one day."

Her eyes were glued to Wash as she backpedaled clumsily, dangerously close to tripping on her own feet, and all Wash could think was, *She's going to fall and the gun is going to go off and she's going to blow her brains out. Jesus, kid, stop moving!*

"Who?" Ana was saying even as she followed the girl, holding out one hand, her other still clutching the bottle of water for some reason. "Who's coming back?"

"Him," the girl said. *"Him."*

"Who? Does he have a name?"

"He knows," the girl said, pointing at Wash with her other hand. The gun shook against her temple briefly but never went away. "He's gone now, but he says to tell you he'll be waiting in Texas. He says not to keep him waiting too long, because he gets bored easily."

"He?" Wash thought. *"He?"*

But even as he asked himself the question, he knew the answer.

Ana glanced back at him for a brief second before quickly

turning back around to the girl. She kept pace with the teenager, matching her step by step, completely unafraid of the gun in her hand.

She's fearless.

Of course she is. She's chasing eleven dangerous men all by herself with nothing but a knife.

"I'll protect you," Ana was saying to the girl. She was almost pleading. "No one's going to hurt you while I'm here. Please. Give me the gun."

"Listen to her," Wash said. "Listen to Ana. We'll both protect you."

"You can't," the girl said, shaking her head so violently Wash was afraid she might accidentally pull the trigger. "No one can. He's in my head. I can't get him out. He's in there now. *Right now*. Talking to me. Telling me to do things I don't want to do. I can't make him stop! He's gone, but he's still here! He's still inside me!"

"We can make him stop," Ana said. "*I* can make him stop. Just give me the gun. Just give me the gun..."

The girl's eyes shifted to Ana for the first time.

For a moment—just a second, maybe not even that long—Wash thought Ana had gotten through to the kid, that she was on the verge of believing.

And then it was gone.

"You can't stop him," the girl said, and stopped moving. She pressed the gun harder against her temple. "No one can stop him. Not even Dad. Or Billy. Or Pete. No one can stop him. He's going to come back for me like he promised, and no one can stop him. *No one*."

"Please, don't—" Ana began, but the very loud *bang!* of the gunshot made sure she never finished her plea.

THIRTEEN

For the second time in as many days, Ana was digging a grave for a stranger when Wash came out of the barn and walked over to her. He passed the house, still being consumed by flames that probably wouldn't stop for another hour or more. The only reason the fire hadn't ravaged the rest of the property was the lack of grass in the clearing to feed it. That hadn't stopped the heat from spreading across the yard anyway, warming up the property significantly enough that Wash considered taking off some of his layers.

Ana tossed the shovel away when she was done, then sat down at a nearby tree to drink from a bottle of water. Her face, like her clothes, was sprinkled with fresh dirt. Their four horses lingered nearby, grazing on the greens that connected the woods to the mostly dirt-floored property.

"I'm getting sick of digging graves for people," Ana said. "I wish I could say I haven't done it before, but that would be a lie. But then, who hasn't dug their share of graves?"

No one, Wash thought. *Absolutely no one that I've met in six years.*

Ana wetted a rag to wipe at her face. "What did you find?"

Wash handed her the photo album he'd discovered on the floor on the second floor of the barn. It was an old thing, frayed at the corners, with the words *Terry Family Album* scrolled in careful cursive across the label. Ana turned the first page and paused at a Polaroid of a family of five that took up the entire sheet—a father, his wife, and their three children, one of whom was the girl who had killed herself less than an hour ago.

"No one can stop him," the teenager had said. *"Not even Dad. Or Billy. Or Pete."*

It hadn't taken much to figure out who was who. Dad, Mom, Billy, and Pete. Wash had flipped through the album but hadn't lingered on any one of them. He didn't like looking at pictures of the dead; they reminded him too much of all the people he had lost.

"Did you find out her name?" Ana asked.

Wash shook his head and sat down next to her under the shade. "Not yet. It didn't look like she'd been inside the barn for very long, though. Maybe less than a day before we showed up."

"You think she was the one who set fire to the house?"

"Who else could have done it?"

Ana didn't answer and continued turning album pages. The family at Thanksgiving and Christmas, the kids dressed up in costumes for Halloween over the years. The girl grew up before their eyes, so vibrant in all the pictures that she practically glowed. It didn't even look like the same person who had just shot herself in front of them less than an hour ago.

"She said 'him,'" Ana said quietly. "You know who she was talking about, don't you?"

He nodded, but kept quiet.

"He's gone now, but he says to tell you he'll be waiting in Texas," the girl had said. *"He says not to keep him waiting too long, because he gets bored easily."*

"Wash," Ana said. "What's going on?"

"It was here, this entire time," Wash said. He stared across the yard at the fire.

"It's the same one? The one you were hunting outside of Harrisonville?"

"It has to be. The girl knew my name."

"Washington..."

"Yeah."

"It told her to wait for you, didn't it?"

"I think so."

"Why would it do something like that?"

"They like to play games. The blue eyed ones. It's almost like their form of torture." He stopped for a moment, before continuing. "They're sadistic bastards, Ana. You don't understand how truly evil they can be until you've stood face to face with one of them. The black eyes are simple and instinct-driven, like children. They don't hate or love you, they just want what we have. The blue eyes are different. They're so different..."

"The girl mentioned Texas..."

"Yeah, she did."

"That's why you're going down there."

He sighed. He hadn't wanted to have this conversation—had done all he could to steer her away from it—but there was no choice now.

"Yeah," he said. "You were right."

Ana went quiet. Maybe she was thinking about everything she'd heard and seen, trying to process something that would make most people run away screaming in terror. She wasn't a slayer, after all, and as capable as she had shown herself to be, Ana was still just another girl from the towns in over her head.

Finally, she said, "What does it want with you?"

"It's personal," he said. "I'll help you find your sister, take out this Mathison fucker, and then we'll go our separate ways. I'm not going to ask you to go after One Eye with me. You won't want to, anyway. It's dangerous beyond belief." He clenched his teeth. "I've already made peace with it."

"Made peace with what?"

"That it's going to be a one-way trip down south for me," Wash said, and stood up and walked away.

He could feel Ana's eyes on him the entire time as he crossed the yard, but he wasn't thinking about her.

I'll kill it, old timer. I'll put it down.

For you, for the others.

Even if it kills me...

"What do you think happened to her family?" Ana asked when they were back on the road.

"I'm not sure I want to think about it too much," Wash said. "They're either dead, or worse. Either way, that family's gone. There's no point in talking about them."

Ana didn't argue, even though he sensed that she wanted to. Instead, they rode on for another ten, then twenty minutes in silence.

Finally, Ana said, "We need to start looking for a place to stay the night. It'll be dark soon."

Wash glanced up at the sky. It was still bright, but he could see hints of darkness on the way. They had spent nearly three hours at the farmhouse, and combined with getting ready at the mountain men's place this morning, had burned away too much traveling time. Night wasn't the danger it once was back when there were more ghouls running around in the shadows than people, but there was no sane reason to risk traveling at night if you didn't have to.

He rode forward until he was moving along next to her. "We'll be coming up to a town called Kanter 11 soon."

"What kind of name is Kanter 11?"

"It was K11 five years ago. I guess they decided to keep the K and spelled it out."

The fact that Kanter 11 was once K11 meant it was a former ghoul town, just like Harrisonville and the hundreds of other places Wash had gone through over the years. The ghouls weren't very concerned with creativity when they renamed the repurposed settlements, with the first letter of the state used followed by a number. So collaborator towns in Alabama started at A1 and went up. It was N1 and up for settlements in Nebraska, and so on. Things got dicey when a state shared the first letter with another state, such as Texas and Tennessee. But then, no one ever accused the night-crawlers of being good at recordkeeping.

"I didn't see anything indicating a Kanter 11 up ahead," Ana said. "How do you know it's out there?"

"It's on my map."

"It wasn't on mine."

"My map is different than yours. When slayers meet up,

we usually spend some time trading information about what's out there. Ghoul activity, potential jobs, quick sands. Stuff like that. I know slayers who've been all the way west to California and east to New York. A few even tried crossing the oceans to see what was still out there."

"What is still out there?"

Wash shrugged. "I don't know. I never heard back from them."

"So they could be dead? Or drowned?"

"It's possible."

"You said quick sands. What's that?"

"Spots that aren't as welcoming as, say, Harrisonville or your Newton. I know it's hard to believe, but not everyone rolls out the red carpet for us."

She smiled. "You're right. That is hard to believe."

Wash grunted. "More places welcome us than not, though. And the ones that don't, well, they change their tune pretty quickly when they need us. When a ghoul gets hungry enough, it goes for the nearest human every time."

"So, Kanter 11, then."

"Beats sleeping out in the open."

"Yeah, let's try to avoid that," Ana said.

Kanter 11 wasn't much to look at except for the stream that ran next to it and was probably its most vital commodity besides its people. There might have been more to the place once upon a time, but these days it was a lone main street flanked by twenty or so buildings that looked in reasonable shape. The place was ringed by trees, and it had taken Wash and Ana two miles traveling through the woods along a hiking trail to find it. If a slayer in Utah hadn't told Wash about its existence, he would have ridden right past it.

"The stream," Ana said, nodding in the direction of the water.

"What about it?" Wash said.

"It might be part of the same one that Marla crossed back at the warehouse."

"Makes sense. There's a lot of lakes around the state, so there would be plenty of connected streams. That's why there's a lot of towns in the area. Silver's good, and so is food, but drinkable water is always priority number one."

They approached Kanter from the south, making sure to stay within view at all times. Soon, they were moving alongside the flowing stream where they spotted a dozen or so people, most of them kids, bathing in the water near the edge of town.

The kids, to Wash's unsurprise, were almost all under five years old, with a few even younger than that. The adults were all women, a couple of them grabbing at their clothes lying on nearby boulders or on the ground when they spotted Wash and Ana approaching.

Ana smiled and nodded at the bathers and got a few positive responses, while the rest relaxed and went back to what they were doing. All except one woman, who climbed out of the water and walked to a nearby tree where she had hung her clothes. She hadn't bothered to cover herself as she made the ten-foot journey, water dripping from her naked skin the whole time. She was tall, with an athlete's build, and was squeezing water out of a patch of long brown hair as she looked over in their direction.

Ana glanced back at Wash. "Be careful there, Wash, don't want your horse to step on your tongue."

"What?" Wash said.

"Don't stare too hard," Ana smiled before turning back around.

The woman pulled a long-sleeved T-shirt from a branch and slipped it on, then did the same to a pair of pants. Ana veered her Tennessee Walker toward the woman, who came over to meet them halfway. She put her hands on her hips and smiled at them, water still dripping from her hair and chin. She had light blue eyes that went from Ana to Wash and back again.

"Hey there, strangers," the woman said. "You guys lost?"

"We're looking for Kanter 11," Ana said.

"You found it." She gestured at the town behind her. "What can we do for you?"

Ana looked over at Wash, and he guessed she was thinking the same thing. The way the woman had spoken, even her pose, indicated she was more than just one of the townspeople.

"You're in charge?" Ana asked.

"I guess I am, but don't tell anyone. Call me Marie," the woman said, and walked over to shake Ana's hand.

Ana shook it, then nodded at Wash. "I'm Ana. That's Wash."

"Wash?" Marie said, maneuvering around Ana's horse to shake Wash's hand. She had an impressive grip. "That's an interesting name."

"It's really not," Wash said.

Marie smiled at him, and Wash returned it.

"We're looking for a place to stay for the night," Ana said. "We can pay for it."

Marie took a quick peek at the bags hanging off their horses before nodding. "Come on in, and let's talk."

"You guys bathe out here all the time?" Wash asked.

"Beats a bucket and a bowl," Marie said. She turned and waved at the others before walking on ahead of them.

Wash and Ana followed on their horses.

Kanter 11 grew larger in front of them, and the more Wash saw of it up close, the better the place looked. It had clearly seen a lot of wear and tear but plenty of upkeep, too. Not that he and Ana had any choice but to find lodging here. A quick glimpse up at the slowly darkening sky confirmed that.

"Where did you folks come from?" Marie was asking Ana.

"North Dakota," Ana lied.

"What're you folks doing all the way down here?"

"Looking for our Shangri-La. You know where we can find it?"

"Your Shangri-La, huh?" Marie said. Wash didn't have to be able to see Marie's face to know she was nowhere close to buying Ana's answer. "You think it's down here?"

"That's what we're here to find out," Ana said. "We're heading into Arkansas after this. Maybe cross through Oklahoma first."

"It'll be the first time I hear anyone call Sooner country Shangri-La," Marie said with a chuckle.

"It won't hurt to take a look."

"Well, I don't know if you'll find your paradise down here or not, but you're both welcome to stay in Kanter for as long as you want. We won't ask for much in return, just what you can spare."

"I'm sure we can work something out."

"I'm sure we can," Marie said, and walked on ahead of them.

Ana slowed down her mount noticeably, and Wash did likewise. They were close enough to the town now that Wash could make out a young woman in her late teens sitting in a rocking chair feeding a baby with one breast, while two young men in their twenties sat on the porch of what looked like an apartment playing checkers. The streets were mostly empty, but there were a couple of trucks and ATVs parked in front of buildings. Whether they still worked or not was another question.

"What are you thinking?" Wash asked, keeping his voice low so Marie, who had lengthened her lead in front of them, couldn't overhear.

"I'm not getting any mountain man vibes from her or this place, but we should be careful anyway," Ana said. She glanced up at the sky, then back down. "Let's not tell them more than they need to know."

"We should also stay together."

"You sure you wouldn't rather stay closer to Marie?"

Wash glanced over and saw her grinning at him. "Is that supposed to mean something?"

"Just that she put on quite a show for you."

"You're crazy. You were there, too."

"Yeah, but the way she was looking at you..."

"Where is this going?"

Ana shrugged and looked forward. "Just remember: You're not one hundred percent. If there are any horizontal aerobics, you need to be careful about your stitches."

"Horizontal aerobics?"

"It's not like I blame you. She's gorgeous. And she's definitely not shy."

Wash sighed. "Are you done?"

"I'll let you know," Ana said, before riding on ahead until she had caught up to Marie. "So, how many people do you guys have in Kanter?"

Wash looked after her and thought, *What was that all about?*

FOURTEEN

"He's gone now, but he says to tell you he'll be waiting in Texas. He says not to keep him waiting too long, because he gets bored easily."

He couldn't get the teenager's voice out of his head, and the knowledge that he had been so close pounded inside his skull over and over.

It was here all along, old timer. Just down the road. Just down the road.

He was still thinking about that missed opportunity as he zombie-walked through Marie's introduction of the town and its one hundred or so population. (He was pretty sure it was one hundred or so.) Marie took them to an old bakery that hadn't been used for a while, and she had to unlock the front door using a key ring that was as big as her entire hand.

The place smelled of mold and abandonment, but that was better than the stink of ghouls hiding in the shadows. A hallway led into an office in the back and the counter was covered in dust, as were the empty display cases in one corner. Fading sunlight filtered in through the two windows behind them, each fitted with security gates soldered into place on the other side.

"It's either this or one of the rooms in the apartments," Marie said. "But there's no privacy there, and the walls are pretty thin." She winked at them. "If you know what I mean."

Neither Ana nor Wash corrected her, and Wash said instead, "What about the horses?"

"We'll put them in the stables on the north side of town. It's secure, and we have two people on guard throughout the night. You can bring your things in here with you, just to be safe."

"What about beds?" Ana asked.

"There's a couch in the back office. It's not a pullout, though, and probably too small for the both of you. I'll fetch someone to bring you pillows and blankets later. You guys can use the floor. More, you know, room."

"Thanks, we'll make it work," Wash said.

"My pleasure. We'll talk about what you guys have in those bags in the morning. Maybe you can part ways with some things we could use."

"You don't want to do that now?"

"Nah. I trust you two." She smiled at him. "Besides, I know where you'll be until morning." Marie opened the door, but before stepping through it, said, "Someone will come and take your horses for you."

"Thanks," Ana said after her.

"See you for breakfast tomorrow," Marie said as she closed the door after her.

Wash walked to the window and looked out through the steel bars. Marie was waving to one of the twenty-something young men Wash had seen earlier, and a lanky figure jogged over. They talked in the streets for a while, Marie pointing back at the bakery, before she headed over and into a two-story white building just a little farther up the road.

Ana had gone to look at the office in the back and returned a few minutes later. "There's a couch back there, but she's right, it's definitely too small for the both of us. It should fit you just fine, though."

"You can take it," Wash said.

"You're the one with the bullet holes. The floor's fine for me."

"I thought we agreed we should stay close?"

"We'll still be in the same building."

"Anyway, the last thing I want is to roll off that couch in the middle of the night."

Ana shrugged. "Up to you. But don't say I didn't offer."

She joined him at the window and peered out. The sun was dipping in the horizon, and they could see the town preparing for it. Calmly. There wasn't anything out there that looked even close to chaos. Kanter had gone through plenty of nightfalls from the looks of it, and the people at the stream were only now starting to file back.

Ana pointed at a red two-story brick and mortar across the street from them, next door to the white one Marie had gone into earlier. "That's probably the apartments. Everyone's going in there."

"Looks like it," Wash nodded.

He watched as people appeared at the windows and began

closing them. Like their windows, the ones outside were also secured with bars. A few had boards instead.

"What do you think?" Ana asked.

"About what?"

"The town."

"It's nothing I haven't seen before. The slayer who told me about the place did some work for them a few years back. He had nothing special to say; in and out."

"I don't see any farms or livestock…"

"There's the stream."

"Fish?"

"There's a lot of fish and not a lot of fishermen culling them. You could live on fish if you had a stream right next door, like Kanter does. And there's the woods. Plenty of food in there if you know how to hunt, which they probably do."

"Marie said there were only a hundred and twenty-one people in town. Half of the buildings are empty, or almost empty."

"They must have lost a lot of people after The Walk Out."

"Did you notice all the women?" She smiled. "The place is overflowing with estrogen."

"I saw that."

"Why do you think that is?"

"You'd have to ask Marie."

"Maybe you can ask her. She might be more forthcoming."

He gave her a curious look. "I feel like you've been trying to say something since we got here. Wanna spill it?"

"She seems to like you, that's all."

"Where did you get that idea?"

"She kept staring at you. And vice versa."

"I wasn't staring at her." He added quickly, "Maybe back

at the stream, but I couldn't help that. Gorgeous women don't climb out of a stream soaking wet in front of me every day, contrary to popular opinion."

She smiled and might have been about to say something when there was a knock on the door.

Wash walked over and opened it for the same two twenty-somethings he'd seen earlier, as they carried a bundle each inside.

"Home delivery," one of them said with a grin. He had dark red hair and freckles and hurried past Wash to drop a thick blanket and pillow on the floor.

His companion was blond and rail thin. "We're gonna grab your horses and take them to the stables, so you guys wanna get your stuff first?"

Wash and Ana did just that, carrying their bags into the bakery before the two young men untied their horses' reins and led them up the road. Sunlight was fading, but neither townsman seemed to be in any hurry.

"I don't see any old men around, either," Wash said, watching after the two from the bakery's front porch. "Just kids, like those two."

"'Kids?'" Ana said. "They're your age, Wash."

"I'm twenty-five."

"Of course you are," Ana said before heading back into the building.

Wash gave the darkening skies a quick peek, then glanced at the windows around him. Some had turned on lanterns while others had closed up and simply gone dark. There weren't that many people still out in the street, but a few were checking the bars over their windows before heading inside.

He turned and followed Ana back into the bakery. Wash

closed the door, then pushed the deadbolt into place before dropping his bags. He took the Mossberg and M4 with him to the corner where Ana had unrolled the blankets and fixed up their makeshift beds. She had laid them out side by side, with about a foot of space to spare.

"Are you still thinking about it?" Ana asked. She had sat down on her "bed" and was taking off her jacket.

"About what?" Wash said. "The girl, the farmhouse, the mountain men, or One Eye?"

"All of the above."

"Yeah." Wash leaned the carbine against the wall to his left (Ana was to his right) and laid the shotgun on the floor. "They're all I've been thinking about. Especially what the girl said."

"Me too." She stared at the door for a moment, her hands wrapped around her knees. "It's gotten a lot complicated, hasn't it?"

He sat down next to her. "It wasn't complicated before when you decided to chase down Mathison and his gang all by your little lonesome?"

She shook her head. "It was a pretty easy decision, actually. It's my sister. I'd go to hell for her. And it'd been pretty straightforward since, but..." She looked over at him and smiled. "Then you came along."

"Hey, you're the one who came to *me*, remember?"

"I know, Wash. I just meant that things didn't quite go as planned, that's all."

"I'm not sure how to take that."

"It's a good thing."

"Is it?"

"Yes," she said, and leaned over and kissed him before he could reply.

She caught him by surprise, but he didn't let that stop him from kissing her back. Her mouth was warm and her lips were amazingly soft and malleable, and it had been a while since he'd inhaled a woman's scent from such close proximity.

Wash was reaching for her when she pulled away and said, "That's enough."

"What?" he said. "Wait—"

"We both need sleep."

"Now?"

She lay down and pulled the blanket over her, then turned over onto her side with her back to him.

"Really?" Wash said.

"Go to sleep. We need to wake up early tomorrow and try to make up ground on Mathison."

"We should talk about this."

"There's nothing to talk about."

"You kissed me."

"Yes, I did. Now to go sleep."

"Just like that?"

"Go to sleep, Wash."

"Easy for you to say, lady."

He lay down and stared at dust flitting across fading sunlight from the windows. Kanter 11 was already quiet when they first stepped inside, but it had gone completely silent now. It would have been the same inside the bakery if not for his slightly accelerated breathing.

Wash pushed up onto one elbow and looked over at her. "What if—"

"Go to sleep," Ana said before he could finish.

"Hear me out..."

"*Go...to...sleep.*"

"Hey, you started this," Wash said, unable to hide his annoyance.

"It was just a kiss. You've been kissed before, haven't you?"

"Of course I have."

"Then don't make more out of it than what it is."

"And what is it?"

"It was a kiss."

"Why did you kiss me?"

"I felt like it, so I did it."

"And that's it?"

"What else is there?"

"You tell me."

"There isn't more." She pulled the blanket higher up her shoulder. "Go to sleep. I want to get an early start tomorrow."

"Hey, woman, you can't just pull something like that and expect me to forget about it," Wash said, but Ana didn't respond.

He tried again:

"Ana..."

Nothing from her, even though he was sure she hadn't fallen asleep *that* fast.

"Goddammit," he said, and turned over onto his back and stared up at the ceiling.

———

After about an hour of trying to go to sleep, it was obvious it wasn't going to happen. Even the usually comforting *tick-tick-tick-tick* of the watch couldn't help him. Ana didn't share his troubles, if the sound of her snoring softly next to him was any indication.

Wash sat up and dug out the sheet of Tramadol and punched out two more pills. He glanced over at Ana just to make sure she wasn't pretending before taking the meds with some warm water. He felt better almost immediately, even though there was a very high probability it was all in his mind. The pain hadn't been too bad throughout the day, but Wash didn't feel like taking any chances.

Wash looked over at Ana again. She had turned over onto her back and her hair, loosened from its ponytail, fanned around her face, a few strays draping over her eyes. There was enough moonlight to give him a breathtaking view of her.

She really was a beautiful woman, and he wondered how he hadn't seen that before. Maybe it was the way she slept—peaceful, without a care in the world, and with that ghost of a smile on her lips—that convinced him he was nuts when he thought she was pretty before, just not *that* pretty.

Wash wasn't sure how he felt about her. About *this* thing between them. This was exactly the kind of entanglement he wasn't looking for, that he had actively avoided since starting his manhunt for One Eye. If he'd wanted a woman, he would have stayed in Harrisonville when the mayor made his generous offer. But he hadn't, because there were other things that took precedence over his libido.

He lay back down and tried to go to sleep. The pills helped, and he could already feel himself starting to drift off. The quiet from outside and Ana's soft and soothing breathing next to him didn't hurt, either. The watch's *tick-tick-tick-tick*, this time, was more effective.

Even as he started to fade, the girl's words came back to him:

"He's gone now, but he says to tell you he'll be waiting in Texas. He says not to keep him waiting too long, because he gets bored easily."

"...he'll be waiting for you..."

"....he'll be waiting for you..."

FIFTEEN

He woke up to Ana sitting next to him in that now familiar-looking Indian style, her hands draped over her knees and her eyes fixed on him. He had a feeling she'd been in that pose for a while and wondered how much of it was because of her *it was just a kiss* kiss from last night.

"What?" Wash said, sitting up and rubbing at his eyes.

"I need to change your bandages and check your sutures," Ana said.

"That's all?"

"That's all."

"You sure?"

"Yes." Then, without missing a beat, "For now."

"What's that mean?"

"It means what it sounds like. Now come on, I want to get this done so we can get back on the road."

He pulled off his clothes for her. "Let me know if you see anything you like."

Ana smiled as she took out the supplies from a bag sitting

nearby. She immediately went to work, unrolling the gauze from around his waist while Wash occupied himself by blinking at the sunlight coming in through the windows. Ana had pulled aside the curtains, and he could see Kanter's citizens going about their business. They were early risers, apparently.

Wash glanced down at his watch. A few minutes after seven. "How long have you been awake?"

"About an hour." She tossed the old bandages and peered at her handiwork on one side, then leaned over to see the other one. "Any pain?"

"Does blue balls count?"

"Really? That's mature." She picked up a clean rag and wetted it with some water. "How long has it been?"

"How long has what been?"

"Since you've been laid. It sounds like it's been a while." Wash couldn't see her face, but he imagined her smiling when she said that.

"What makes you think that?"

"I don't know; the way you keep harping on a simple kiss."

Wash grunted. "It hasn't been that long. Last week in a place called Jones City, just north of Harrisonville. Did you pass by it?"

"I did. Saw a lot of pretty girls there."

"Why did you think I spent a few days there after I was done working?"

"Did you, now?" she asked. He wasn't sure if that was actually a question, though.

"That's right, I did."

"What a playboy," Ana said as she cleaned his side, concentrating around the sutures before leaning over and doing the same to his back. "What are all those girls in Jones City going to say when you don't show back up after this one-way trip of yours to Texas?"

The question caught him off guard. Wash thought they were just having fun, going back and forth, and then she had to hit him with *that*.

"I don't know," he said. "I didn't tell them. You're the only person who knows what I'm doing out here. What I'm really doing."

She sat back, putting the towel away and picking up the roll of gauze, while catching his gaze. "I'm the only one you've told?"

He nodded.

"Why me?" she asked.

"I don't know." Then, with a satisfied smirk, "I wouldn't read too much into it, if I were you. It was just something that happened."

She rolled her eyes, then picked up a pair of scissors. "This might hurt a little bit."

"It didn't hurt last time."

"Yeah, well, you weren't being an asshat last time..."

Marie showed up about an hour later while they were getting ready to leave. She invited them to breakfast, but they'd already eaten from the mountain men's stash and declined. For the night stay, Marie took some supplies, but nothing they couldn't do without. She also asked for a box of 9mm bullets, even though Wash hadn't seen anyone in town walk around with a weapon since they arrived yesterday.

"Before we go, can I ask you something?" Ana said as Marie was about to leave with her payment. "Before us, did anyone come through here? Eleven men and four women? They would have come through about a week ago."

Marie didn't think about it for very long before shaking her head. "No one like that. You're the first couple that's been through here for about four months now."

"Are you sure?"

"I'd remember a group of eleven men and four women from a week ago."

Ana nodded. "Thanks."

"Friends of yours?"

"Acquaintances."

Marie nodded, even though Wash didn't think she bought that explanation. "I'll be sure to keep an eye out for them. In case, you know, they come back this way."

Maybe that's not such a good idea, Wash thought, but Ana said first, "It might be a good idea to avoid them if they do end up back in this direction."

Marie looked at her for a moment before turning to Wash. Then, "So, not friendly acquaintances?"

"No," Ana said.

"Thanks for the heads-up."

Ana nodded.

"You sure you guys don't want to stay longer?" Marie asked. "We can all use a little more rest. Some of us more than others, I'm guessing."

"We can't," Ana said. "We have to get going."

"To find your Shangri-La."

"That's right." Ana smiled. "It's not going to find itself."

Marie returned her smile. "Kanter's doors are always open,

if you folks should come back this way. We can always use more supplies."

Thirty minutes later, Ana and Wash were back in their saddles and riding out of town. They saw more people in the streets than yesterday, with more kids under five years old. A few of the young women were cradling infants. They entered Kanter from the south and left through the north using the same dirt street.

They were just beyond the town when the same two twenty-somethings from yesterday stepped out of the nearby woods. They were packing sidearms and rifles and had a white-tailed deer dangling from a branch between them. Wash exchanged a nod with the two as they rode past.

"That's the first townspeople with guns I've seen," Ana said.

"You noticed that, too, huh?" Wash said.

"Hard not to. Even those milquetoasts in Harrisonville knew enough to arm themselves." She glanced behind them back at the town. "They don't have much, do they?"

"They have enough."

"My point is that they don't have a lot, and they don't care. After everything they went through—everything we've all gone through in the last six years—maybe this is what paradise is. A small, nondescript town next to a stream, with no cares in the world."

Wash smiled. "You thinking of switching homes?"

"Maybe. After what those people in Newton allowed to happen..." She gritted her teeth for a moment before finishing. "Maybe."

They continued through the woods until they'd found the dirt road they were on yesterday. Wash breathed easier once they were beyond the canopy of trees and underneath open skies. For some reason, he had expected Kanter 11 to be more than what they'd found, or what he'd been told about it. After the run-in with the mountain men, then later with the girl at the farm, he just expected trouble in Kanter as well. Ana might have felt the same way from the relieved look she gave him once they were finally moving south again.

It took another two hours before they finally stopped at a gray asphalt highway. It wasn't much—two lanes separated by a fading yellow divider—but it was the first hint that there was more to Kansas than woods, collaborator towns, and back-country roads.

"State Highway 49," Ana said. "We can take it across the Kansas-Oklahoma border, then figure out what road to take once we're on the other side. I think Mathison will avoid the big cities, and we should, too."

Wash nodded. "That's a good idea."

"So it's true. About the cities." She looked over at him. "It's been a while since I've been out here, but we've heard stories..."

"Depends on what stories you're talking about."

"Bad ones. Really bad ones."

"Oh. Those."

"So they're true?"

"Mostly, yeah. And the ones that aren't, aren't too far from the truth."

"You've been back inside them since The Walk Out?"

"Not because I wanted to." He frowned. "They're not happy places, Ana. Best to avoid them at all costs, if possible."

Ana nodded. "We'll take 49 south for as long as we can, then switch to another highway when we near Oklahoma

City and Norman. Go around them instead of through them."

State Highway 49 was flat to the ground and flanked by walls of trees on both sides. They traveled on the shoulder just in case they had to quickly dart back into the woods for cover. The first road sign they came across told them Oklahoma was still ten miles south, which meant they would easily cross the border before the end of the day.

Wash's side was feeling better, but he took two more of the Tramadol anyway just to make sure it remained that way. Ana either didn't see him do it, or she didn't feel like arguing about it if she had.

About five miles later, Ana stopped her Tennessee Walker on the shoulder.

Wash moved his big orange-brown over to join her. "What is it?"

She nodded at a sign in front of them. It was rectangular and had an arrow on one side pointing left toward an over-grown trail. The sign was green with faded yellow letters, but Wash could still read most of it and was able to figure out the rest: *Pond Creek Campsite.*

"Campsite?" he said.

"Mathison likes to stop at places like campsites and RV parks to rest during the day. That was how I picked up their tracks outside of Harrisonville. They have the gear for it."

"We should take a look. It won't take that much time, and if nothing else, there's the creek. We can refill our bottles."

Ana rode forward, then turned left into the covered trail. She leaned in her saddle to bat at low-hanging tree branches and leaves in her path. Wash pulled his shotgun out of its holster and followed behind her.

Voices.

They heard it after fighting through the trail for about a hundred yards. It was almost impossible not to. There was more than one man, and they were laughing. Booming laughter, as if they were having the time of their lives.

Ana stopped and glanced back at Wash. He nodded, confirming what she'd heard, and saw the combination of dread and anticipation on her face. They climbed off their horses and tied them to a nearby tree.

Wash was unslinging the M4 to give her when Ana shook her head.

"Take it," he whispered.

"No," she whispered back. "It might not be them, and I don't want to scare whoever it is."

Another round of laughter from in front of them, and Wash thought, *Those don't sound like the kind of people who'd be scared so easily.*

But he whispered back instead, "I'll circle around, but I won't show myself. If it's friendlies, I'll wait for your signal to come out, *after* you've warned them."

He expected her to argue, but she nodded. "Wait for my signal, okay?"

"Be careful."

"You too."

They went in separate directions—Ana continuing forward on foot and Wash moving off the covered trail. He slid his way around trees and through thickets. It was impossible to be completely silent, but he did his best while still maintaining some speed.

It was easy to tell where the campsite was—about fifty or so yards to his left. All he had to do was listen to the raucous laughter as whoever was out there continued to enjoy themselves. He counted two, maybe three distinct voices talking back and forth. They weren't loud enough that he could decipher every word they were saying and the thick trees and bushes between him and them didn't help.

After moving for a few minutes, he changed directions and started angling toward the camp's location. After another minute of walking, he started to glimpse a clearing in front of him through the trees. The voices were also becoming clearer, and the laughter even louder.

Wash slung the shotgun and replaced it with the carbine. The Mossberg was good for a crowd, but not if he had to distinguish between enemies and friendlies in one contained location. The M4 on semiautomatic would give him better target selection, and the thirty rounds would come in handy if a gunfight broke out. If all else failed and he needed to cover a lot of ground, he could always switch to full-auto—

"Wash!"

He forgot about his wounds and broke off into a sprint. He immediately regretted it, but he kept going anyway because that was Ana who had just shouted out his name.

The clearing was right in front of him, and Wash burst through a bush with some thorns and onto the other side, lifting the rifle as he slid to a stop.

Two seconds became an eternity as he surveyed the clearing:

Three men standing around a pit with a smothered fire looking across the grounds at Ana on the other side. Two of the men were clutching bottles in their fists while a third was holding what looked like a turkey leg. They were all armed, and shotguns and rifles leaned against the logs they had been sitting on.

Wash had tossed aside stealth for speed and knew he had made way too much noise, so he wasn't surprised when two of the men instantly turned around to look at him as he revealed himself in the open.

Then Ana was screaming, "Shoot them, Wash! Shoot them!"

He pulled the trigger.

SIXTEEN

"Slow is smooth, and smooth is fast."

The Old Man's words ricocheted back and forth in his head even as everything else faded into the background.

The campsite. The three men inside it. The pathetically put-together tent next to them. The wind picking up and tossing ashes from the dead fire. A bottle falling, then shattering as its owner dropped with a hole in his chest.

"In a firefight, the guy who shoots first doesn't always shoot last. It's the guy who shoots truest. To get there, you have to practice until it becomes muscle memory. Slowly at first, until it becomes smooth as butter. Slow is smooth, and smooth is fast, kid. Remember that."

Slow is smooth, and smooth is fast, Wash thought as he turned slightly to the left and pulled the trigger again, even as the second man reached for his sidearm.

Wash didn't know if the man would have gotten to his weapon faster if he'd dropped the bottle clutched in his left hand first. But that was a moot point as a pinkish red cloud sprayed the crisp morning air and the man stumbled and fell, slamming the side of his head into the log he'd been sitting on seconds ago, then rolled off to the side.

"Avoid the gunfight if you can, but if you can't, make sure you end it. Never, ever leave a man with a gun standing once the bullets fly. Finish it and move on. Next!"

Wash tracked the third man who had taken off. His target was still holding onto the turkey leg as he fled; he also hadn't gone for his holstered sidearm. As far as Wash could tell, the man hadn't even made an attempt for the pistol before running.

"Wash!" Ana shouted.

Her voice thrummed in his ears even as he followed the man's progress, Wash's forefinger tightening around the trigger. The target was moving surprisingly fast for someone of his size—six-two, at least, and well over two hundred pounds. Crunching autumn leaves scattered under his boots. The man was bundled up in cargo pants and a thick winter coat, and when he glanced over in Wash's direction while still in midstride, Wash got an eyeful of a mask of fear looking back at him through his rifle's scope.

"Don't shoot!" Ana shouted.

Ana's words registered almost too late, but he was able to process it in time to pull the reticle down even as he squeezed the trigger, and his target seemed to trip on an imaginary obstacle before spinning in the air and falling back down to the ground.

"Don't shoot!" Ana shouted again as she raced toward the fallen man.

"Don't shoot?" Wash thought as he lowered the carbine.

First "Shoot them!" and now "Don't shoot." Make up your mind, woman!

Wash hurried over to the two men he'd dropped, while Ana rushed over to the third one. Wash had gotten him in the shoulder—if Ana's words had come just a split second too late, the round would have gone through his head—and the man was grabbing it while rolling around on the ground clenching his teeth in pain.

"Stay down," Ana said to him. "Stay the hell down, Travis."

The man named Travis had other ideas, and began reaching for his sidearm. Wash was about to shoot him again, but Ana beat him to it. She kicked Travis in the shoulder—the same shoulder Wash had shot him. The man howled in pain, and in that moment probably didn't even feel Ana stepping on his extended right arm—the same arm that had been reaching for the gun—to pin it to the ground.

"Don't make me tell you twice," Ana said.

Glad she's on my side, Wash thought as he finished walking over to the other two men.

The first one was on his back, lifeless brown eyes wide open and staring up at the cloudless sky. He was dead. Wash had shot for center mass, but he'd gotten the man in the heart instead.

I'll take it.

The second one was still alive, both hands folded across his chest where the 5.56 round had punched through his sweater. His mouth opened and closed like a fish out of water, sweat covering his forehead. He was trying desperately to keep the blood from pumping out of his chest, but Wash had seen that kind of wound before, and without proper treatment, it was only a matter of time.

The man's lips quivered as he struggled to talk. "Finish it. For God's sake, finish it."

Wash shot him in the forehead, remembering the Old Man's words as he pulled the trigger:

"Never, ever leave a man with a gun standing once the bullets fly. Finish it and move on. Next!"

"Next," Wash said quietly before looking over at Ana.

She was still standing over Travis, his pistol in her hand, and looking in his direction. If she had any objections to him just killing a man in cold blood, he didn't see it on her face or in her eyes.

"You okay?" he asked.

She nodded and looked past him. He followed her gaze to the tent nearby.

"I'll clear it," Wash said and headed over.

He had to walk over four backpacks, all of them bulging with supplies, in order to get to the tent. It was beige and worn from use, and though it looked big enough for at least three people, Wash knew from experience it could be disassembled and stuffed into a backpack and still have plenty of space. Whoever had put it up hadn't done a very good job, though, and Wash was afraid the canopy might fall apart when he pulled down the front zipper and stuck his carbine inside.

A face covered in dirty brown hair peered at him, its owner huddled as far into the back of the small tent as they were able. Small, thin arms were clutched around bent knees as the woman hid behind her hair. She was nude and hyperventilating, her chest heaving with every pained breath.

Wash backed his way out of the tent.

He glanced across the campsite at Ana. She hadn't moved and was watching him with an almost blank expression, barely able to contain herself as she waited for him to speak. She had Travis's sidearm dangling from one hand, but he wasn't sure if she even remembered the wounded man was there.

"You should come here," Wash said.

Ana nodded and hurried to him. Wash walked over to meet her halfway, one eye looking past her at Travis, still lying on the ground clutching his wounded shoulder.

"What's inside?" Ana asked.

"It's a girl," Wash said. Then, before she could ask, "It's not Emily."

She looked at him, and Wash wasn't sure if that was relief or disappointment on her face. "Are you sure?"

"Brown hair."

"Oh."

Wash nodded at Travis. "Is he one of them? Mathison's men?"

"Yes," Ana said, and walked to the tent.

Wash continued on to Travis, who had managed to sit up. Blood trickled down his arm, and he was trying to grit away the pain while staring past Wash at his two dead friends. Or, at least, Wash assumed they were friends. Traveling companions, if nothing else.

The campsite was split into different sections, each with their own fire pit and large moss-covered logs arranged in a semicircle around them, as well as wooden benches for dining. The grass had gotten tall throughout the area, but it would still be years before *Pond Creek Campsite* was completely reclaimed by the thick woods that surrounded it.

"You're pretty fast, for a big man," Wash said.

Travis looked over at him. "Not fast enough."

"No one's ever fast enough."

"You murdered Duncan."

It wasn't hard for Wash to figure out who Duncan was. The *murdered* part gave it away.

"He asked for it," Wash said. "Literally."

"Bullshit," Travis said. "You're a fucking killer."

"I never said I wasn't."

"Who are you?"

"The guy with the rifle," Wash said, and sat down on a log about ten yards from Travis.

Travis looked past him again, but this time toward Ana. Wash glanced over to check on her, but she was already inside the tent.

He turned back to Travis. "You're one of Mathison's guys."

Travis didn't answer.

"So what happened?" Wash continued. "Why'd you guys split up?" He gave the woods around them a quick glance. "Or is he still around here somewhere?"

"He's gone," Travis said. "Been gone for two days now."

"Gone where?"

"Gone."

"Texas," Wash said. "Brownsville, Texas, to be precise."

The sudden flash of surprise in Travis's eyes told Wash that Ana's information had been correct after all.

Wash smiled. "Yeah, we know all about Brownsville."

"How the fuck do you know that?"

"Loose lips sink ships." He looked back at the two dead men, then at the half-empty bottles of liquor they'd dropped. "Where'd you guys get Johnny Walker and his buddy Jim Beam over there?"

"You can find anything, if you look hard enough."

"What was the occasion?"

Travis kept quiet.

Wash looked back at the tent, remembering the sight of the girl inside it. "Never mind. I figured it out."

"Who are you?" Travis asked. "You from Newton?"

"No, I'm not from Newton."

"Then who the fuck are you?"

"Just a guy who owes someone his life," Wash said.

"Her name's Teresa," Ana said about thirty minutes later. "Mathison's people killed her husband when they took her. She has a three-year-old waiting for her back in Newton."

She glanced over at Travis, sitting on the grass with his legs tied in front of him and his arms similarly bound, but behind his back. He was leaning back against one of the logs, with a bandage wrapped around his wounded shoulder. He looked in pain, but neither Wash nor Ana cared enough to help him alleviate it. He kept looking over at the two men that Wash had killed and left to lie where they fell nearby.

"The other two are Duncan and Chris," Ana said. "Were Duncan and Chris, now. They were Mathison's people, too."

Wash checked on Teresa, sitting on the wooden bench on the other side of the camping grounds. She was dressed in one of Ana's shirts and pants, but Ana only had one pair of shoes so the woman had to stay barefoot. She was devouring the contents of an MRE bag that Travis and the other two were carrying around in their packs like someone who hadn't eaten in days. And maybe that wasn't too far from the truth, by the looks of her.

"How is she?" Wash asked.

Ana shook her head, and Wash wondered how often she had been thinking about Emily ever since they stumbled across the campsite. Because her sister was still out there, in Mathison's hands, and Wash didn't want to think about what they were doing to her now. If he felt that way, he couldn't imagine what was going through Ana's mind.

"What did he tell you about Mathison?" Ana asked, looking at Travis.

"I was saving that part for you," Wash said.

She nodded, then walked over to Travis with Wash beside her. As they neared him, Travis looked up and swallowed. For such a big man, he appeared amazingly small at the moment. The bandage around his shoulder wasn't exactly a great example of textbook field tourniquet in action, but then Wash hadn't been concerned with aesthetics when he put it on the man.

"Where is he?" Ana asked when she stopped in front of Travis. "Where's Mathison?"

"He's gone," Travis said. "To Brownsville."

"Then why are you and the other two still here?"

"We parted ways."

"When?"

"Two days ago." He smirked. "He's got a two-day head start on you, lady. You'll never catch up to him. I don't think he's even on that highway out there anymore. Mathison's smart. Too smart for you. He wouldn't make it *that* easy."

Ana ignored his taunts and said, "Why?"

"Why what?" Travis asked.

"Why did you and the others part ways with Mathison?"

"What are you going to do to me?"

"Answer the question."

"Tell me what you're going to do to me first."

"Wash," Ana said.

Wash drew the kukri from its sheath. "Evade another question with a question, and I'm going to chop off your finger. Keep doing it, and I'll chop off another one. You get me, Travis?"

Travis swallowed again. "You wouldn't do that. I'm no use to you dead."

"Who said anything about killing you? You know how long a man can go without his digits?"

"You're bluffing."

"Only one way to find out," Wash said, and grinned.

Travis looked away from Wash to focus on Ana. "You won't get any answers from me until you call off your wild dog."

"What happened with you and Mathison?" Ana asked again.

Travis hesitated. He glanced from Wash to Ana, then over at Duncan's and Chris's bodies.

"Wash, take one of his thumbs," Ana said.

"Okay, okay, Jesus Christ," Travis said. "Jesus Christ..." He gathered himself, before starting. "We decided—Duncan, Chris, and me—that we didn't want to go back to Texas. That was always Mathison's thing, not ours. He agreed to let us go our own way."

"And Teresa?"

"He gave her to us as a going-away present."

"How nice of him," Wash said.

"Yeah, that's Mathison; he's a regular humanitarian, all right," Travis said, though there wasn't anything that even sounded like humor in his voice.

"So he's still going to Brownsville?" Ana asked.

Travis nodded. "As far as I know, yeah."

"And she's still with him? Emily?"

"Again, as far as I know, yeah."

"Where is he now?"

"I already told you, I don't have any idea. It's been two days since we said adios. He could be in Texas by now, for all I care. It's not like we got phones to keep in touch, you know?"

Wash could see that Ana had more questions—most of them probably about her sister—but she didn't ask them. Either she didn't want to know, or she already knew and didn't want the confirmation.

"What now?" Travis asked. "What're you going to do to me?"

"I'm not going to do anything to you," Ana said.

"I don't understand..."

"Wash," Ana said.

Travis's eyes widened as he finally understood. Wash almost felt sorry for the guy. Almost. But then all he had to do was look across at Teresa, buried behind her dirty hair as she spooned food into her mouth like a wild child who hadn't eaten in days, and all of that empathy went away.

"Hey, come on, we had a deal," Travis said. "Didn't we? Didn't we?"

"No," Ana said. "And if you don't know where to find Mathison, then you're no use to me."

She turned away before he could say anything else to her, and walked over to where Teresa sat.

When Wash looked back, Travis was staring at him. No, not staring, but *pleading* with his eyes. "Look, it wasn't my idea. All of it. None of it was my idea. It was Mathison all the way. He's the real bad guy here. I was just going along with it. I mean, I had no choice, you understand? Mathison is fucking insane. Did she tell you that? That guy is fucking *insane*."

"Where do you want it?" Wash asked.

"What?"

"Where do you want it?" Wash asked again as he put the machete away and drew the Beretta and thumbed back the hammer.

"Don't do this..."

"I won't ask again."

Travis shook his head violently and tried to get up, but that was difficult with his legs and arms bound, and he spent more time trying not to fall than actually making any progress. "Please, don't do this. I can help you find Mathison. I was just fucking around earlier. I know how he thinks. I can help you get her sister back. Fuck Mathison. That motherfucker's always been nuts anyway. Let me help you. I can help you. I can *help you*."

"Oh, we'll get her back," Wash said. "Don't you worry about that."

Wash pulled the trigger and was already walking back to where Ana was sitting with Teresa before Travis's body had slumped to the ground behind him.

Ana looked across the campsite, her eyes meeting his. She nodded wordlessly, and he returned it.

Three down.

Eight to go...

SEVENTEEN

"*So you're killing for her now, huh?*" Imaginary Old Man asked.

I'm doing what I have to do. You taught me that, didn't you?

"*Be careful, kid. It's a slippery slope. Once you start, you might not be able to pull yourself out of the hole.*"

I don't have any choice.

"*Don't you?*"

No, I don't...

Wash stepped through the bushes with the empty bottles of water in his hands. They weren't going anywhere for a while, so he had gone in search of the creek that was promised in the campsite's name, but he had come up empty. He did find a ditch that looked as if it once held water, but that was years ago. After another thirty minutes or so of fruitless searching, he gave up and returned to the camp to find Ana crouched over one of Mathison's men. Chris, since Duncan was the one with the hole in his head.

"Where's Teresa?" he asked.

"She's in the tent, getting ready," Ana said.

"So how's this gonna work?"

"I'm going to give her one of the horses and some of our supplies. She'll have to get home on her own."

"You mean one of *my* horses, don't you?"

She smiled, but it was a little bit more forced than usual. "Should I have asked first?"

Wash shook his head. "No. But *will* she be able to get back home by herself?"

Ana glanced over at the tent. They could just make out Teresa's silhouette on the other side moving around. "I think so."

"You don't sound too sure."

"I can't afford to go back with her." Ana sighed and stood up. "The best I can do is point her in the right direction. I told her about Kanter 11, about Marie, and she's got a map from these asshats to help her find her way. That's the best I can do for her," Ana finished, but what Wash saw on her face was, *"Because Mathison is still out there with my sister, and God only knows what he's doing to her now."*

Wash nodded at Chris. "Find anything useful?"

"No. They have another unopened bottle of whiskey in their pack, if you're interested."

"Maybe later, when we're celebrating."

"What will we be celebrating?"

"Getting your sister back."

Ana pursed her lips but didn't say anything.

"And we will get her back," Wash said.

"I know I'm asking a lot from you." She looked down at the two bodies, then over at Travis. "I know this isn't easy."

"Tell me the truth. This was always the reason you wanted me to come along, why you saved my life. So I'd owe you."

"I didn't set you up to get shot by the mountain men, if that's what you're implying."

"No, but you took advantage of it."

"By saving your life." She didn't look away from him, and he didn't see any regrets in her eyes. "Yes, I took advantage of the opportunity when it presented itself. I needed someone like you, Wash."

"'Someone like me?'"

"The first time I saw you, you were sitting in a tree, in the middle of the night, waiting for ghouls to come out. It was never about the horses. It was always about you."

Wash grunted. "You could have just asked."

"Maybe, but I couldn't take that chance. Besides, would you have said yes?"

"I don't know, but I would have leaned toward helping."

"Would you have really?"

"Yes." Then, off her genuinely surprised look, "They're evil men, Ana. I was taught not to allow evil to happen if I can stop it. And I can stop this, so I am, even if it is taking me off course. I can't just look the other way. I guess I'm just not built that way."

"'The only thing necessary for the triumph of evil is for good men to do nothing.'"

"I don't know about the 'good men' part..."

"It's a quote from Edmund Burke."

"Was Edmund Burke old and cranky, and liked movies about space aliens and ghost hunters way too much?"

Ana smiled. "Maybe not ghost hunters..."

"But I guess all of that's moot anyway, since you did save

my life. What kind of asshat would I be if I just ignored that part?"

"And you just saved mine."

"Nah, this doesn't count."

"Doesn't it?"

"No. But I'll let you know when we're even."

"Okay."

Teresa emerged from the tent behind them. She had washed her face and hair with water and barely looked like the same woman he had seen earlier. She was clutching a backpack to her stomach and looked tentatively at them, as if too afraid to speak first.

"Ready?" Ana asked.

Teresa nodded but didn't say anything. He hadn't heard her say a single word—at least, not while he was around.

"Come on," Ana said, and held out her hand toward Teresa.

The younger woman walked over and took it, and they walked over to the horses. Ana had already prepared the American Paint for the trip, Wash saw.

"Remember what I told you about what's between here and Newton," Ana said to Teresa. "Try to follow the map as closely as possible. Stop at Kanter 11 before you continue on to Nebraska. They're good people over there; tell Marie you're our friend."

Teresa nodded but kept silent. From the way she was walking, like she was on automatic pilot, Wash wondered if she actually heard a single thing Ana had said.

While Ana got Teresa ready to travel, Wash went through the dead men's packs and catalogued their inventory. By the time Teresa was gone and Ana had walked back over to him,

Wash had found a half-full box of 9mm to replace the one he'd given Marie, along with an equally half-full box of 5.56s. All three men were carrying AR rifles, and one of those was apparently chambered for 7.62 rounds because Wash pulled out an almost empty box of just that caliber. There were knives, more MREs, and the bottle of Jack Daniels Ana had mentioned.

"God, I hope she makes it back to Newton," Ana said quietly, looking after Teresa.

"You said her husband's dead?"

"Yes."

"Does she know that?"

"She saw it happen the night they took her. They killed him in their house." She glanced over at Duncan's lifeless body. "She said it was him."

Wash stood up with the bottle of liquor and box of 5.56s stuffed into one of the packs, along with the MREs that were already inside. He made a mental note to enjoy one of the meals before leaving the campsite. There were, after all, only so many nuts a man could eat. He had tossed the rest to lessen his weight.

"Travis said they split from Mathison two days ago, that they've been here since...enjoying themselves," Wash said. "That means Mathison's got about two days' head start on us."

"It could be worse."

"How so?"

"They could be traveling by horseback instead of on foot. That means there's still a pretty good chance we can catch up to them before they reach Texas."

"And then what?" he almost asked, but then all he had to do was check the three dead bodies and get his answer.

"We'll catch up to them," Wash said. "We'll get Emily back."

She looked over at him and nodded. "I know we will."

They returned to State Highway 49 and immediately pointed their horses south. They rode for two hours straight without stopping, and when they did pause for any length of time, it was to drink some water and let the horses feed. His stomach was full again after the generous calories provided by a bag of MRE, and he had enough renewed strength that Wash didn't have to dip into his dwindling Tramadol supply. Which was a good thing, because he had a feeling he might need them later.

Ana remained in the lead while he pulled the Morgan behind them. They were making good progress, and Ana seemed anxious to keep moving as fast as possible, though he was pretty sure she wasn't overtly aware of it. What she was probably very aware of, though, was that Emily was out there and she was *close*.

They passed two signs, one old and one relatively new, pointing to towns off the state highway, but they rode past both without stopping. Wash recognized one of the names from his map, but the other one was new. He made a mental note to update his map later when he had some free time.

If Mathison was even a little bit smart, he would be avoiding towns just as he had since leaving Newton. The man would be opting instead for campsites and isolated wooded areas to rest, which was how Ana had been able to keep track of him since Nebraska. Wash and Ana stumbling across Travis and the other two had been dumb luck, but the problem with luck was that it never lasted for very long.

Not that Wash voiced those doubts as they picked up their pace while still sticking to the shoulder. There weren't a lot of chances of being run over by a vehicle since any car out here would be heard long before they were close enough to be of any danger. It was more from habit; that, and the closer proximity to the trees meant they could dart for cover at a moment's notice. Wash was still wary of traveling so out in the open after the ambush outside of Harrisonville. The softer shoulder was also easier on the unshod horses.

They had just passed an old road sign indicating that the Kansas-Nebraska border was two miles up ahead when Ana pulled up short. Wash did likewise and instantly saw the reason why she had stopped:

Thin wisps of white smoke rising into the air in front and to the right of them.

They exchanged a quick look, and Wash imagined she was thinking the same thing he was: The girl, the suicide, and One Eye's message to Wash.

Then there was that old saying: *Fool me once, shame on you. Fool me twice, shame on me.*

"Are you getting the same bad vibes as I am?" Wash asked.

"Yeah," Ana said.

"We should keep going."

Ana shook her head and bit her lip. She was as conflicted as he was—maybe even more, given what was at stake for her. "We're not too far from where Travis and the others made camp. And Mathison was headed this way..."

"You really think he'll still be this close? Remember what Travis said. They split up two days ago."

"He could have been lying."

"I don't think he was. He had no reason to."

"Even if he wasn't a lying bastard, Mathison and the others are still on foot. There could be a lot of reasons why they would slow down or even stop for a while."

"Like what?"

"For one, they don't know I'm chasing them. They think they're out here all by themselves. I'm sure they would have taken precautions after Newton, but now?" She shook her head, and Wash thought she was trying to convince herself more than she was him. "There's no reason for them to be in any hurry. Texas and Brownsville aren't going anywhere."

Wash concentrated on the smoke. It was lazy and didn't have the telltale signs of a blazing fire. "Could be chimney smoke or an outdoor fire pit. Doesn't look like a blaze. Not thick or dark enough."

"We have to make sure," Ana said, before nodding with as much confidence as she could muster. "We have to make sure, Wash. I can't risk passing her—*them* by. Not when I'm this close."

"I guess I'm not going to talk you out of it."

"I know you're still freaked out by what happened at the farmhouse..."

"Aren't you?"

"Yes, I am. But we can't ignore this. Even after everything that's happened, I have to make sure of *everything*."

He sighed. He could hear it in her voice; Ana had made up her mind, and he wasn't going to talk her out of it.

Right. Like you ever had a chance to talk her out of doing anything, buddy. Let's face it: You're not the one leading the charge here, she is. And she has been since day one.

He sighed. "All right, but this time you're taking this." He unzipped his main pack and took out the 1911 model Colt he'd used back at the warehouse, and handed it to her. "No arguments. Not after what just happened back there."

She stared at the gun but didn't reach for it.

"Ana..." Wash said.

"I'm really not a very good shot, Wash. I told you that, right?"

"You don't have to be. Put it behind your back, under your clothes. Your jacket'll hide it. Don't use it unless you absolutely have to."

"But if it's on me, and someone finds it..."

"If we run into Mathison, do you really think you can talk your way out of it? I know you're good, but are you *that* good?"

She didn't answer.

"Mathison is a different animal," Wash said. "You know that."

She nodded. "I know."

"So I need you to take this."

"You *need* me to?"

"Yes. I need you to, Ana. If you have to use it, aim for center mass. The chest. The biggest area on the human body. Once you start shooting, keep shooting until they go down. Understand?"

"Yes."

Wash handed the 1911 to her again, and this time she took it, still reluctantly.

"If there's any shooting to be done, I'll do it," Wash said. "But I can't leave you out there unprotected if something were to happen to me."

She put the gun away behind her back. "Maybe one day you can teach me how to use it properly."

"It's a date."

She smiled. "It's been a while since I've had a date."

"You and me both."

"Then I guess we better make sure it happens," she said, before turning her Tennessee Walker around and pointing it toward the right side of the road. A few seconds later, she had slipped past the tree line.

He followed her off the road, at the same time moving his M4 from behind his back to in front of him. The new position would save him about a second (maybe two) if he should need the rifle, and in a straight-up face-to-face gunfight, an extra second (or two) was an eternity.

EIGHTEEN

This time it wasn't a farmhouse being engulfed in flames, and there were no suicidal teenagers with revolvers waiting to greet them. The scenery couldn't have been more different. Not that that did anything to stop the feeling of a gnat nipping at the edge of his peripheral vision, that familiar gut instinct that *something wasn't right.*

It was a log cabin in the woods, maybe just two bedrooms in the back and a great room up front, given its size. Something glinted on the rooftop, and Wash thought, *Solar panels?* The longer he looked, the more convinced he was that the gleaming objects were solar cell collectors. They didn't cover the entire roof, but enough to provide some juice. Solar panels were a smart move, and as long as you went to great lengths to conserve power, there was no need for fuel or generators. That, though, also immediately brought to mind the mountain men's setup.

Be careful. Be really, really careful.

There wasn't much to look at around the cabin, and

besides the birds around them, the only other sound was the natural flow of a small stream nearby. There was almost a football field of clearing between the tree line and the house, but the distance was much shorter from the side of the house to the woods—maybe just half that. Two windows flanked the building's front door, the interior hidden behind curtains. A stack of firewood sat next to the door with an ax jutting out of the ground next to the pile. As he had guessed, the smoke they'd spotted from the road was coming from the chimney.

There were no signs of people, which contributed to the surrounding's idyllic vibe. That should have eased Wash's paranoia some, but it only put him on even higher alert. Maybe it was the events of the last few days reminding him not to let his guard down even for a second. The last time he did that, he'd gotten shot.

Let's not do that again.

Ana stood next to him, their horses tied to a tree about twenty yards farther back in the woods to keep them out of sight. They were well hidden enough that Wash didn't think anyone from inside the cabin could spot them across the yard—especially from the front—even if they did know exactly where to look, which they didn't. The lack of grass between them and the house was a problem because it meant no cover for their approach. And Wash had a feeling Ana wasn't going to just leave here without first knocking on that door.

His side tingled, but he wasn't sure if that was the wound acting up or his sixth sense reminding him (as if he needed any reminders) that there was something very wrong about this place. He didn't know what it was, exactly—it was hard to put his finger on any one thing—but everything just looked too damn...perfect.

Nothing's ever this perfect. Nothing.

Ana may have been feeling the same paranoia because she hadn't moved or said a word since they arrived more than ten minutes ago.

Finally, Wash said, "We're going to have to make a decision, Ana. Do we go out there and knock on the door or take off?"

She didn't say anything but also didn't take her eyes off the cabin.

"You're feeling it, too?" he asked.

"What?"

"That something's not right."

She didn't answer right away, but after about five seconds, said, "Where is everyone? Someone had to have started the fireplace."

"Probably inside. Curtains are drawn."

"That doesn't make any sense, either."

"What's that?"

"The curtains."

"I don't understand..."

"It's still daylight, Wash. It's actually a perfect day. Who would cover up the windows on a day like this?"

"Good catch," Wash said. He hadn't seen that. He'd seen everything else that was wrong with the cabin *except* that. "No rebars over the windows, too."

It was the first thing he noticed about the place—there was no security of any type over the exterior of the windows. The door, he could understand, because it took a lot to break down a wooden door, but the window glass was easy to break by even the weakest of ghouls.

"Maybe they're so hidden they haven't run into any issues with keeping people out," Ana said.

"I don't know about that. People who are smart enough to put solar panels on rooftops wouldn't ignore simple security."

Ana looked around. "Do you see any horses?"

"No. You?"

"No. Or any type of transportation. But someone was chopping wood not very long ago."

"More wood for the fireplace, I guess." He paused, then, "All right. We're not going to get anywhere hiding in here."

"You have a plan?"

"Let me take a look at it first. I'll recon the place, see if I can spot anything on the other side."

"How long's that going to take?"

"Why? Are you in a hurry?"

She glanced up at the sky. It wasn't dark yet. Like she'd said, it was a perfect afternoon, and it would be a few hours before the first hints of nightfall even appeared on the horizon.

"About an hour," Wash said. "That should allow me to move without being seen. When I'm sure it's safe, we can—"

Ana stepped out from behind the trees and into the clearing.

Goddammit, woman, Wash thought as he watched her walk calmly across the field toward the lone building.

He unslung the M4 and positioned it in front of him for an easy lift and shoot. He also took a couple of steps back behind a large tree that provided him with thicker cover but also allowed him to peek out (hopefully) unnoticed.

Wash watched Ana in front of him. She walked calmly forward, her hands visible at her sides. If she were even the least bit scared or reluctant, he couldn't see it in the way she moved. Of course, he also couldn't see her face at the moment, but Wash imagined it would look neutral—or whatever look she wanted him to see—

Here we go!

Ana had walked ten yards—*eleven*—when the cabin door opened and a thin figure stepped outside. It was a woman, and she was holding a bucket in both hands in front of her. Whatever was inside must have weighed a ton, because she was clearly straining even as she turned right toward the stream.

Ana had stopped as soon as she saw the woman. Frozen, really, out there in the open.

Wash flicked the safety off his carbine and lifted it slightly, forefinger next to the trigger guard while his left hand wrapped around the pistol grip. Just over a hundred yards separated him and the cabin—and the woman in front of it. Wash had taken shots at much longer distances without the benefit of an ACOG.

He was getting ready, trying to get control of his breathing, when Ana began running—right at the cabin and the girl.

"Emily!" Ana shouted.

The girl with the bucket stopped and looked over. A second later, the metal pail dropped from her hands and a large volume of water splashed the dirt and grass. But unlike Ana, the girl didn't move. Wash was too far away to get a proper look at the girl's face, so he couldn't be sure what was happening.

"Emily!" Ana shouted again.

Wait, did she just say "Emily?"

The reality of what she'd shouted hadn't registered with him in the first instance, but it did the second time around.

Emily. Ana had shouted the name *Emily*. That was her sister!

I guess it was a good thing we didn't keep going!

Ana was running full stride across the yard now, even as the girl remained rooted in place. Damn, she was fast. Wash didn't even know Ana was capable of that kind of speed. It was impressive. What else could she do that she was keeping from him? She was already at the halfway point and not even slowing down a bit, as far as Wash could tell.

Wash lifted the ACOG and got a good look at the girl— and the shock on her face as she watched Ana racing toward her.

What the hell is she doing?

For a moment Wash thought Emily didn't recognize her own sister, which would explain why she wasn't moving *at all*. But then that didn't quite jive with the almost horrified look on the younger sister's face as she watched Ana get closer, and closer.

Something's wrong. Something's wrong!

That "something" showed itself when the door behind Emily flung open and a second figure stepped outside. This time it was a man, and he was big enough that he filled out the open doorframe and towered over Emily even though he was still a few yards behind her.

Ana's feet instantly dug into the ground as she slid to a sudden stop, and Wash could see her hand reaching backward.

The 1911. She's going for the 1911!

Wash switched his crosshairs from Emily to the large man as he lumbered out of the cabin, and suddenly there was a gun in his fist.

Shit!

Wash was half a heartbeat from pulling the trigger when Emily turned and threw herself at the man, slamming her much smaller body into his large arm. The gun in the man's hand bucked and a shot rang out, either because he had squeezed the trigger or Emily had created an accidental discharge. Either way, the round sailed high over Ana's head even as she instinctively ducked in front of them.

Then Emily was in front of the large man, her body moving across Wash's optics as he tried to line up a shot. He tilted the reticle upward, searching for and finding the man's forehead, even as Emily's blonde hair flailed back and forth.

He focused on the target's face.

It was ugly. Square-shaped, with a massive jaw and a large nose that had been broken more than once. He had a goatee, but there was nothing on top, and sunlight reflected off his domed head.

Mathison? Wash thought.

Whoever you are, you're a dead man.

Wash's finger was on the trigger and he was pulling it, the crosshairs perfectly centered on the man's forehead, when voices boomed from his right side.

He immediately swung the M4 in that direction as two figures, both clad in black and green camo, raced out of the woods with their own rifles.

Dammit!

They ran toward Ana, pointing their guns at her while Emily and Baldy continued to struggle at the cabin. Not that it was much of a fight, because the man simply raised his hand and the girl went flying to the ground.

"Emily!" Ana shouted.

Ana was raising herself back up from the ground as the

two men swarmed her, their rifles pointed at her head. They were so close to Ana (*Too close*) that if one of them pulled his trigger, she was dead. But they didn't shoot her; instead, one of them turned around and looked in the direction of the cabin.

The big man was stomping toward them while Emily tried to pick herself up from the ground. She looked hurt, or just stunned.

"Don't shoot!" Baldy shouted as he stalked toward Ana. "I want her alive!"

Well, you're not getting her, Wash thought and refocused his rifle on Baldy, while quickly crunching the numbers in his head.

Three targets. Two at just over fifty yards, and a third getting there soon enough. Easy enough shots with an ACOG-mounted M4. Hell, it wasn't even going to be a fair fight. It was almost too easy—

A flurry of activity in the background drew his scope's focus, and Wash jerked the rifle slightly back toward the cabin as men burst out of the door. Emily, nearby, recoiled as they rushed past her.

Shit. Spoke too soon.

There were five of them, but only three had rifles. Not that the other two were unarmed, because they were all wearing gun belts and the ones without a long gun had pistols in their hands. They ran after Baldy (*That's gotta be Mathison*) and ignored Emily completely as she picked herself up, staggering a bit to maintain her balance.

Wash recrunched the numbers in his head:

Eight men. All armed. He could take out the two closest to him, then Mathison—*if* that was actually Mathison—next. That would leave five. He could probably pick off one or two more before the rest got smart and either retreated back into the cabin or fanned out to make it harder on him. They would definitely return fire, and big tree in front of him or not, Wash wasn't going to be able to dodge bullets from five separate guns firing at once.

And then there was Ana, still on her knees with her hands behind the back of her head as Mathison's two camo-wearing thugs crowded around her. The two men were constantly moving, never staying at one place for more than a few seconds. Wash was in the wrong position to open up on full-auto. To do that, he'd have to take out the closest two, then Mathison, then quickly move to a better spot so he didn't hit Ana while picking off the others.

And then there was Emily standing like a statue in the background.

Shit.

Shit, shit, shit.

As the five men neared him, Baldy turned to face them and said something, gesturing calmly as he did so. He was giving orders, that much was clear, and the men jumped to obey by spreading out. Two of them began running in Wash's direction.

And the hits just keep coming.

Wash took one, then two steps back even as he played the different scenarios in his head. But it didn't matter what tactics he considered, because it kept coming back to the same thing:

Eight men. All armed. And Ana and Emily in his field of fire.

Eight men. All armed. And Ana and Emily in his field of fire...

Goddammit.

He kept moving until he'd put enough distance between him and the tree line that he could turn and hurry back to the horses. He glanced back one last time and could just barely make out Ana through the trees and bushes between them.

She was still on her knees as the two men in camo pointed their rifles dangerously close to her head. Baldy was also there, standing with his hands on his hips in front of her. *Lording* over her.

"*Don't be a fool,*" Imaginary Old Man said inside Wash's head. "*Recognize when you're outclassed and live to fight another day, kid.*"

Live to fight another day, Wash thought as he quickly untied the horses' reins and led them back, back into the woods.

NINETEEN

"Cut your losses. You got the horses. You got the supplies. And you got One Eye waiting for you in Texas. You promised me you'd go and kill the bastard. You promised the others, too. But more importantly, you promised me. *A man is nothing if he can't keep his promises, kid. I taught you that, remember?"*

It was the Old Man's voice in his head, but it wasn't really the Old Man saying those words. It was Wash's imagining of what the old timer would have said if he were here right now.

"So she saved your life," Imaginary Old Man continued. *"You more than paid that back at the campsite with Travis and the other two bozos. What, exactly, do you think you still owe her?"*

The Old Man was right. He had paid Ana back; he'd taken out Travis for her, and he was pretty sure she would have been toast if he hadn't. He'd put three men into the ground, not that he was having second thoughts about what he'd done or anything. Travis, Duncan, and Chris were animals. Wash would snuff out their lives a second time if presented with the same choice, knowing what they'd done to Teresa.

"She's not going to make it out of that cabin alive. Mathison is going to waste her," Imaginary Old Man said.

He's going to do more than that.

"Yeah, but it's not your fault. You did your best. Beyond the call of duty, kid. Time to cut your losses and move on. Next!"

Except Wash didn't move on, because he couldn't. And he didn't believe the Old Man would tell him to do so if he were actually here. The old timer believed in justice, and if presented with a choice to cut bait and run or do what was right, he would always choose the right path.

So why did I just imagine him telling me to get the hell out of Dodge?

Because you want to believe he'd say that, to justify your own cowardice, that's why.

Maybe it was a little bit of cowardice—or was it common sense? He didn't know, but he spent about an hour thinking about it, watching the sun dipping beyond the tree canopies doing so.

Another hour, maybe less, before nightfall.

That was fine. Night didn't present him with the same kind of dangerous rush that it used to. Ghouls were no longer the threat they once were since The Walk Out. They were smaller in number and manageable. The four outside of Harrisonville hadn't taken very much effort to dispatch. Wash had faced more than that at once, all alone, and left without a scratch.

"Yeah, but you didn't have holes in you during all those other times, kid."

That reminded him to pop the last two Tramadol. He

almost tossed the sheet, but remembered that Mathison's people could still be searching for him in the woods, and shoved it back into his pack instead so as not to leave a trail. He didn't know how good these guys were, but there was little point in throwing them a bone.

He had moved a good two miles back from the cabin just to clear space for himself to think without being accidentally stumbled upon. That, and to get ready for what was coming. He'd spent a lot of that time trying to justify abandoning Ana, even coming up with the Old Man's imaginary argument.

It hadn't worked.

The problem with nightfall wasn't his safety—Wash had long ago lost any fear of the darkness—but the horses'. There were no buildings to keep them in and no abandoned houses to be found in the woods since they left Kanter 11 this morning. His choices were to return to Kanter or risk the animals out here as he made his move on the cabin.

And he had to do it at night. Not now, not while Ana's capture was still too fresh in everyone's minds. Mathison and his crew would be too wired after this evening. All eight of them.

Eight. There had to be all eight of them around, didn't it? A few more couldn't have broken off like Travis and the other two had done.

No, there had to be all eight of them.

He needed to give them the rest of the day to calm down, for their adrenaline to run its course. But that was it. He couldn't wait longer than one day. God only knew what Mathison would do to Ana. *If* he hadn't already shot her like he'd been fully prepared to do earlier, and would have undoubtedly succeeded, if Emily hadn't stopped him.

Emily...

The girl had thrown herself at Mathison, but before that she had come out of the cabin by herself with the bucket of water. She'd been walking like a free woman, not someone who had been torn from her home and marched across two states. The sight of Mathison following her outside had surprised both Wash and Ana.

What the hell was going on back there?

Not that it mattered to him right now. Ana was the important key. Wash had promised to help her get her sister back, and regardless of what the sister's motivations were, it was still Ana who held his marker, and a man always paid back what he owed. *That* was something the Old Man always said, not this fake version Wash had been using to try to convince himself to turn tail and run.

He got ready for the night by carefully selecting his tools. He had a choice between the Mossberg and the M4, and decided to go with the shotgun for its effectiveness at short range. After all, if everything went according to plan, he'd be seeing Mathison and his boys up close and personal. Buckshot was the way to go for that occasion.

Wash hid the bulk of his supplies where they wouldn't be found by man or nightcrawler, then left the horses standing free, because tying them up during the night would have been cruel if something were to stumble across them. What were the chances the animals would still be here when he came back?

Probably about as good a chance as you surviving this and getting to Texas, buddy.

He sighed at the somber thought before starting on his journey back to the cabin. The woods were already darkening around him, the last glimpses of sunlight quickly fading, and with that a noticeable drop in temperature. Wash barely felt it, a combination of his thick thermal clothing and the adrenaline pumping through his veins at the prospect of the violence yet to come.

"You're nuts, kid," Imaginary Old Man said. *"You're going to get yourself killed. One against eight. And every single one of them a cold-blooded murderer. I thought I taught you better than this."*

Wash grinned and thought, *Yeah, you did, old timer. That's why I'm going back. This is all your fault.*

He had never been shy about killing, and the Old Man saw the killer in him a long time ago and turned it into something decent, maybe even "good," if that definition could be stretched. But Wash didn't think he was good. Or decent. He just was.

And right now, he was going to kill a lot of people, not because he wanted to, but because it had to be done.

"Do what you have to do, but make sure you stick by your decisions," the Old Man had said. *"The only thing worse than a man who doesn't act is one who does and then tries to run away from his choices."*

He thought of the Old Man's words as he crouched near the clearing and watched the cabin from a distance. His only companions were the animals in the trees and the melodic *tick-tick-tick-tick* of the automatic watch on his left wrist.

There were no guards standing outside the cabin and no signs of Mathison's men anywhere in the area. Wash had been careful about his return, approaching his target from a different direction and stopping frequently to listen for telltale signs of human presence other than his own. He'd been out in the wilds long enough to know what ambushes looked like, and there were none in his path. At least, none that he could detect.

Day had completely given way to night thirty minutes earlier, but the birds still chirped and a lonely owl made its presence known about thirty yards behind him. He hadn't spotted (or smelled) ghouls in the area. Not yet, anyway. Right now he was only concerned with menace of the human variety, but he was fully prepared for the other kind, too.

The cabin itself was pitch dark, with no source of artificial light of any kind coming from within or outside. Wash took out the ACOG he'd removed from the M4 and peered through it.

I guess they're not so dumb after all, he thought when he saw the wooden boards over the windows.

He hadn't seen them earlier when he was last here with the curtains pulled over the windows. Instead of repurposed security rebar for security, the homeowners had instead fastened blocks of wood that could be opened and closed as needed from the inside. They were closed right now.

Using the ACOG's magnification, Wash could detect lights emitting from tiny slits along both front windows and the doorframe. He didn't think the cabin would be empty, but there had been some creeping doubts when he saw how utterly pitch dark the building was to the naked eye. For a second or two, he had entertained the terrible possibility that Mathison had abandoned the building and taken off before Wash could return.

He lowered the scope and stared at the cabin.

He guessed two bedrooms plus a great room up front and a

kitchen on the side. Then add a fireplace for the chimney. That wasn't a whole lot of space for eight grown men and the three women they still had in their possession. Unless, of course, it was just Emily and something else had happened to the other two captives. Even then, Wash was looking at nine people—ten now, including Ana—crammed into a space-challenged property.

It would have been easy to smoke everyone out. Tossing an incendiary down the chimney would have accomplished that. He had a feeling that as tightly sealed as the cabin was right now, no one would notice his approach. The smoke alone would get everyone running out of there, and then he could pick them off one by one. It wouldn't exactly be the fairest fight in the world, but what was fair when life and death were at stake?

Of course, the presence of Ana and Emily (and possibly the other two captives) took that strategy off the table. He was left with a much more dangerous option, but at least he still had one. A lot of it, though, would depend on how much Ana had already told Mathison about him, if anything at all.

Nothing. She wouldn't have told them anything, because she would know better. Ana wouldn't take away his element of surprise, his one advantage.

Then again, she might have, if she didn't think he was coming back to rescue her. That was entirely possible. How much faith did she have in him? Was five days enough for her to believe he wouldn't just abandon her at the first opportunity? He was, after all, going to have to face eight armed men just to keep his word. Only an idiot would take on that kind of challenge.

I guess I'm an idiot.

He didn't see any other choices. It was either follow through on the plan he'd come up with on the way back here or retreat and figure something out later, but the latter meant leaving Ana in Mathison's hands for another day.

He couldn't do that. Not after seeing what Travis and the others had done to Teresa. What could they have been doing to Emily all this time? To the other two girls since Newton? Or to Ana, right this very second?

Emily was the wild card. He could count on Ana—she'd more than proven that over the last few days—but the sister was another story.

He replayed the image of the teenager coming out of the cabin earlier today. Was she going to fetch more water? But the bucket she was carrying was already full because of the way it splashed the ground when she dropped it. It didn't make any sense. If she wasn't a captive anymore, why didn't the kid run when she saw Ana? It almost looked as if she had chosen to stay. With Mathison?

Then there was the status of the other two girls. Assuming they were even still there.

"Yeah, that's Mathison; he's a regular humanitarian, all right," Travis had said about his former leader.

Wash didn't believe that for a second. He'd crossed paths with plenty of guys like Mathison, like Travis, and the other two from the campsite. They were opportunists who would have been doing the same thing—if perhaps on a smaller scale —if The Purge hadn't upended society and made law and order obsolete. The state of the world had just given them the opportunity to fully embrace their depravity.

"The only thing necessary for the triumph of evil is for good men to do nothing."

It was a good quote, one that Wash had never encountered before. If the Old Man knew it, he'd never said it to him.

Wash didn't consider himself a "good man" by any stretch of the imagination, but he wasn't a despicable piece of shit, either. And that was exactly what he would be if he abandoned Ana and Emily and the other two Newton captives now.

Yeah, there were eight of them. So what?

You're probably going to die. You know that, right? What about Texas?

Fuck Texas, he thought, and felt better.

He wasn't sure why exactly, but just saying it out loud— even if it wasn't actually *out* loud—made his decision all the more final.

He remained crouched within the safe space of the woods and watched the cabin under the moonlight. There continued to be no activities inside or outside, which lent credence to his theory that Ana hadn't said a word about him, and Mathison's men hadn't found tracks of him in the woods when they were searching earlier. If they knew he was out here—if they knew he even existed in the first place—wouldn't they take more precautions? But if they thought Ana had come here alone, there would be no reason for them to expect him tonight.

"That's a lot of ifs, kid," Imaginary Old Man said inside Wash's head. *"What did I tell you about putting your life in the hands of hypothetical situations?"*

I don't have any choice, old timer.

"Of course you do. Stop lying to yourself. You have plenty of choices. You just chose this one."

Maybe you're right.

"I'm always right," Imaginary Old Man laughed.

I hate it when he's right, Wash thought as he got up and began moving through the woods, sticking to the trees and keeping a generous distance from the clearing on his left.

The air around him grew colder, and his breath formed white clouds. He hadn't felt the chill before, but it was impossible to ignore it now.

As he skirted the clearing, always keeping the cabin within sight at all times between the trees, Wash felt the familiar building up of adrenaline. It coursed through him, starting from the soles of his feet and traveling all the way to the top of his head. He embraced the overwhelming sensation, just like he did all the other times.

He was well camouflaged in the shadows, a place he had forced himself to become comfortable with years ago. You had to be, when you stalked creatures that lived and thrived in the darkness.

I'm coming, Ana. Stay strong.

I'm coming...

TWENTY

Tick-tick-tick-tick ...

The cabin was one story and constructed with hewn logs that interlocked at the corners. Moonlight gleamed off the solar panels on top, giving it the appearance of an unmoving surface of a calm lake. The windows were five feet from the door on both sides and five feet to the edges. The building was low to the ground, with no porch, and the closer he got to it the more he was convinced it was newly built, possibly in the previous few years, which would make it a post-Purge construction. It made him wonder what happened to the previous tenant. Or, to be exact, what Mathison did to them before he took over.

As he skulked around the darkness getting a better look at the cabin from multiple angles, Wash eyeballed the house as being almost as wide as it was long. There was a single window along the side, and like the windows at the front, this one was also covered by a board from the inside. The cabin's spaces were probably halved—the living room and kitchen at the front and the bedrooms in the back.

Wash finally stopped moving and went into a crouch while staying well within the shadows. He was fully blended into his almost pitch-black environment as he gazed out across the clearing at the rear of the cabin.

Fifty yards or so separated him and his target, with a lone door in the middle. There were no lights back here, either, but a little bit more moonlight than at the front. The door seemed to almost glow invitingly through the lens of the ACOG, the result of lights from inside peeking through the slits underneath and along the doorframe.

Wash glanced down at his watch. 10:11 p.m.

He'd spent the last three hours methodically making his way around the cabin, and the only side he hadn't gotten a good look at was the one that faced the stream. What were the chances there was anything out of the ordinary over there?

He unslung the Mossberg and held it in front of him. The shotgun had an LED flashlight attached alongside the barrel. It was turned off at the moment, but he felt good knowing he had the option of bringing light into the world whenever he needed some. The 12-gauge had a capacity of nine, and the shell carrier gave him an additional six rounds with which to reload it.

He still had the Beretta 9mm in his right hip holster. That was another seventeen in the magazine, and one in the chamber. Eighteen in all, and it was a lot easier—not to mention faster—to reload a sidearm. There were two spares for the sidearm in his back pocket, within easy reach. He had a backup piece behind him—a Glock 19. That gave him fifteen more bullets to fall back on.

If all else failed, he had the kukri on his left hip. For up close and personal. If and when he had to switch to the machete, it either meant Wash was almost done with what he needed to do, or *he* was almost done. Either way, it would be the signal that this whole crazy plan of his was at its end, or pretty damn close to it.

The rest of his arsenal was in the pouch just over the kukri; more gifts from the mountain men's armory. He could have brought more but had to prioritize for weight. He was already too heavy, and that had shown in the negative impact on his side. The extra painkillers he'd found in Ana's backpack had helped with that, and his wounds had mostly numbed over since he began scouting the cabin. Mostly.

The night around him remained as still and dark now as it had been when he first arrived back at his target. Without the ACOG, he couldn't see any traces of light at all, which he guessed was the point. The builders had clearly designed the place to literally go dark at night so it wouldn't attract attention.

A shaft of yellow light flashed in front of Wash's eyes as the back door opened and a lone figure stepped outside.

Wash tensed and tightened his grip on the Mossberg's forend.

Here we go...

The man left the door open behind him as he glanced around briefly before starting to unzip his pants. A lightbulb, likely the fruit of the solar panels on the roof, created an almost halo effect around the back of the cabin. The man found a spot in the shadows as he began urinating, so even with the ACOG, Wash had to mostly guess at the man's appearance. He might have had the same build as Baldy; Wash couldn't be certain. The man had also turned slightly, giving Wash an unnecessarily perfect view of the stream of urine arcing out from his crotch area.

After what seemed like five minutes, but was probably closer to one or two, the man zipped himself up and gave the surrounding woods a sweeping glance. A few seconds later, he turned around and disappeared back into the house, closing the door after him. Darkness once again swamped the rear of the cabin.

Wash glanced down at his watch again.

It was still too early. His original plan didn't call for action until at least well past midnight, when all or most of the cabin's occupants would either be asleep or getting close.

"*Shock and awe,*" the Old Man used to say. "*Hit them fast, hit them hard, and take away their will to fight. That's how you win a war. Next!*"

That's how you win a war, Wash thought. *Hopefully I can keep the civilian casualties down at the same time—*

The loud *bang!* of a gunshot interrupted his thoughts.

Wash stood up slightly just as two more—*bang! bang!* —rang out.

They were coming from *inside* the cabin.

Aw, hell! Wash thought, and was on his feet and running across the field before he knew he had made the decision.

Forty yards...

He was moving as fast as he could, but it didn't seem to be nearly fast enough. His legs felt like they were stuck in quicksand even as a third gunshot—*bang!*—crackled.

Thirty-five...

His side was starting to throb again, and all Wash wanted to do was stop for a moment—a second, okay, maybe sixty seconds—and make sure he wasn't bleeding down there. For all he knew, that wetness he was feeling around his waist was blood and not the condensation from the cold sticking to his clothes after being still for so long in the woods.

Thirty...

He was starting to slow down. He knew it was happening despite his best efforts. His legs were becoming heavier, his breath starting to hammer against his chest. He dug deep and found some willpower and pushed on, even as the throbbing increased. But he didn't let that stop him and forced his legs to piston harder, faster...

Twenty-five...

He'd made it halfway to the cabin, running out in the wide open, and no one had come out of the back door a second time or appeared from the sides to prove that all of this had been a trick to lure him out. Granted, firing off guns inside a house wasn't the most obvious of traps, but he'd seen crazier—

The *pop-pop-pop* of automatic rifle fire coming from the cabin interrupted his thoughts. It continued for a good five or six seconds, and during that time—

Twenty yards...

Fifteen...

He was almost there, so close that he could smell the ashes of the long-extinguished fireplace drifting from the chimney. Or was that something else? Another smell? Maybe—

The continuous clatter of rifle fire was answered by single gunshots from a handgun. And all of it was coming from the house directly in front of him.

Ten yards...

Was he listening to two sides exchanging gunfire? That was the only possible explanation. What else could it be?

There!

Wash aimed the shotgun at the door and fired even as he continued moving forward, his momentum slowing down but never stopping completely. His second shot went higher than the first, at about where a deadbolt would be just over the lever. Both shots were so loud he thought Marie back in Kanter 11 could probably hear them.

He'd put both shots where they needed to be, and the door was swinging open by itself as Wash stepped through, shouldering it open faster while racking the Mossberg at the same time.

His heartbeat hammered against his chest, his breath forming thick cloud bursts in front of him. All the running and adrenaline was coming to the forefront, pushing him forward even if every ounce of him wanted to turn and run. Or stop and drop, and lie down for a long time.

Get in there! Get in there!

He was just barely inside the cabin when he was confronted by a patch of brown hair and a man's turned back. Wash saw it all clearly with help from the squiggly lightbulb on the ceiling almost directly over the man's head; it wasn't LED-bright, but it was more than enough to show Wash that there was someone *standing right in front of him.*

And that man was in the process of spinning around and giving Wash a glimpse of the AK-47 in his hands.

The *boom!* from the Mossberg sent two dozen .24-inch lead balls into the man's back and side and dropped him like a sack of lifeless meat.

In the next two and a half seconds, Wash saw:

Three more men standing at the other end of a back hall-way, hidden from Wash's view until now. They were all armed —two of them holding AR rifles while a third, standing between them, clutched a large silver Desert Eagle handgun.

Mathison.

Or, at least, the man who Wash had concluded was Mathi-son. It was Baldy, and he towered over the two that flanked him. Mathison looked every bit like the alpha dog that he was, even more so now in the midst of his men—six-six with that bald head and his immaculately-trimmed goatee.

Wash's eyes dropped to Mathison's left hand, currently pushed against his waist. His fingers were covered in blood, and there was a trail from where he stood to the bedroom in front and to the left of Wash. There was a second bedroom to Wash's right, directly opposite the first, but Wash didn't pay any attention to it because its door was perfectly fine and not riddled with bullets like the one to his left.

The three men stood just beyond the corridor, and all their attention had been focused on the bullet-riddled door when Wash burst inside and dropped the man with brown hair. Now, all three pairs of eyes were trained on him.

"The fuck are you?" Mathison said, just before Wash racked the shotgun. He didn't have to lift the weapon—it was already aimed and ready.

Mathison was the first to react out of the three, lunging out of the hallway opening on the first *clack* as the Mossberg's forend slid back and a spent cartridge flicked out of the weapon's side. The other two were in the process of jumping in the other direction on the second *clack* as the shotgun's slide snapped forward, just a split second before a second thun-derous *boom!* filled the cabin. Flecks of blood sprayed the air, but there were no signs (or sounds) of bodies falling, and Wash thought, *Fuck!*

Wash racked the shotgun and took a step forward when a new face appeared in the opening in front of him, leaning around the corner to get a look. He fired again, but his target jerked his head back in time, and Wash only managed to obliterate a large chunk of the hallway wall and filling the living room on the other side with splintered wood.

"Wash!" someone shouted from behind the door to his left. "Is that you?"

That voice...

Sonofabitch, Wash thought as he worked the forend to load a new round into the Mossberg.

"Ana?" Wash shouted.

"Yes!" the voice shouted back. "You came back!"

He grinned, all the while keeping his eyes fixed on the opening in front of him. He could see into the living room, but his angle was badly limited to what was in front of him. There could have been an army amassed in the other parts of the room, hidden by the walls, and he wouldn't have known it. But he could see the door directly in front of him just fine, which meant there wasn't a chance anyone could use it to run outside and try to flank him from behind.

"You came back!" Ana shouted from the bedroom to his left. And it was her. It was definitely her.

A flicker of movement as a pair of hands—no, *two pairs* of hands—suddenly appeared in the opening in front of him, both clutching rifles aimed awkwardly in his direction. It was just the hands and no signs of their owners, and Wash knew what they were going to do before they did it.

Shit!

He dropped to the floor, reaching down with the shotgun just before his chest (*Your side, idiot, your wounded side!*) could slam into the boards. At the same time, Mathison's men opened fire in front of him.

Shit shit shit!

Both hidden figures were swinging their weapons side to side, their bullets chopping into the thick wooden walls above Wash's head. *Above* his head. Hundreds of splinters, big and small, zipped like heat-seeking missiles around him, even more falling in sheets over his body.

The shooters kept firing, clearly determined to empty their magazines, but neither men had done very much to correct for Wash's new position—flat on his stomach on the floor, barely an inch from the steel-toed boots of the dead man he'd killed when he first entered the cabin, and who still lay in front of him.

Wash kept the Mossberg in front of him, aimed and ready for the first head—

Bingo.

A man with long blond hair tied back in a ponytail with a scar over one cheek poked out from behind the right side wall. He appeared just underneath one of the firing rifles. The man's eyes widened at the sight of Wash with the shotgun aimed right back at him.

Wash pulled the trigger, and the face turned to mush against a bloody torrent of buckshot, and a body *thumped!* to the floor.

The rifles finally stopped firing and disappeared.

Wash took the opportunity to rack the shotgun and climb back up to one knee when he heard Ana's voice shouting from behind the closed door in front and to the left of him: "Wash, are you still alive?"

"Fuck yeah!" he shouted back.

"We're leaving, Wash!"

"Leaving?" he thought. How was she going to "leave" the cabin? She wasn't going to come out of the bullet-riddled door and expect him to cover her, was she?

No way. She's too smart for that.

Right?

And she'd said *we,* which could only mean Emily was in there with her. If not Emily, then one of the other two captives.

No, it had to be Emily. Ana wouldn't abandon the cabin without Emily.

Wash glanced at the bedroom door to his right. It had remained closed throughout this entire ordeal.

"You hear me?" Ana shouted. "We're leaving now!"

And how exactly are you going to do that? he thought, but of course didn't shout out loud because Mathison and his men were obviously listening in. It was impossible for them *not* to hear the back and forth between Wash and Ana.

Then it occurred to him.

The window. The one on the side with the wooden blocks that was designed to be closed and opened by someone from inside the bedroom.

"Wash!" Ana shouted. "Did you hear me?"

"Go!" he shouted back. "Go now!"

Wash hurried the rest of the way up from the floor, the 12-gauge still aimed at the other end of the corridor with one hand—waiting, hoping for another head to appear for him to pop—while his left snapped open the pouch on his hip. There, round and cold to the touch. He pulled it out while keeping himself slightly low to the ground, ready to jump back down should Mathison's men decided to try the same tactic twice.

It took some fumbling around, but he managed to hold onto the shotgun's pistol grip and keep it aimed while he pulled the pin with his teeth. Wash sucked in a big breath and tossed the canister underhanded toward the opening. It sailed, white plumes of smoke already expelling from the top on one side as it left his hand in a wide arc.

He returned both hands to the shotgun as the canister landed, bounced, and kept rolling toward the living room beyond, spewing clouds of tear gas that quickly consumed everything in its path. He heard shouting, coughing, and swearing almost right away.

Wash said a silent *Thank you, boys* to the mountain men as he backed up. His eyes were already starting to burn, his skin tingling, and that encouraged him to move faster, to get as far and as quickly away from the spreading fog as possible.

He didn't have to look back to know where he was going. He hadn't gone that far into the hallway. Plus, the cold outside was drawing him out step by step—

A figure appeared in the smoke, trying desperately to wade through it. Then two more stumbled behind the first. He wasn't sure what they were doing—trying to get away from the smoke or pursuing him?

Wash fired, and the first and closest figure collapsed to the floor. The other two staggered back into the smoke before Wash could pick them off, too.

"Wash!" Someone was screaming his name from *outside* the cabin. "Come on!"

That's my cue!

Wash stepped outside, felt damp ground under his boots,

and only took one hand off the shotgun to grab the door and pull it closed. Of course it couldn't slam shut, because he'd taken out the latch and deadbolt earlier. While it didn't close flush, it was just good enough, with smoke filtering out through the two holes from his shotgun blasts.

"Wash!"

He spun around and saw Ana and a second figure, Emily, standing in the open. They were almost halfway to the woods and were looking back at him. Ana gestured wildly with one hand while her other, he saw, was holding a handgun.

"Wash, come on!" Ana shouted.

He turned and began jogging toward them, the fresh, cold air helping him to fight against his brief exposure to the tear gas. More importantly, he was still alive, and Ana and her sister were free.

All in all, it was a hell of a good night.

Not that he thought for one second the night was over.

It was just getting started...

TWENTY-ONE

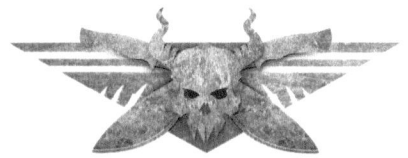

"Avoid the gunfight if you can, but if you can't, make sure you end it. Never, ever leave a man with a gun standing once the bullets fly. Finish it and move on. Next!"

Wash wished he could have done just that, but he didn't have the option. Even after taking down—how many? Two? Three?—of Mathison's men inside the cabin, there was still the big man himself—and whoever was left. That was too many, and he had lost the element of surprise.

It was time to run.

White smoke vented from all four sides of the cabin and out the chimney. It was quite a sight, the clouds a stark contrast against the black of night. Wash could already hear voices, shouts, and doors banging as Mathison's men flooded outside, either in pursuit or to escape the tear gas. Either way, they were coming, and it wouldn't take them long to figure out which direction he and the sisters were headed.

Wash turned around and followed Ana and her sister Emily as they raced through the clearing and toward the trees on the other side. They were running fast, but then they could afford to. He was the one with bullet holes in him. He gritted his teeth and picked up speed, shoving fresh shells from the carrier into the Mossberg as he did so. He still had the Beretta and could have switched to it, but there was no point in wasting the extra seconds he'd bought himself since fleeing the cabin.

The sisters were twenty yards ahead of him, but he was catching up. Which was surprising, because he didn't think he was running *that* fast—or was even capable. He must have been doing a better job than he thought; either that, or the sisters were moving slowly on purpose to let him catch up.

Once he ran out of room to slip in more shells, Wash glanced over his shoulder. The voices had faded, but he didn't for a second believe that would be the end of the chase. It hadn't even begun yet.

And it was coming as long as Mathison was alive. What were the chances the shrouded figure that he had put down before he darted out of the cabin was Mathison? If it had been the man, then there was a chance the others wouldn't pursue—

The *pop-pop-pop* of gunfire coming from the left side of the house was the answer to his question.

The ground erupted around him, and bullets *zipped!* over his head. Wash ducked instinctively, just low enough to still maintain his stride. Ahead of him, the sisters never stopped running, though Ana did glance back.

"Go, go, go!" he shouted at her.

She might have nodded before looking forward, and, one hand gripping Emily's wrist, seemed to pick up even more speed.

Well, that answers that: She was definitely moving slow for my benefit earlier. That's awfully nice of her.

More gunfire, the loud clatters of rifles all coming from behind him. More than one person was shooting, from the sounds of it, but it would have cost him two or three seconds to slow down and look back to confirm that, and he couldn't afford even one of those seconds. The dirt to his left and right flicked at his fleeing form, pelting his pants legs and some bouncing off his shoulders and cheeks. But dirt, while annoying, didn't kill you.

Wash kept his head low and ran for all he was worth. The trees were in front of him, so tantalizingly close that he could almost feel their shade.

All he had to do was reach them.

All he had to do was run faster.

All he had to do was get there before one of Mathison's men—maybe even the man himself—managed to get in a lucky shot.

Gee, that's it?

Ten yards...

Five...

Ana and Emily had vanished into the wall of shadows even before the branches started snapping in half and chunks of bark filled the air from the torrent of bullets. He wasn't sure if they were aiming at him and missing, or if they were also trying to hit the sisters. Not that it mattered. Bullets didn't have people's names written on them, and even if they did, they wouldn't care anyway.

Better branches and bark than me!

The fact that he was still running was a miracle, one that

he had every intention of prolonging as Wash leapt the last few yards and—

He crashed through the tree line and hit the ground in a tuck and roll. It was a stupid move, but he'd done it without thinking, and let out a howl of pain as his side screamed in opposition to the ill-conceived stunt.

Jesus Christ! Don't ever do that again, you idiot!

He was having trouble scrambling back on his feet when warm hands clasped over his left arm. Wash glanced up at Ana, hovering over him, that familiar smile on a face that was fanned by her amazingly brilliant red hair.

"You okay?" she asked.

"I don't know. Am I?"

He stumbled to his feet and patted himself down. He had time because Mathison's men had stopped shooting once he made the tree line. Wash was thankful for the adrenaline; while it didn't completely dampen the pain, it did keep enough of it at bay that he was able to remain on his feet even though he did sway erratically for a few seconds after standing up.

"You're good," Ana said. She sounded out of breath. "I don't see any blood."

"Thank God," Wash said. "I didn't think I was going to make it."

"You and me both. When did you get so slow?"

He gave her a sharp look and saw her grinning back at him.

He softened and chuckled. "I must have inhaled more tear gas back there than I thought."

"Yeah, that must be it."

"Annie, they're coming," a voice said from in front of them.

Wash looked over at Emily, hugging her chest with her arms. He hadn't realized it before, but she was wearing a one-piece silk nightgown with spaghetti straps that looked like they might slide off her small shoulders at any second.

And so was Ana, standing next to him.

"What?" he started to say.

Ana shook her head and hurried over to where Emily stood. The younger sister seemed to be trembling, trying to warm herself by rubbing her arms up and down with her hands. Wash didn't blame her, considering what she was wearing. And, like Ana, she was barefoot.

What the hell was going on back there?

"Em's right, they're coming," Ana said. "We have to go!"

The sisters turned and hurried through a thicket, and Wash stumbled after them. He didn't say anything, but his mind was trying to process what he was seeing now and what he had seen back in the cabin.

Mathison's men surrounding the bullet-riddled bedroom door. They had clearly been shooting at it. Then there was Mathison himself, standing there with a bleeding side. How had he gotten that way? Ana, probably. But how had Ana gotten her hands on the gun that she was still clutching now as they fled through the woods?

But all of that was going to have to wait, even if it killed him not to know the answers. Right now, it was about survival, about putting as much distance between them and Mathison's people as possible. Besides, Wash thought he already knew the answer anyway. Maybe not the hows, but he was pretty sure about the whys.

Two beautiful women in silk nightgowns, a bedroom that turned into a shooting gallery, and Mathison with a bleeding side...

"Yeah, that's Mathison; he's a regular humanitarian, all

right," Travis had said. He had meant it sarcastically, of course, because there was nothing remotely humanitarian about the man. Hell, Wash had a hard time believing there was anything *human* about Mathison, and he hadn't even gotten to know him all that well.

Well enough to know the world's better off with him gone. That's all I need to know.

He glanced back just to make sure their pursuers weren't already on his heels, but didn't see anyone back there.

Any minute now...

He turned and hurried after the sisters. They were ten yards in front of him, Ana up front with the gun in one hand and the other one pulling her sister along. The girl looked way younger than nineteen and skinnier than Wash had thought when he first saw her from a distance earlier today. Emily seemed to be always on the verge of falling or losing her balance, but never did. Her feet, like her sister's, were already covered in dirt from the soles all the way up to their ankles. Of course, being barefoot didn't seem to be slowing down Ana even a little bit.

She's a survivor, that's why. Even if I die in this place tonight, she'll keep going, finding ways to keep Emily alive, too.

He admired her. Not just for everything he had seen her do, but everything else he hadn't seen but saw the results of. Stealing that knife from one of the mountain men, then using it on them to launch their escape. And now, escaping from Mathison's clutches.

As if sensing him staring, Ana glanced back and caught his gaze. "Are they coming yet?"

"I don't see them," Wash said. "Stop for a minute."

They did, and while the sisters took the opportunity to

catch their breaths, Wash turned around and listened. All he could hear were the birds and owls and their slightly (*too*) loud breathing.

Wash finally shook his head and turned back to Ana. "I don't hear anything."

"Me neither." Instead of joy, there was just confusion on Ana's face. "What's taking them so long? They were right behind you."

"Maybe they're regrouping. Getting their shit together before they pursue. That's what I would do if I were in charge."

He saw something on Ana's face—a question that she wanted desperately to ask but was too afraid to say out loud.

"What is it?" Wash said.

"Did you get him?" Ana asked. "Did you get Mathison? Tell me he's dead, Wash. Please tell me he's dead. If he is, the others might not come after us."

The question made Emily stare at Wash, too, as both sisters waited for an answer. The expression on Ana's face was mirrored in the little sister's.

"That depends on which one was Mathison," Wash said.

He described Baldy, and Ana nodded. "That's him." Then, "Did you get him?"

"I can't say for sure. I took a couple of shots at him, but the motherfucker's faster than he looks. He was already bleeding when I saw him, though. Was that you?"

"I couldn't finish him off," Ana said.

"But you shot him?"

"Yes. And you're right, he is faster than he looks."

Ana's face morphed into steely determination, but Wash thought he saw the world collapse in Emily's eyes. The sisters had similar features, and although Emily was taller than Ana by a few inches, she seemed actually smaller in every way. That had a lot to do with her thin frame and drooping shoulders, and there was an undeniable look of hopelessness on her face that wasn't anywhere on Ana's at the moment.

"We need to keep going," Wash said. "We need to put as much distance between them and us as possible while they're still regrouping. We might not get another opportunity once they start."

"Come on," Ana said to Emily, and the sisters were moving again.

Wash hurried over until he was moving next to them, with Ana and her sister to his right. "Where did you get the gun?"

"It's his," Ana said.

"Mathison?"

"Yes."

Wash added that new information to the puzzle he'd been trying to solve. "You almost got him."

"Almost."

"What happened back there?"

She shook her head but didn't answer.

"Ana..." Wash said.

"Can we talk about this later?"

There was something in her voice; it wasn't quite annoyance, but maybe...fatigue? If she was tired, it wasn't slowing her down any. Wash actually had to pick up his pace just to keep up with her. So did poor Emily on the other side.

"We need to get out of here," Ana said. "I need to get Emily to safety."

Wash looked around them at the dark woods and thought, *I'm not sure there's any safety around here, Ana,* but he was pretty sure neither sister wanted to hear that, so he kept it to himself.

Ana was looking over at him. "Thank you."

"For what?" Wash said.

"Coming back for me."

"Did you have any doubts I would?"

"I wasn't sure."

"You didn't tell them about me?"

She shook her head. "They didn't know about you in the first place, so I kept it that way. Just in case I was right and you did come back for me."

"Oh, ye of little faith."

"It's not my lack of faith. It's experience."

"With men?"

"With human beings in general."

"Well, I'm different."

"And I'll remember that from now on. For everything you've done. For me, for Emily."

"It's not over yet."

"I know, but it's a good start. It's a better start than I could have hoped for when the night began."

Wash wanted badly to ask her what had happened back there at the cabin. How had she and Emily ended up in the same room as Mathison? Why were they in nightgowns? How had she managed to get her hands on his gun?

But he didn't ask those questions, because she was right. This wasn't the time.

Snap! from behind them.

He stopped and turned around, Ana and Emily doing the same next to him. All three of them went deathly still, and he thought Emily even stopped breathing altogether.

"What?" Ana asked, dropping her voice to barely a whisper.

He shook his head. It could have been anything. Man or animal.

"Wash?" Ana whispered.

He was about to answer when he heard it again—and this time more than once:

Snap! Snap!

They were far away, but getting closer.

Wash turned around. "They're coming. Let's go!"

TWENTY-TWO

"Where are we going?" Ana asked after about five minutes of walking, then running, then walking some more through the woods without once stopping to catch her breath.

Now that's a good question, Wash thought, because he didn't know. He'd been asking himself the same thing for a while now.

"Wash?"

The problem was that the woods looked a lot different at night than they had during the daytime. There were too many shadows, too many patches of darkness, and too much of a canopy that only sporadic shafts of moonlight were able to pierce and light their way. He had difficulty seeing more than ten or so yards around him at any one time.

"Wash!"

He had lights on his shotgun, but Wash had left it off. The bright LED would have certainly given their position away to Mathison's people. He didn't think they were losing them by any stretch of the imagination by staying in the dark, but he didn't feel like giving them more clues to their whereabouts, either. They were coming, but that didn't mean he should make it easier on them.

Even if there were plenty of lights to see with, it wouldn't have mattered. It had been easier when he'd scouted the cabin, because all he had to do was keep the clearing to his left as he moved from one spot to the next. But now he was going deeper into the woods, and there wasn't anything that even looked familiar. One tree was the same as the other tens of thousands they'd passed, and the persistent knowledge that Mathison's men, somewhere behind them, were getting closer weighed heavily on his mind.

"Goddammit, Wash, answer me," Ana said.

He shook his head. "I don't know."

"You don't know?"

"I don't know."

"We're lost?" Emily asked. Her voice was so much softer than Ana's. Weaker, more vulnerable.

"Not, not exactly," Wash said.

"Not exactly how?" Ana asked.

"Not exactly," he repeated.

Wash glanced back at the mess they'd made as they lumbered their way from the cabin. Snapped branches, broken twigs, and ruined bushes. Any man with two eyes would be able to easily track them even with the little light.

Well, that's not good.

"'Not exactly' is not good, Wash," Ana said from in front of him.

"Yeah, I know," Wash said.

"Where are the horses?"

"I had to leave them behind."

"Leave them behind where?"

"I have no idea. I didn't exactly have time to map out the area before I went back to rescue you."

"So you're saying that you don't know where they are?"

"That's what I'm saying. They're probably long gone by now anyway."

"You left them to roam free?"

"Had to. It would have been cruel to tie them up out in the open at night. And I couldn't bring them back here with me."

"I guess you did the right thing."

"Glad you approve."

He glanced down at the gun in her hand. It was a 1911 model Remington, similar to the one he'd given her before, but this one was matte black, whereas the other one was silver. The fact that she had a gun was the good news; the bad was that the Remington came with very limited ammo capacity.

"How many shots did you fire back there?" he asked.

Ana shook her head. "I don't remember. I wasn't exactly counting. Why?"

"That model has seven plus one. Eight bullets."

"Eight? That's it?"

"Yeah."

He took the gun from her and knew there was a problem as soon as he felt the weight. He ejected the magazine anyway and frowned. She was down to two rounds—one in the pipe and one in the magazine.

"Hey," Ana said when Wash threw the gun into a nearby bush. "What the hell, Wash?"

"Relax. I got you covered."

"You better have."

"What did I say about having little faith?"

"You'd get more if you didn't go around throwing my guns away."

"I thought you hated guns."

"I do, but not when they can save my life. Like now."

"Like I said, relax." He took the Glock out from behind his waist and handed it to her. "It's fully loaded, unlike the other one."

"How many is loaded?" Ana asked, taking the gun.

"Fifteen rounds."

"How many did the other one have?"

"Less than fifteen rounds."

"Then I guess you did the right thing. Again."

"Glad you approve. Again."

"Just tell me first next time."

"Yes, ma'am."

He pulled two magazines for the Glock from the pouch he carried at his side and held them out to her.

"I, uh, don't have anywhere to put those," Ana said. He thought she might have actually blushed a bit when she said it, but it could have just been the limited light causing him to see things. After all, Ana didn't blush. Right?

"Yeah, I noticed that," Wash said. "I guess you'll tell me how you ended up in that getup later, too?"

She pursed a smile. "Add it to the list."

"Here, I'll take them," Emily said.

The younger sister took the magazines from him. She had said so little since they began fleeing the cabin that the sudden sound of her voice surprised Wash. She might have been taller than Ana, and if he was being honest about it, prettier in a lot of ways, but there was a fire to Ana that overwhelmed her little sister.

"You sure?" Ana asked her. "I know you don't like guns."

"I don't have to like them, just hold onto them for you," Emily said. "Just like when we were kids."

Ana smiled at her, and Emily returned it. There was nothing forced about their reactions, and Wash imagined this was what they were like back in Newton before Mathison was even a figment of their nightmares.

It was a nice moment that was quickly broken by voices coming from behind them. They were still not close yet, but they were gradually getting closer.

"Go," Wash said.

They started moving again.

"Wash..." Ana said.

"Yeah?" Wash said.

"You figured out where we're going yet?"

"Nope."

"I was afraid you'd say that."

"Just keep walking until we can't walk anymore."

"I've said it already, and I hate to repeat myself, but Wash, that's not much of a plan."

"I know."

"*Do* you have a plan?"

"Not yet."

"Does that mean you will, soon?"

"Um..."

"Wash..."

He shook his head. "I'll let you know when I think of one. Until then, let's just keep moving."

She nodded, and he could see her biting her tongue. He didn't blame her. *"Just keep moving"* wasn't exactly the best plan in the world when people with guns were chasing you.

"Are you okay?" she asked instead.

He nodded. "I'm fine."

"I mean, your side."

He had forgotten about his wounds, but being asked about them suddenly brought back reminders by way of a flurry of pain.

Ana saw it in his face. "Wash..."

"I'll be fine after this," Wash said.

He dug out two of the half dozen painkillers he'd put into his cargo pants pocket for just such an occasion. He swallowed them down in one gulp and saw Emily wincing on the other side of her sister.

"What's that?" Ana asked.

Wash shrugged. "I don't know, but they seem to be working."

"How many have you taken so far?"

"Two earlier today. These two make four."

"Four is a lot..."

"Not when you're running for your life."

She put her hand in his pocket and took out one of the pills. It was white and triangular, with writing on both sides: The number 8 on one and the letters *P* and *D* on the other.

"Dilaudid," Ana said, and put it back into his pocket. "They're just as addictive as the Tramadol."

"I'd rather be addicted than dead," Wash said.

"I'm serious, Wash."

"So am I."

He glanced back at the trail.

The *massive* trail that even a blind man could follow right to them.

Dammit. We should have been more careful. I should have been more careful.

Now what?

He looked back at Ana. "Did you kill anyone back there?"

"I shot Mathison..." she said.

"But did you *kill* anyone? For sure?"

She shook her head. "Mathison was the only one in the room with us." She gritted her teeth. "I tried to end him, Wash. I really tried. But I told you I'm not a very good shot, right?"

"But you did manage to hit him."

"He was standing in front of me when I pulled the trigger. And he's still alive."

"Why didn't you shoot him in the chest?"

"That *was* where I was aiming, but I must have hesitated. Did you see where I got him?"

"In the side."

"Well, at least I'm not completely useless."

He grinned to himself. He could call Ana a lot of things, but *useless* was definitely not one of them.

"How many did you get back there?" Ana asked. She added, with some hopefulness in her voice, "You did get some, right?"

"Three that I'm sure of," Wash said. "Maybe four, but that might be wishful thinking. The problem with buckshot is that they spread too much, even over a short distance."

"So where does that leave us?"

Another good question, except this time Wash had the answer. He didn't like it. In fact, he hated it, but there was no other choice.

"You and Emily keep going forward," Wash said. "Try to

find the highway that we used yesterday and head back to Kanter 11, if you're able."

Ana gave him a confused look. "You mean 'us,' right? You, me, and Emily."

"No. I mean just you and Emily."

"What about you?"

"They're coming, Ana. Four of them. Maybe five. But definitely four. Sooner or later, they're going to catch up. We can't outrun them, and we can't lose them. Not in here. Not like this."

"What are you saying, Wash?"

"I'm saying, you and Emily keep moving and don't stop, don't look back, and whatever you do, *don't come back* for me. Understand?"

"Wash..."

He opened his side pouch and took out a small tactical knife in a sheath and handed it to her. "The blade's silver-coated. And it never runs out of bullets."

She stared at it, then at him, before releasing Emily's wrist to take the knife. "Wash..."

He grinned at her. It wasn't entirely forced, and he thought it was mostly semi-credible. "Look, I'm not trying to get myself killed here. I have something to do in Texas. You know that. But they're going to catch up to us eventually. When that happens, we'll probably be tired and barely standing. This way, we have a fighting chance."

"But just you?"

"No offense, but I have a way better chance by myself. I can't worry about the both of you and fight at the same time."

That last part wasn't a total lie, but he didn't think Ana fully bought it.

"I need to be able to move without having to worry about two chicks in nightgowns," Wash said. "As fancy and sexy as you look at the moment, Ana, it's just not very conducive to gunfights, you understand?"

She smiled at him. It was a halfhearted attempt, and he thought she knew it, too.

Ana walked over and put her arms around him in a hug. When she pulled back, he was ready to let go, but she kissed him first.

It wasn't like the first time, back at Kanter 11. There was a real urgency to her lips and her mouth this time, and he couldn't help but lose himself in them. Their taste, their wetness, the warmth that flowed from her to him as if they were transferring their life energy to one another.

But eventually it had to end, and when it did, Ana placed her forehead against his and whispered, "Don't die, Washateria."

He grinned. "That's the plan."

"I mean it."

"So do I. Have faith."

"I do. In you." She pulled away. "Find us, okay? We'll be waiting for you. *I'll* be waiting for you."

She released him and turned to go without another word.

"Thank you," Emily said softly to him, before Ana tugged at her wrist and the sisters vanished into a patch of shadows in front of him.

After a few seconds, there was no evidence they were ever there.

Wash stared after them anyway, at the same time trying to think what the Old Man would say if he were here. The truth was, the old timer was too smart to ever put himself in such a precarious situation.

Face it, old timer, it was always going to end in a place like this. We both knew it. One dark woods looks the same as any other. So why not here?

He turned around, then went into a slight crouch, the Mossberg draped over one knee. He was carrying a much lighter load now that he didn't have the extra pistol and spare shells to lug around. Wash wasn't entirely sure if that was a good thing, though. Speed was great, but not at the cost of dwindling ammo.

He sucked in a deep breath, then held it before closing his eyes and opening up his senses to the world around him.

It was cold.

It was dark.

But it wasn't quiet, because they were coming.

He didn't have to see them to know it. He could hear them. They weren't talking, but they weren't being shy about trampling over twigs and batting branches out of their path. He thought he could even hear their breathing.

Haggard, out of breath, and...*anxious.*

They were moving slowly, which he guessed they could afford to, because they didn't even have to try to track his and the sisters' trail. They had left a hell of a mess. If he were smarter, he would have done something about that earlier.

Then again, if he were smarter, he wouldn't be here right now.

Enough. Face the present. Face the enemy.

Get ready...

He crunched the numbers in his head.

Five men. Maybe four, if he were lucky.

(*Yeah, right.*)

Four or five, they would be armed. That was a dead certainty.

And one of them was Mathison. Big, ugly, bald Mathison.

Somewhere behind him, still moving, were the sisters. Ana and Emily.

"Find us, okay? We'll be waiting for you. I'll be waiting for you."

Wash opened his eyes.

"Hell, who wants to live forever anyway?" he whispered to the darkness, before getting up and moving farther back into the shadows.

TWENTY-THREE

They were coming, all five of them. Or maybe there was just four. But four or five—did it really matter? Not in the slightest, when it was just him versus them.

Nine shells filled with lead buckshot...

Just as he had expected, they were being careful, if not entirely silent. He was somewhat impressed with their plodding progress.

Eighteen 9mm bullets tipped with silver...

But he guessed they could afford to be slow and methodical because they knew exactly where he and the girls had gone. All they had to do was follow the trail of broken branches and twigs on the ground.

Two spare magazines with seventeen 9mm apiece...

Mathison would be among them. Wash didn't for one second think Baldy would skip the hunt. He remembered the look on the big man's face when he saw Wash in the cabin. There was no fear, no hatred, just annoyance that things hadn't worked out the way he had planned.

One very, very sharp machete...

What exactly had gone down in that bedroom with Mathison and the sisters? Wash guessed he would find out if he survived this. It probably had a lot to do with why both Ana and Emily were still running through the woods right now, barefoot, wearing silk nightgowns. It didn't take a genius to put two and two together.

Four, possible five men. All armed.

He wished he could have brought more rounds for the 590A1, but the additional shells would have added even more weight, and he'd already been carrying too much already. The two spares for the Beretta would come in real handy once he had to ditch the shotgun, and Wash was pretty sure that was coming. As for the kukri strapped to his left leg...well, the longer he could delay reaching for it, the better.

A branch snapped.

A twig broke in half.

Then someone coughed, the sound muffled because the man had covered his mouth just in time.

That, though, led to a chain reaction, and two others coughed after the first.

Come on, everybody, let's all cough together!

He might have chuckled quietly. It was an absurd thought, but then what wasn't absurd about what he was doing tonight?

Wash tuned them out and concentrated instead on the smooth *tick-tick-tick-tick* from underneath the sleeve on his left hand.

Tick-tick-tick-tick ...

He willed his heartbeat to slow down.

Tick-tick-tick-tick ...

He relaxed his fingers around the pistol grip of the Mossberg. The shotgun was cold, mirroring the elements around him. Wetness covered the leaves hanging off branches above his head, their drops landing occasionally on his shoulders in the last twenty or so minutes he had been sitting there waiting...and waiting.

Tick-tick-tick-tick ...

He didn't have to see them to know they were close.

So, so close.

Tick-tick-tick-tick ...

He could smell them, too. Gunpowder and smoke. The tear gas from the cabin still clinging to the fabric of their clothes. Every breath they took either through their mouths or nostrils was impossibly loud, as were the drops of sweat that fell from their faces despite the cold night air. He wasn't even sure how that was possible.

Tick-tick-tick-tick ...

Five men. Possibly four. Heavily armed men, he was sure of *that*.

Tick-tick-tick-tick ...

They were almost on top of him, and all Wash could think of was the Old Man and what he had said that day when Wash picked up a gun for the first time in his life.

"This thing kills people. Men, women, children. Married, single, divorced. Old, young, or ancient. It doesn't care. It kills people. It snuffs them out. Takes away everything they got or will ever get. Remember that when you hold it. Remember that when you load it. And remember that when you pull the trigger."

He remembered all those things as he stood up, his back scraping against the bark of the tree he'd been hiding behind, the precious *tick-tick-tick-ticks* of the watch in his ears the entire time. He spun left, coming out from his cover, and hoping he'd guessed correctly.

Everything began moving in slow motion, from the clouds forming in front of his face to the two men in front of them. Both were wearing thick coats—one in something that might have been fur, the collars high and hugging the sides of his neck—in the process of moving through a stream of moonlight that had managed to penetrate the thick canopies above. They cradled rifles with gloved hands and they were separated by five feet or so, the one farther in the back standing slightly to the left of his comrade.

The man closest to Wash was short and stocky, and one side of his face was covered by a fresh gauze pad. He was blinking rapidly, wiping at the eye on the exposed part of his face, when Wash appeared in front of him less than ten feet away. The man froze, pale and cracked lips starting to open as he began the process of forming words—

The first *boom!* sent balls of lead into the man chest-first and knocked him down.

His partner ducked as stray buckshot *zipped!* around his head, but that move meant he couldn't immediately return fire. Not that he didn't try, but he was clumsy and not ready, just as Wash had hoped.

Wash racked the shotgun, swung slightly, and fired again. The second man collapsed behind a bush even as blood and shredded flesh flew from his face.

Flashes of movement erupted from Wash's left peripheral vision, but Wash was already turning and running, sliding back the forend to reload another cartridge into the Mossberg as he did so.

Run run run!

The explosive *pop-pop-pop* of automatic rifle fire scattered whatever animals that hadn't taken off when Wash unleashed his first two shots. He wasn't worried about innocent little creatures at the moment. He was only concerned with himself.

Faster, faster, faster!

His feet, in midstride, gave out underneath him, and he somersaulted forward and would have slammed face-first into the damp ground if he didn't drop the shotgun and reach forward with both hands to preserve himself. He managed to tuck and roll (*Second time's the charm!*), landing on the back of his neck instead of his face, and pain screamed through every part of him as he slid headfirst into a bush. He kept going, sliding like a maniac, and came out on the other side covered in leaves and broken branches.

What the hell?

Had he tripped on his own legs? A branch sticking out of the ground? Maybe one of those innocent critters trying to flee the onslaught of bullets?

No, none of those things, because he was bleeding. There was a hole at the front of his right leg, two inches above the kneecap. Blood oozed out of it, along with the second hole in the back of his leg.

He'd been shot. One of the bullets had clipped him. He hadn't even felt the pain, but then maybe he was too busy trying to deal with the fire burning from his side—

Voices shouting, overlapping, and *way too close*.

"Where is he?"

"Over there!"

"I don't see him!"

"There!"

"Where? Where?"

"There!"

Gunfire followed the last *There!* and the bush Wash had slid through was cut down to half its size against a tidal wave of bullets.

He didn't dare scramble to his feet, because that would have gotten his head shot off. Instead, he began crawling away, reaching down for the Beretta as he did so. The shooting continued, the rounds coming fast and furious. He wasn't sure if there was anything left of the bush he'd crashed into, but there must have been some because they hadn't hit him (*again*) yet. The ground erupted, specks of dirt flicking at his face and clothes.

A voice, shouting, *sounding even closer than before.*

"Hold your fire! I said hold your fire, goddammit!"

Was that Mathison? Maybe. It wasn't as if Wash had gotten a good bead on what the man sounded like back at the cabin. He'd only heard Mathison's voice once when the man had asked, almost nonchalantly, *"The fuck are you?"*

Whoever it was that had made the command, it took a while—Five seconds? Six?—before the shooters finally obeyed.

Thank God!

Footsteps, coming fast.

Wash rolled over onto his back, lifting the Beretta at the same time a figure lumbered through what was left of the bush—

A brief half-second of recognition as the man realized his mistake.

Wash fired, aiming for the man's large chest, and kept squeezing the trigger until the black-clad human being collapsed in front of him, slamming face-first into the bullet-pocked ground less than two feet from where Wash lay.

His legs kicked at the dirt, and Wash turned back onto his belly before scrambling up to his feet. He took off, legs pistoning, hoping the man's partners (How many were left now? Two? Three? He'd lost count, dammit!) were still far enough away that they couldn't pick him off—

The *boom!* of a shotgun exploded in his ears just before the round followed. It struck him in one of his shoulder blades, and Wash spun like a top in midstride.

He wasn't sure which part of him hit the ground first—his outstretched hands (The Beretta! What happened to the Beretta?) or his head. Whichever did, he barely felt the contact before he was already up on his knees even as the entire length of his back burned with a raging flame that began spreading to the rest of his body.

He spent a second—more?—trying to figure out why he was still alive. He had clearly heard a shotgun blast and something had hit him from behind, so why wasn't he dead? It had to be some kind of slug round, because buckshot would have sent lead balls into more than just one spot near his shoulder blade.

Voices, followed by heavy footsteps, *coming up behind him fast.*

This time Wash's head was spinning too fast and the fire was burning through every inch of him, lessening his ability to decipher the voices. He somehow managed to reach out, find the gnarled trunk of a tree, and use it as leverage to pull himself up on two wobbly feet.

Why am I still alive?

"Don't kill him!" a voice shouted. "Not until we get the girls back. Go, see if you can find them."

"By myself?" another voice asked.

"You see anyone else here? Beside, you're the tracker. It's your job. So do your fucking job."

"Shit, man, it's just us now. Forget the girls."

"What did you say?"

"I..."

"Go. *Now*."

"Yeah, okay," the second voice said.

Wash managed to remain on his feet (*How?*) and turned around, using the tree for support. His vision blurred, but he somehow found a way to peer through the haze at a figure standing in front of him holding a pump-action shotgun. The man was huge, and it was impossible to miss the domed head and goatee.

Mathison.

He was somehow even uglier up close. The cheekbones were too high and the nose too big and too flat. The forehead was too wide and his neck, possibly the size of Wash's thigh, too sinewy and unnaturally shaped. He had bad teeth and wore a bandoleer of shotgun shells across his chest. The rifle slung over his back looked like a child's toy, as did the gun in the holster on his right hip. Wash could see fresh scars along one side of his cheek, so the man hadn't managed to avoid Wash's fire back at the cabin completely unscathed.

"Still up, huh?" Mathison was saying. "I guess they don't make LTL ammo like they used to."

LTL?

Mathison kicked at something on the ground, and it flicked past Wash's head. It was a bean bag, small enough to fit into a shotgun shell.

LTL. Less Than Lethal.

Bean bag rounds.

That's why I'm still alive. That's the only reason I'm still alive.

He forced himself to refocus on Mathison, standing less than ten feet from him. Too far for a (desperate, at best) punch or a kick, but maybe just right for the kukri still in its sheath on Wash's left hip. Of course, he'd have to get his hands on the machete first, which was difficult at the moment with both palms flat against the trunk of the tree behind him; that was the only thing keeping him from collapsing right back down to the ground. Compared to the pain burning its way through him, the blood dripping out of his right thigh didn't even compute.

And where were his guns? The Beretta was gone, and so was the shotgun. He was down to the machete, something he had hoped wouldn't happen but always knew was inevitable. It had served him well for a long time, so why wouldn't it again?

Except this time there was a man with a shotgun to contend with, even if the ammo in his weapon was the non-lethal kind. Those bean bags didn't kill, but they sure as hell had dropped Wash like a ton of bricks earlier, and would no doubt do so again. Or kill him this time if Mathison shot him anywhere close to his wounded side. Just the thought of that made Wash grimace with discomfort.

"Where are they?" Mathison was asking. "They're mine. Both of them. They belong to me now. I took them fair and square."

"Fair and square?" Wash thought. *You're one sick fuck, you know that?*

But he couldn't make himself say the words out loud. It was hard enough just breathing and trying not to choke on whatever it was that was crawling its way down his throat. His chest heaved, and his legs threatened to come undone. If it weren't for the tree, he would be lying on his face in a pool of his own blood right now.

"Well?" Mathison said. "What do you have to say for yourself?"

He heard Mathison's question, but his focus had slipped away from the man and gone over his shoulder. He wasn't entirely sure what he was seeing at first, but then it became clearer as *it* moved closer, slowly emerging out of a heavily shadowed part of the woods.

About fucking time, Wash thought, and grinned.

It was a ghoul, and it was moving straight for Mathison.

TWENTY-FOUR

He knew it would happen sooner or later. Knew that all the shooting at the cabin, then later in the woods, would bring them out of hiding. If they weren't around the area, they would be drawn over like moths to a flame. A roaring, raging flame. Sound traveled these days, and the continuous thunderclaps of gunfire were a clear signal that man was around.

Man and the blood in their veins.

He wasn't too surprised that it had taken the first ghoul this long to appear. Six years ago, at the height of The Purge, the minute after the first gunshot would have seen a flood of the creatures swarming the vicinity. Those days were long gone and the nightcrawlers were massively reduced in numbers, so it took them longer to cover more ground.

But they were still out there, and sooner or later, he knew they'd show up.

And they did, finally.

Or one of them did, anyway.

It had to just be one, didn't it? When I needed them the

most—when I finally *need them around*—all I could get was one lousy undead asshat.

He grinned at the word *asshat.* Ana's favorite descriptor.

Ana. Had she gotten away? Her and her sister? Did they make it out of the woods? Were they still running for their lives right now? He'd given them enough time. He *hoped* he had, anyway. What he wouldn't give to know if they'd made it or not. He already had too many regrets. The biggest one of them all was that he'd never reach Texas. He'd never find One Eye and take its other eye.

"He's gone now, but he says to tell you he'll be waiting in Texas. He says not to keep him waiting too long, because he gets bored easily."

The girl at the farmhouse had said those things, but it was One Eye's voice that came out of her mouth.

I guess you'll have to wait a little longer, you piece of shit. How does forever sound?

But it wasn't over yet. It was close to the end, but he wasn't there yet.

Not quite yet.

Wash stared at the ghoul as it walked slowly (*God, why is it so damn slow?*) toward Mathison. It was ugly and frail, and against the hulking size of a man like Mathison, impossibly pathetic. The moonlight gleamed off its domed head, so it had that in common with the human piece of shit standing in front of it. Its hairless, pruned body seemed to ripple as it moved awkwardly forward on deformed legs. It was slightly hunched over at the waist, looking more insect than man.

It wasn't much (God, was it not much), but it was all Wash had.

How sad is that?

"*Pretty damn sad is the answer, kid,*" Imaginary Old Man answered.

Gee thanks, old timer. Glad you're here to lift my spirits!

If Wash hadn't seen the creature, he would have smelled its presence. The cool, crisp night had turned thick with rot, the ghoul's decaying stench fouling everything around it with its mere existence.

Wash's eyes snapped back to Mathison. Did he know? He had to know, didn't he? He had to be able to smell the night-crawler back there, even if he couldn't see or hear its approach. How could he not? Wash's senses were on fire, and his back throbbed from the spot where the bean bag had struck him, and he could still smell the creature easily.

Then Mathison grinned at him.

He knows...

Baldy lifted one forefinger to his lips, and in his best Elmer Fudd impression, "Shhhh. Be vewy, vewy quiet."

What the hell is he doing?

The look on Mathison's face only added to what Wash already thought of the man. Dangerous, reckless, and out of his mind.

He's insane. He thinks it's a game.

God, I want to kill this motherfucker so bad...

The nightcrawler had gotten halfway to Mathison when he turned and shot it. *Boom!* as the bean bag punched its way through the undead thing's chest and blasted out of its back, splattering thick, black blood across the grass. The monster glanced down at the gaping hole in its torso, then back at Mathison, just before it lunged at him.

Wash grinned, thought, *That didn't work out quite as you planned, did it, Mathison?*

Bang! as Mathison drew his pistol—the large Desert Eagle—and shot the creature at almost point-blank range. The gunshot was so ear shattering that Wash thought it might have been even louder than the shotgun blasts from earlier.

The pistol round entered the middle of the ghoul's face and exited the back, shattering the skull in its path with barely any resistance, before the large caliber round disappeared into the darkness beyond. The nightcrawler flopped to the ground and lay still, its body resting at an odd angle with its legs bent underneath it like it should have hurt. A lot. But of course Wash knew it didn't, because the black eyes didn't feel pain anymore.

So much for being saved by a monster. What was I thinking?

He pictured the Old Man grinning and shouting, *"Time to save yourself, kid!"*

Good call!

Mathison's back was still turned to him when Wash pulled one of his hands away from the tree that was keeping him upright and drew the kukri. It slid freely from its sheath, and he tightened his finger around the handle, unsure of his own grip. The combination of bleeding and pain from being struck by the bean bag was still wreaking havoc with his senses, and he couldn't be 100 percent certain of anything.

Wash got the machete out as Mathison was turning around. The big man stared at him for a moment, then looked down at the blade, before turning dark brown eyes back up to Wash's face.

Mathison chuckled. "What're you gonna to do with that pig sticker?" The man calmly slid his Desert Eagle back into its holster, unslung his shotgun, and racked it. "I think you need to get down on your knees and beg me not to kill you."

"That'll be the day," Wash said. It came out as more of a growl, and he couldn't be sure if Mathison had even heard it, because *he* barely heard it.

"Tough guy, huh?" Mathison said.

I guess he heard it.

"Tough enough," Wash said.

"I guess we'll have to test that theory out."

"I'm going to kill you."

"You won't be the first to try—or the first to fail." Mathison lifted the shotgun and aimed it at Wash's chest. "You're lucky I still need you alive, boy, just in case Kelly can't find where you stashed my girls. I'm betting he can, though. Guy's a natural tracker. Born and raised in the woods. But just 'cause I might need you breathing don't mean I need you standin', too."

Get ready, get ready, Wash thought as he mentally prepared himself to push off against the tree with everything he had.

Was there a chance he could do something dramatic, like twist and avoid Mathison's shot? Probably not. At least, not from the seven or so feet that currently separated them.

Looks closer to eight. Or ten...

Wash wasn't convinced he would make it two or three feet, never mind the entire way when he did push off the tree, before he would end up on his face against the ground. He had almost no feeling in either leg. He could see the blood dripping from one thigh but didn't actually feel it happening, which was a bad sign.

A very bad sign.

"So?" Mathison said. "You gonna to do something with that pig sticker or not—" He stopped short and took a quick step back, before throwing the shotgun down—

What the hell?

—and quickly pulling out the Desert Eagle with one hand, while drawing a Ka-Bar knife from a sheath along his left hip with the other.

Wash couldn't understand what was happening. Was Mathison going to fight him hand to hand? Then why did he take out his sidearm—

Oh.

The air had shifted again. It had done so a few seconds ago, but Wash hadn't noticed until now. Slowly, the rotting stink of week-old garbage invaded his nostrils, and he heard the *tap-tap* of bare feet against the soft, damp earth.

Wash pushed slightly off the tree, tightening his grip on the kukri, and turned around just as they raced out of the dark at him.

Ghouls!

He swung with the machete purely on instinct and lopped off a head at the neck as the others came out of the shadows behind it, like little malformed children with arms outstretched to hug him.

Wash was stumbling and didn't know how he was even still on his feet, if just barely. Maybe it was because every part of him knew that if he fell now he was done, that there would be no way back up because they would be all over him.

So he didn't fall (*How am I doing this?*) and kept backpedaling even as one of the creatures leapt at him, its thick spittle splashing Wash in the face. He grimaced through the disgust and chopped, and got it across the shoulder blade. The machete kept going, cutting through flesh and weak bone, and severed the nightcrawler into two pieces.

A massive *bang!* from behind him.

Wash went still and waited for the pain, for the unbelievable torture of being struck by a large caliber bullet at close range. It was going to hurt way more than the bean bag had.

Except it didn't. Nothing hit him because Mathison *hadn't fired at him.*

He wanted to glance back to see what Mathison was shooting at, but he had a feeling he already knew the answer. The thick stench in the air was all the evidence he needed. It was now coming from everywhere, which meant *they* were everywhere.

But he was only concerned with the ones in front of him. They trampled over the remains of the halved ghoul, seeking the quickest path to their goal: *Him.*

Wash stumbled back some more, even as gunshots continued from behind him, each one seemingly louder than the last. So loud, in fact, that every ghoul in the area would have heard them if they hadn't already been drawn over by all the shooting previously.

But Mathison shooting at nightcrawlers meant he wasn't shooting at Wash, and right now that was all Wash cared about. The second Baldy's gun went quiet was when Wash was in really deep, deep trouble. Not that he wasn't already in a lot of trouble.

Wash slashed with the kukri and raked the closest ghoul across the face. He had struck too soon and just barely gotten the creature as it was in mid-lunge. It was a minor wound, and although it sliced off a piece of the thing's already mutilated nose, it shouldn't have killed it. It shouldn't have been anything but an annoyance. Except it was more than that because the kukri's blade was partially made of silver and that was all it took—contact with their bloodstream, and the ghoul fell.

But the undead thing hadn't settled on the ground for more than a heartbeat before the four behind it crushed its corpse under their feet.

Wash continued backpedaling, every step sending painful electricity through his body. His vision continued to get worse, and the ghouls were starting to blur, looking more like charred and black stick figures lumbering out of an unnatural fog.

He willed every ounce of him to remain on his feet, because he couldn't afford to fall. Not now. Not *now*.

Bang! from behind him, this time so close (and loud!) that he wondered if he hadn't inadvertently stumbled into Mathison's field of fire.

Then again—*bang!*

And again—*bang!*

Don't run out of ammo, Mathison. Don't run out of ammo, you piece of shit!

Because it wasn't just the ghouls in front of Wash that he had to worry about. It was the ones behind him that he couldn't see. The only reason they weren't coming for him yet was because of Mathison's presence. He was closer to them, and the ghouls always went for the easiest prey.

Don't you run out of ammo, Mathison. Don't you run out of ammo, you slimy, miserable excuse for a human being!

He hacked at a ghoul as it reached for him from barely two feet away and its arm flew off at the elbow joint. The creature's eyes—already solid black—became even more lifeless (*Is that possible?*) as it pitched forward and slammed into the ground in front of him.

That left three more, already stepping over their dead to get to him.

Shouldn't have wished for too many earlier! Wash thought as he slashed again, putting everything he had into the swing.

TWENTY-FIVE

Mathison's Desert Eagle was still thundering behind him.

Again and again and *again.*

He found comfort in their earsplitting crashes, in the knowledge that the man himself was still back there killing ghouls with his silver-tipped bullets. And as long as Mathison was back there, he was drawing the other creatures to him and keeping them away from Wash.

Keep shooting, Mathison. Keep shooting!

But there was something weird about that last shot. It hadn't sounded like the others. It had sounded more...distant. Not by much, but enough to be noticeable. Unless, of course, Wash was imagining it. After all, every part of him was screaming, so could he really trust his hearing right now?

God, let me be imagining it.

Please, please, please.

He risked a glance (he had to, he just had to know!) and found Mathison backing away from him while shooting and stabbing with his Ka-Bar. He was surrounded by ghouls—even *more* than the three in front of Wash at the moment. There had to be at least a half dozen of the spindly things, and they were converging on him as if Wash didn't even exist.

Better him than me!

That was the good part. The flip side was that Mathison was leaving him to fend for himself, and each step he took led him farther away. Soon, Mathison might not be the closest living thing to the ghouls anymore. Soon, it might end up being Wash.

Sonofabitch!

Wash guessed he should be thankful Mathison hadn't sent one of those large rounds in his direction. He wouldn't have survived being shot by a Desert Eagle. Very few people could, but especially someone who was already badly hurt like he was. God, he was leaking blood everywhere, and he was pretty sure his side had opened up and was bleeding again, but he just couldn't afford the second or two (or ten) it would have taken to pull up his shirt to check.

Who cares if you're bleeding if you end up dead in the next few seconds!

Wetness flicked at his forehead, and Wash swung the kukri again, catching a ghoul as it came within a foot of biting his face, its arms outstretched to grab a piece of him.

But he'd swung the machete wrong—it was a combination of being weak and swinging too hard to make up for that weakness, all the while being slightly off-balance—and hadn't taken the time to aim. The curved blade went in from the side of the creature's neck and straight down in a diagonal slash, chopping its way past the chest just before it became lodged in the ghoul's ribcage.

Shit!

Wash tried to pull the machete out but only succeeded in lifting the lifeless dead thing clinging to its sharp blade up from the ground. Maybe if he weren't wounded or so weak, or barely standing and moving on pure fumes, he might have been able to jerk the kukri free.

Shit shit shit!

The two remaining ghouls charged, breaking off from their head-on approach to go around the dead nightcrawler. He was sure they hadn't planned it; the black eyes weren't that smart. They had no head for tactics and acted purely on a primal instinct to feed.

And right now Wash was the key to satiating their hunger. He could see it in their dark, hollowed eyes, in the thick saliva that flitted from the jagged things that were once teeth but were now broken and cracked spikes jutting out along the sides of their open mouths.

Wash frantically grabbed the dead ghoul by the shoulder with one hand, the other still clinging to the handle of the kukri, and swung the creature into one of the attacking night-crawlers. His plan was to use the dead ghoul as a battering ram —hit one, then the other—but instead he lost his grip on the machete as it flew out of his hand.

No no no!

But something good came out of the loss. The sharp edge of the machete, still embedded in the dead ghoul, slashed the arm of the attacking nightcrawler as they collided, and both creatures fell to the ground in a twisted pile of clacking bones and entwined limbs.

Except Wash didn't have any chance to wallow in his accidental victory because the last ghoul pounced, its slim frame crashing into Wash and driving him back, back!

He lost his footing and went down, and the creature fell right on top of him. It was so weak, so thin and skinny and barely weighed anything, and if he had his legs under him, Wash would never have allowed himself to be taken like that. But he *didn't*, and all he could think was, *Don't let it bite you. Jesus, don't let it get its blood into you!*

He punched the ghoul in the side of the head with a balled fist and caved in a part of its brittle skull. Not that the blow did anything to make the creature jump off him or even hesitate. Instead, it opened its mouth to reveal those same jagged teeth covered in layers of dripping black liquid and leaned toward Wash's face.

He grabbed it by the throat with his left hand, every motion causing unnatural agony to rip across his frame. He might have screamed out once or twice (or a dozen times), but he couldn't keep track. He kept it at bay (*Its teeth! Watch out for its teeth!*) with his left hand while he hit it again with his right, aiming for the same spot.

When that didn't seem to have any effect on the ghoul, Wash struck it in the cheek.

Then again, and again, and *again*.

Through it all, he couldn't help but notice that the night around him had gone deathly quiet. There were just his own gasps and the unnatural sound of the creature's bones breaking apart against every one of his desperate blows pounding in Wash's ears.

Mathison had stopped shooting.

Mathison had stopped shooting!

He had done that either because he was dead or he'd run out of bullets, or both. Without Mathison, there was no one left to help whittle down the ghouls in the area. Wash didn't even know how many were left, if any. He'd seen a dozen of them converging on Mathison earlier. Had there been more? He only knew for certain that there had been enough that the entire woods reeked of vomit, and it was all Wash could do not to gag.

But he didn't, because everything he had was being used to keep the ghoul from getting closer, even as the creature's legs fought for purchase against his own while its hands kept trying to reach for him. Wash had it at arm's length, and thank God the ghoul's arms were deformed and shorter and it couldn't make up the difference. Instead, it flailed away at his chest and arms, and if it had nails at all, it would have raked bloody strips across Wash's exposed skin.

He was keeping it back, but it wasn't going to last forever. Time wasn't on his side. It didn't matter how many times he hit it or how long he held it in place, because sooner or later he would tire. His arms would turn to mush and his strength would be sapped, and the creature, with its skull cracked a dozen spots over, would never, ever tire. Even as its left eyeball threatened to pop free from its socket, the damn thing kept moving, kept trying to push against his left arm, kept *coming*.

And it would keep coming, and coming, and he wouldn't be able to kill it. He didn't have anything. Not even a silver knife. Right now he would settle for a rock, but he didn't even have that. All he could do was hold it back and pray—

He heard a strange gurgling sound and turned his head to the right. There was a pile of bodies next to him—ghouls, thick black blood oozing out of holes in their chests and faces and severed limbs. Mathison's handiwork.

Except it wasn't the corpses that Wash focused on.

It was the *lone figure* walking toward him.

Oh, shit.

It was a ghoul, dragging one of its legs behind it, black eyes glinting in the moonlight as it zeroed in on him.

Oh, shit!

He didn't know where it came from or why it was late to the party. Maybe the fact that it was moving so slowly, pulling one leg behind it, was the reason it had taken the creature this long to reach them when all of its other brethren were already here. Maybe that was why the monster was alive and the rest were dead.

No, not *all* dead. The one on top of him was still very much alive, still fighting, still trying to lean forward and bite a chunk out of Wash's face. It wouldn't stop squirming against his outstretched arm and it kept pushing, and pushing...

Wash looked over at Leggy.

"Leggy?" Did you just give the undead ghoul a name?

He wanted to let out a laugh at the absurd thought, but he could barely afford the strength to gasp for each breath.

And Leggy was still coming, pulling that grotesque broken leg behind it.

Slowly. Slowly...

Bang! as the bark on a tree at least ten feet behind Leggy exploded.

Except nothing happened to Leggy itself. The creature kept coming, oblivious to the bullet that had almost taken its life (*again*).

Wash swung his head back to the left.

Ana!

She was standing nearby with the Glock in both hands, the gun aimed at Leggy. She was squinting behind the iron sights, trying to line up a shot.

"The chest!" Wash shouted. "Shoot it in the chest!"

"I'm trying!" Ana said, and fired again.

Wash glanced back at Leggy.

It was still coming.

She'd missed *again!*

"The chest!" he shouted.

"Shut up!" Ana shouted back and squeezed the trigger a third time.

Leggy flinched when the bullet creased its shoulder —*barely*—and took a lump of flesh along with it. But a graze was all that was necessary, and the ghoul stumbled for a bit, as if drunk, before falling sideways to the ground, its bad leg sticking out at an impossible angle from underneath its bruised form.

Wash turned back to Ana, saw the shock on her face. He would have grinned if he thought he was in the clear, but he wasn't. Snappy, the other ghoul (*Are you serious right now? Stop giving them cute names, you dummy!*), was still on top of him, still trying to get at him. It was oblivious to what had happened to Leggy or even Ana's presence. It just didn't care.

Ana hurried over and pointed the gun at the creature, the Glock trembling dangerously in both her hands.

"No, no, don't!" Wash shouted.

"What?" Ana said.

"You'll miss!"

Ana gave him an annoyed look, but she didn't pull the trigger.

"Closer!" he said.

"How much closer?"

"Closer!"

The ghoul finally glanced up when Ana approached them, and for a moment Wash thought it would go for her. But all it did was look back down at him and snap its teeth and lean in some more.

"Do it!" Wash said.

"Are you sure—" Ana started.

"Do it!"

She fired, and the round entered one side of the ghoul's head and exploded out the other, covering parts of Wash's right hand and the grass nearby in a shower of black blood, chunks of bone, and shredded flesh.

Wash sighed and held the ghoul up with both arms before rolling away. It landed back on the ground next to him because he hadn't gotten more than a few feet from his original spot before the pain was too much and he had to stop to breathe.

Ana stepped over the dead creature and kneeled next to him. He didn't have to ask her how he looked, because her face told him everything.

"Mathison," Wash said.

"What?" Ana said.

"Mathison...

"What about him?"

"He's alive..."

Her expression changed, but instead of fear, there was just anger.

That's my girl, Wash thought.

Ana picked up the gun she'd placed next to them and glanced around. "Where is he, Wash?"

"I don't know. He boogied."

"Boogied?"

"Ran off."

She looked back down at him. "I didn't see him when I came back."

"He might still be around..."

She shook her head and put the gun back down. "Forget about Mathison. Let's concentrate on keeping you alive first."

"Emily?"

"She's safe. Everyone's safe, except you."

"Didn't I tell you not to come back?"

"I had to."

"But I told you *not* to."

"I don't give a shit what you told me. And stop that!"

He hadn't realized he was moving, trying to get up, until she put one hand on his chest and pushed him back down. She clasped her other hand over his right thigh to stop the bleeding (he had forgotten about that), before feeling along his side. When she pulled her hand back, the palm was damp and bloody.

"Bad?" he asked.

She smiled. "No."

"I don't believe you."

"You want to know why it's not bad?"

"Why?"

"Because you promised you wouldn't die on me, that's why. So it's not bad, because 'bad' means you're about to die, and you're not going to."

"That makes no sense."

"Shut the hell up."

"I'm just sayin'."

"And I said to shut up. I'm going to keep you alive because you still have to go down to Texas, remember? One Eye. Remember him?"

Wash nodded. Or thought he did, anyway.

"That's right, it's still down there," Ana said. "It's still waiting for you. And you have to go and kill it. Remember?"

"I remember..."

"Good. So you can't die. Not on me, and not on that blue-eyed prick. You still have to take out its other eye."

"Yeah, I do..."

"So we're in agreement. You're not going to die here."

"I'm not going to die here..."

"You're goddamn right you're not going to die here."

Even as he heard her voice, her face was becoming blurry. It wasn't just her, but also the trees and branches and canopies above her, too. He wouldn't have been able to focus on Ana at all or know where she was in all that mosaic if not for her bright red hair, gently blowing in the cold breeze.

"Wash," Ana whispered.

"Yeah?"

She leaned down, and, cupping his face in her bloodied hands, kissed him briefly on the lips.

I like this, Wash thought. *I could spend the rest of my life doing this.*

She pulled back slightly, her eyes focused on his. "Okay?"

He grinned. "Okay."

Wash closed his eyes and concentrated on the *tick-tick-tick-tick* from his wrist. That, and the warmth of Ana's hands on his cheeks, the sound of her soft breathing over him.

"It's not bad," he heard her say. "It's not bad at all. We can fix this. We can fix this..."

He smiled. He wasn't sure if she was trying to convince him or herself, but he'd be damned if he didn't believe her anyway.

Wash let go and drifted, the *tick-tick-tick-tick* of the watch keeping time in his ears the entire way...

TWENTY-SIX

"You should be dead."

But he wasn't.

"But you should be."

And yet...

"That's beside the point."

What was the point?

"The point is, you screwed up. Royally. You took on a fight that wasn't yours. You went up against overwhelming numbers. You...should...be...dead."

Yeah, yeah, Wash thought as he opened his eyes and stared at a spider spinning webs in the rafters above him. The arachnid looked bright brown with seemingly glowing yellow patches, but it took Wash a while to attribute those properties to the beams of sunlight splashing across it as it worked diligently. If it knew he even existed, the spider never bothered to acknowledge him.

But I'm alive.

Aren't I?

He was, even if he was sore and just keeping his eyes open proved difficult. He blinked away the pain as best he could, but couldn't ignore the heavy and persistent throbbing coming from his side, his right leg, and pretty much every other part of his body that had the capacity to feel anything.

But I'm alive.

I'm alive...

It took him a while to figure out where he was. A room, on a queen-size bed (or was it a king?) with a thick fur blanket on top of him. It was warm and comforting, and he didn't feel like getting up. He didn't *want* to get up. But he did, forcing himself to rise slightly before sliding back until he was sitting against the headboard.

A bedroom with flowery wall patterns, sunlight coming in from his left. He glanced over in that direction and glimpsed figures moving outside. He was on the second floor of a building. Noises from below as people went about their business, the din of activity drifting through the closed window with iron bars across it on the other side.

Where was he?

Wash lifted the blanket to get a better look at himself. He was wearing cotton pajamas, and when he lifted his shirt, saw fresh bandages around his waist. He didn't have to pull down the pajamas to know there was more gauze around his right thigh. He could feel it down there over the heavy fabric.

He looked around the room again, taking everything in as fully as possible. A dresser in front of him; a shelf stacked with bedsheets and pillowcases in a corner. A nightstand to his right—

Tick-tick-tick-tick.

The watch. It was on top of the nightstand, next to a roll of fresh gauze and a handheld vanity mirror.

Wash reached over and picked up the automatic, grimacing slightly with the effort, and slipped the watch on.

Tick-tick-tick-tick.

Four beats per second. No more, no less.

He grabbed the mirror next and took a look at himself. His face was covered in stubble and he'd seen better days. His eyes were puffy, and someone had cut his hair while he was asleep. Unconscious? Half-dead? One of those. He ran his fingers through the short cut, then scratched at the facial hair for a moment. All things considered, he'd come out of the Mathison fiasco pretty well.

"You almost died," Imaginary Old Man said in his head, with just enough of an edge to let Wash know that he was being chastised.

But I'm not.

"You should be."

But I'm not, he thought, putting the mirror back on the nightstand.

He was tired and everything ached, and being awake hadn't done much to ease the discomfort flowing from his side and leg. Wash lowered himself back down and pulled the blanket over him, and although the room was flooded with bright sunlight, he had no trouble going right back to sleep with the *tick-tick-tick-tick* of the watch in his ears.

It was dark outside his window when he opened his eyes again, but any alarm bells in his head quickly faded when he saw Ana sitting at the foot of the bed, smiling at him.

"I'm alive," Wash said.

"Of course you are," Ana said. She got up and walked the short distance to sit on the bed beside him. "I told you I wasn't going to let you die on me, and I always keep my promises."

He put his hand over hers. For some reason, he expected her to pull away, but instead Ana covered his hand with her other one.

"Mathison," he said, and let the rest trail off.

"Don't worry about it," Ana said.

"What happened?"

"I got him."

"How?"

"After I made sure you weren't going to die on me, I went looking for the bastard. He wasn't that far from us. Maybe thirty yards, sitting against a tree. He'd been bitten multiple times and was bleeding out, almost dead when I found him."

Wash watched her face as she told the story, how calm and unemotional she looked. But he knew better. After everything Mathison had done—to her town, to her sister, and to her—there was no way Ana wasn't full of emotion then and now. She just hid it well, that was all.

"He asked me to put him out of his misery," Ana continued.

"Did you?"

She shook her head. "I made sure he knew I was there the whole time, that I would survive him. When it was over, I finished him off so he couldn't come back."

"That's...hardcore."

"Yeah, well, fuck him." She lifted his hand to her lips and kissed it. "He almost killed you."

"There was another guy..."

"Kelly."

"Is that his name?"

"*Was* his name," Ana said. "We ran across each other when I was coming back for you. I slowed down after we left you and tried to hide our tracks, but he still found us. Too bad for him, as it turned out."

"You shouldn't have done that."

"Shut up, I'm telling a story."

"Sorry."

"Anyway. I heard him coming. I hid and waited until he got closer." She shrugged. "I used the knife you gave me."

Damn. Remind me never to get on her bad side.

"The cabin," Wash said.

Ana nodded. "Pauline and Maggie. They were in the other bedroom the entire time you were there. Did you see them?"

He shook his head.

"Well, they heard that commotion you made," Ana smiled. "They were shaken and scared when I found them, but they'll be okay. They're here with us now. Safe and sound, along with Emily."

"Good. Good..." Wash looked around at the room. "Where are we, by the way?"

"Kanter 11."

"Kanter?"

"Emily found your horses. Well, one of them. The big orange-brown. We put you on it and brought you back here. The only reason you didn't bleed to death on the way over was because Kelly had a first-aid kit on him."

"Thank God for Kelly."

"Yeah, thank God for Kelly."

"What about the other horses?"

"We couldn't find them. I think we were lucky to find one."

"I hid our supplies in the woods..."

"Where?"

"I don't know the exact location, but I could probably find it again if I go back there in the daytime."

"That's going to have to wait until you're fully healed. Even then, I'm not sure it's worth going back for."

"Supplies are hard to come by, Ana."

"We can argue about it when you're better."

"Is that what we're doing? Arguing?"

She shook her head. "We're talking, now. We can argue, later."

"Yes, ma'am." Just being reminded of his injuries made him wince a bit. "How long have we been here, anyway?"

"Three days."

"Three days?"

"Technically, two nights and three days."

"Where's your sister?"

"She's sleeping in a room across from this one. Pauline and Maggie have their own room downstairs."

"How is she? Emily?"

Ana bit her lip and didn't answer right away. Then, "She'll survive. Em's tougher than she looks."

You both are, he thought, but said, "She's lucky to have you looking out for her."

"If I were a better sister, I'd never have let her be taken in the first place."

Wash tightened his grip on her hand. "You couldn't have seen it coming."

"That's the problem, Wash; I did. I just couldn't convince the others. But I saw it coming." She frowned. "I saw it coming, and I still let it happen." She shook her head. "That's not going to happen again. Never again."

He nodded, when a jolt of pain made him grimace.

"Pain?" Ana asked.

"Yeah..."

Ana walked over to the dresser and came back with a bottle of water and some pills. "This'll help."

He didn't bother asking what the pills were and washed them down with the water. He closed his eyes and took a breath.

"You trust her that much, kid?" Imaginary Old Man asked.

Yes. Yes, I do.

When he opened his eyes back up, she was hovering over him, watching him curiously. Her red hair, getting longer every day, hung around her face, and he didn't think there was anything more beautiful in the world.

She smiled. "Come on. I'm pretty, but I'm not *that* pretty."

He smiled back. "Yeah, you are."

She leaned down and kissed him, the taste of her as inviting as anything he had ever experienced in his life. It took a while before she pulled slightly back, the tip of her nose still so close that he could have just raised himself slightly off the bed and gave it a peck. And he was tempted, but was afraid any sudden movements were only going to introduce more unnecessary pain.

"You have no idea what I want to do to you right about now," she whispered.

"What's stopping you?"

"You might die, for one."

"I'm willing to take that risk."

She kissed him on the forehead. "But I'm not."

She lay down on the bed next to him instead, then scooted close enough that he could put his arm around her. She maneuvered the blanket until it was covering both of them, the warmth radiating from her body the most natural thing in the world.

"Go to sleep," she whispered. "We'll pick this up again tomorrow."

"Tomorrow?" he asked, unable to hide the excitement in his voice and not caring if she heard it.

"Or the night after. Or the night after that. But eventually."

"I'm not sure I can wait that long."

"Yes, you can," she whispered and leaned her head against his shoulder. "Good night, Washington."

He smiled. "Good night, Anastasia."

And it should have been a good night, but it wasn't.

He dreamt of the Old Man.

And of the others.

And he dreamt of the girl at the farmhouse, except instead of the girl's voice it was One Eye hissing at him:

"He says not to keep him waiting too long, because he gets bored easily."

He woke up in the middle of the night to the sound of Ana breathing softly next to him, her warm body still pressed against his underneath the blanket, and the ever-present *tick-tick-tick-tick* of the watch.

Sleep wouldn't come no matter how many times he closed his eyes and tried to force it.

An hour passed.

Then two...

Tick-tick-tick-tick...

He stared up at the ceiling, at the house spider as it clung to its web, its brown and yellow colors visible against a stream of moonlight.

The arachnid was oblivious to him as it sat on its web and waited.

And waited...

Tick-tick-tick-tick...

———————

"Are you sure you want to be doing this?" Marie asked.

He nodded and climbed into the Quarter Horse's saddle. There wasn't very much pain; either that, or the pills he'd taken before leaving the room were doing their job. "She'll be angry, but she'll get over it. She'll get over me."

"I don't know about that. She's been at your side since they brought you back here. I don't think she's left your room more than an hour in all that time."

Wash didn't know how to answer that, so he opted to stay quiet. Instead, he picked up the orange-brown's reins and turned the animal toward the stable doors. "Tell her I'm sorry, but this isn't something I can put off."

"We talked, you know."

"About?"

"You. I have a feeling she already knows you weren't going to wait until you got better."

"I am better."

"There's 'better' and then there's 'better,' Wash."

"Sounds the same to me."

"My point is," Marie said, "I think she was preparing herself to leave with you when the time came."

"I know," Wash said. "That's why I'm doing this. This way she won't have to decide between me or taking her sister and the others home. I can't do that to her. I won't."

"So this is all for her?"

"For her, for me. Does it matter?"

"Maybe. Depends on your perspective, I guess."

"It doesn't matter to me," Wash said, and hoped it was at least convincing.

The truth was, it did matter to him. It mattered a lot. But he couldn't tell Marie that. She wouldn't understand anyway. Even Ana wouldn't, despite everything they had been through. It had to be this way. It just had to.

I'm sorry, Ana, but you don't want to go where I'm going. Even I don't want to go there, but I have to.

I have to...

"What is this thing that you need to do so badly that it can't wait?" Marie asked.

"You don't want to know, Marie. Trust me, it's better if you don't know." Wash paused, then, "Thanks for taking care of them for me while I was out. And thanks for these," he added, patting the bags of supplies. "I owe you. And I always repay my debts."

"It's not your debts I'm worried about. You're still kind of yellow around the gills there, Mr. Slayer man."

"That's what the pills are for."

Marie sighed. "I guess there's no point in trying to talk you out of this very, very stupid thing you're about to do."

"You could try, but you'd just be wasting your breath."

"So the only thing left to say is, good luck."

"You too."

Marie nodded at a twenty-something man, who walked over and pushed the stable doors open. Soft morning sunlight flooded inside. In less than thirty minutes the entire town would be awake, along with Ana.

"Don't be a stranger," Marie said, and patted the horse on the rump. "If you change your mind, you know where to find us. We're not going anywhere."

Wash gave her a smile and a nod before turning around and riding through the doors, then into the bright street outside.

He turned north in the road and gave the big orange-brown a swift kick in the flanks. The animal picked up speed, and soon they were racing against the sunrise to make it out of Kanter 11 before he changed his mind.

I'm coming for you, you bastard. Ready or not, I'm coming for you...

www.ingramcontent.com/pod-product-compliance
Lightning Source LLC
Chambersburg PA
CBHW020237180626
46810CB00006B/2231